Dating Outside Your DNA

Dating Outside Your DNA

KAREN KELLEY

KENSINGTON PUBLISHING CORP.
www.kensingtonbooks.com

BRAVA BOOKS are published by

Kensington Publishing Corp.
119 West 40th Street
New York, NY 10018

All Kensington titles, imprints, and distributed lines are available at special quantity discounts for bulk purchases for sales promotion, premiums, fund-raising, educational, or institutional use.

Special book excerpts or customized printings can also be created to fit specific needs. For details, write or phone the office of the Kensington Special Sales Manager: Attn.: Special Sales Department, Kensington Publishing Corp., 119 West 40th Street, New York, NY 10018, Phone: 1-800-221-2647.

ISBN-13: 978-0-7582-2576-4
ISBN-10: 0-7582-2576-8

First Kensington Trade Paperback Printing: December 2009

10 9 8 7 6 5 4 3 2 1

Printed in the United States of America

To Trevor Chase Wheeler

Dreams do come true
Always believe in yours

Chapter 1

Roan Hendrix couldn't believe his ears. What the hell was Joe trying to pull? His frown deepened. "You want me to do what?"

"Train her," Joe Beacon said, leaning forward in his chair. With one finger, he pushed his glasses a little higher up the bridge of his nose. "One-on-one," he repeated.

When Joe called him to his office, Roan had hoped his boss was going to let him return to active duty. The total opposite had happened, and he wasn't happy about it.

"I don't do one-on-one. At least, not at work," Roan said.

At home was another story. Like Michelle last night. She was having a little R & R between flights. He really liked her idea of rest and relaxation.

Not that they'd rested that much, but he'd damn sure felt relaxed this morning when he rolled out of bed. Who knew his day would start off so good, only to turn to crap by late afternoon.

What Joe was asking was different from the way he normally trained agents. Roan didn't work on a personal level with anyone, especially Nerakians. They were a strange breed, to say the least, and he still hadn't gotten used to them.

Hell, he didn't think they were that good in the first place, but they were given preferential treatment because of their so-called special abilities. He'd take a street cop with a dose of good old-fashioned gut instinct over a Nerakian any day.

"Lyraka is different."

Roan crossed his legs. "I've heard that crap before."

"She's not full-blooded Nerakian. Her father is an earthling."

He raised an eyebrow. Okay, Joe had his attention. "I didn't know there were any half-breeds old enough to train, but it makes sense they would mate. The ones I've run across make no bones that they like a good roll in the hay."

"Now you're being crude," Joe admonished.

"Just stating facts. Chocolate and sex are the only things they seem to care about."

"That's not true and you know it."

Yeah, he did, but he'd been in a particularly foul mood since Joe told Roan that he wanted him to stay at the training center a little longer. Now Joe was giving him this new assignment. Roan wanted to get back into field work and out of training. He was starting to feel trapped, and that didn't set well with him.

A leg injury he'd sustained a few months ago had kept him on the sidelines. The doc still wouldn't release him for full duty even though Roan felt fine. He had a feeling Joe was behind some of it.

"Train her, and I'll get you the release you've been wanting," Joe said.

"Are you serious?"

"Yes."

"She must mean a lot to you. Is she that good?"

"You can't imagine." Joe handed Roan a manila envelope. "This is everything I have on her. I know it's not much, but read it tonight."

Roan was still skeptical, but believed Joe when he said he would get him the release. Hell, he'd do just about anything to get back to active duty. He believed there was more to training this chick, though. "What's the catch? There has to be something wrong with her."

Joe shrugged, a little too casually, if you asked Roan.

"Like I said, her abilities are different, stronger than the average Nerakian, but she needs to learn discipline and control."

She was half Nerakian and half earthling, how strong could she be? He assumed she was a warrior so he wouldn't have to actually do that much. A few weeks of his time and he'd be back getting his hands dirty. He could handle that.

"Okay, it's a deal. When do I get to meet her?" He'd known Joe for quite a few years. At one time, Joe had been a kick-ass agent, but when the elite force was formed, Joe had taken over recruiting people who had the potential to be the best of the best. Roan knew it took a lot to impress Joe. So yeah, he was curious.

Joe beamed. "You get to meet her right now." He pushed a button on his intercom. "Go get Lyraka and ask her to come in."

A few minutes passed before the door opened. Roan didn't move from his chair. Nerakian women were beautiful, but it hadn't taken him long to realize they had strange ideas about things.

And they took everything literally. He didn't have that much patience when it came to explaining every little detail. Women from Earth were more to his liking. They knew the score. He slowly turned in his chair, expecting to see a beautiful woman.

There were very few times in his life he'd ever felt as though the wind had been knocked out of him. This just happened to be one of them. She didn't look like most Nerakians. Warriors were darker—dark hair, dark eyes, dark clothes. Healers had long blond hair and usually wore green flowing robes, and man, were they a pain in the ass. He'd only met one, but that one had been more than enough. Each Nerakian had a different look that immediately said what their role on Nerak had been.

But this woman was different. God, was she different. His heart had already begun to pound, and the palms of his hands to sweat just looking at her. She was a walking, talking billboard of every man's sexual fantasy—him included.

How the hell was he going to train her? She'd be nothing but a distraction to any team that she was on.

Crap, he felt as though Joe had sucker punched him. No wonder he'd wanted one-on-one training for her. Roan glared at him. Joe met his gaze head on, then gave a slight shake of his head. Yeah, Roan knew what Joe was trying to say—not here, not now.

Why the hell hadn't he explained everything before she came in the room? Easy, because he'd known Roan wouldn't have agreed to train her—too much distraction. She was the kind of woman that got men killed.

Man, this assignment was going to be a pain in the butt. Roan could see that already, but he slowly uncurled his body from the chair and came to his feet. He might be an asshole sometimes, but he was still a gentleman. He nodded his head. The gesture wasn't that friendly, but hell, he was still in shock. And pissed at Joe because he could've warned Roan before the woman came in the room.

"Lyraka, sorry to keep you waiting. Please, have a seat," Joe said as he also stood. "This is Roan. He'll be your instructor."

She glanced Roan's way, then quickly sat in the other chair.

Yeah, she was different all right. He studied her. There was nothing specific to pinpoint what she was supposed to do in life. She didn't carry herself with the self-assuredness of most Nerakians, either. Not that she came across as afraid, only wary, as though she didn't easily trust.

She had the darkness of a warrior, like she tanned at the beach every weekend. Her hair was short and black. Her body lean, but with curves in all the right places.

It was her eyes that drew a man in and kept him from looking away. They were pale blue—hypnotic, and fringed with long, thick lashes. Bedroom eyes. The kind of eyes that conjured visions of two people in bed, naked bodies pressed against each other.

Roan quickly cleared his throat, and the images in his mind. He needed to stay focused on the matter at hand.

Joe had said Lyraka was only half Nerakian so that would explain why she didn't look like other warriors. But did she have the skills of a warrior? If he had to start from scratch, it would mean he was stuck at the training center longer than he wanted.

He mentally shook his head. Of course she had skills. Joe wouldn't send someone to him who didn't at least know the basics.

Lyraka glanced in Roan's direction. How could she not when his presence filled the room. He was the tallest man she'd ever been around. Not that she'd been around that many. Her mother, Aasera, had seen to that.

She guessed him to be at least six-four. His hair was as dark as hers, but his eyes were a clear, penetrating green and they seemed to look into her very soul. That was unnerving in itself. But it was more than that. He was the sexiest man she'd ever seen.

And he was going to be her instructor? This wasn't good. Not at all. Was Mr. Beacon unaware of a Nerakian's need for sex? Sure, she was only half Nerakian, but she'd noticed the impulses were getting stronger every day.

Nervously, she looked away, and then forced herself to smile at Mr. Beacon as she crossed her legs.

It didn't help. She could still feel the body heat radiating from Roan. This wasn't going to work. How in the world was she going to learn anything from him when all she wanted to do was drool all over him? All her life she'd been around artistic types—writers, painters and poets. They always wore dreamy expressions, lost in their own world. But Roan was . . . was . . . muscle, and hard planes and . . .

No, she wouldn't go down that path. She wasn't here for

sex. Excitement, adventure—that was what she craved. She had a feeling Roan didn't sit idly by and watch the world pass. She imagined he would be the type of man who lived his dreams and adventures. She took a deep, steadying breath. Everything would work out just fine. She would be on a team so it wasn't as though she would be alone with him.

At least he was sitting again. His presence didn't quite feel as though it were swallowing her. It was much easier to concentrate on why she was here. She was going to be an elite agent, fighting crime and . . . and putting away the bad guys. Anticipation flittered through her.

She was going to actually do the things she'd only read about in adventure books while growing up at the colony. She'd devoured all the books in the local library, and watched all the secret agent movies she could get her hands on. It was hard to believe she was actually here, and soon she would start her training.

Her gaze strayed toward Roan and she saw that he was checking her out. That was unexpected and unnerving. She quickly looked forward again. Of course he would check her out. He was an agent. Duh. They did stuff like that.

"How was your trip?" Mr. Beacon asked.

"Long," she said as she returned her full attention back to him and off Roan.

Mr. Beacon looked different from the man who'd stayed at the colony. Not as relaxed, but that had only been a cover for him. No wonder he couldn't paint. The man didn't have an artistic bone in his body.

No, Mr. Beacon had chanced upon Lyraka's mother one day, and suspected she was Nerakian. He'd begun to watch her more closely, even renting one of the cabins, hoping to one day recruit her.

After her mother returned to Nerak, he'd recruited Lyraka instead. She'd jumped at the chance to train for the elite force of agents who kept the world safe.

Had she made the right choice? Roan hadn't said or done anything, but he made her nervous the way he seemed to study her every move. She was getting the distinct impression that he didn't even like her. There hadn't been an ounce of welcome in his expression.

Now she was being ridiculous. The trip had been tiresome from East Texas to Colorado, and she wasn't the most experienced driver in the world. She was exhausted, nothing more. The man didn't even know her.

"You're special, Lyraka," Mr. Beacon continued. "For now, I don't want you mingling with other Nerakians, or anyone else for that matter."

Dread washed over her. She closed her eyes for a moment. This was going to be just like her life at the colony. Always watched, always having to be careful of what she said or did so no one would suspect she was part alien. This was the one place she thought would be different. She knew she wasn't like other earthlings, or other Nerakians, but she was tired of being alone.

She made a quick decision and came to her feet. "You know what life was like at my mother's colony, the isolation." She shook her head. "I thought it would be different here. I was wrong." She started to turn away.

"It's only until Roan can teach you how best to use your . . . unique abilities," he hurried on. "Give it a chance, at least. I promise you won't be isolated for long."

She looked at Mr. Beacon, but could see nothing deceiving in his expression. He'd been good at fooling everyone at the colony while he'd studied her mother, though.

But he'd been more than just a guest at the colony. He'd been like a father to her, and had even taught her to drive. She suddenly felt as though she were being tugged in two different directions.

"Please, just give this a chance. That's all I'm asking."

She watched his expression, but saw only sincerity. Maybe

she wouldn't completely trust him, or Roan, but then, she didn't have much of a choice. It was either stay here or make the drive back to the colony. Did she really want to leave? If it did work out, then all the better. "Okay, for a while."

"Good," Mr. Beacon rubbed his hands together. "I know it's late, and you've had a long day. Rest tonight. Tomorrow morning will be early enough for you to start." He turned to Roan. "I took the liberty of having your things moved, and Lyraka's as well, to Building F. I thought it would be better if you had as few interruptions as possible. You'll find everything you need when you get there."

"Remind me later to thank you," Roan said.

His deep voice was like a rush of hot air washing over her. It was raspy, and had a way of touching her in places that hadn't been touched in a long time. She fought down the tingling sensation that quickly spread over her body as her Nerakian blood heated. She would control her sexual urges this time. She would.

Her one and only night of sex had ended in disaster, and she didn't want to repeat the experience. She had a feeling she'd scarred the man for life. Poor Rick.

He'd run back to his cabin before they could finish, but what she had experienced had only whet her appetite for more. Except Rick had been gone the next morning. Since that disaster, she'd tried to keep all her sexual thoughts under control.

Lyraka glanced Roan's way. She could tell by the way his jaw twitched that he wasn't happy about the situation. What was his problem? She wasn't that thrilled, either.

Damn it, she'd hoped for more freedom and the ability to do as she pleased while in training. Rather than show her disappointment, she raised her chin and met his frown when he looked her way. She wasn't afraid of him.

Well, maybe a little. He was really big . . . and had lots of sexy muscles.

Joe came to his feet. "I'll check your progress in a few days."

Roan stood. She did the same. So this was it. The beginning of a new life.

She chewed her bottom lip.

But no sex. Her gaze moved to Roan. She would just take a lot of cold showers. And hope they worked.

Chapter 2

Lyraka followed Roan outside to an olive green Jeep that was parked in front of the building. She cast one last glance at the building before she stepped off the curb. It would have been nice training with other people, and probably safer—for him.

Roan climbed in on the driver's side, tossing a manila envelope into the backseat. Lyraka slid in on the passenger side. Even with a gear shift between them, he was way too close to suit her. When she inhaled, she caught the spicy scent of his aftershave. It was a little too nice, a little too pleasant. She subtly moved closer to her door.

"I won't bite," he spoke gruffly, breaking the silence.

No, but she might.

Roan would be training her. She would need to get used to being around him. Easier said than done. His presence filled the Jeep.

"I didn't think you would bite," she told him. "Most earthlings aren't cannibals."

He snorted. She wasn't sure if it was meant to be a laugh or not.

"You don't like me very much, do you?" She might as well bring her thoughts out into the open. She wanted to know why he disliked her so much. She hadn't done anything to him.

He met her gaze. "You're a means to an end," he said, then returned his attention to the road.

"What exactly does that mean?"

"That as soon as you're trained, I get to go back on active duty."

"Why can't you do that now?"

"Do you always ask this many question?"

"No."

He chuckled at her words. The sound was different from the snort of a moment ago. It rippled over her in small waves of excitement. Her nipples tightened in response. This wasn't good. She glanced his way. His shoulders were less tense than they had been when he'd first climbed behind the wheel. Angry was better, safer.

"I was out of commission from an injury. I go back to active duty when I finish training you."

"But you don't want to train me," she guessed.

"I don't, you're right. I think you'll be a distraction more than anything."

"A distraction?"

"Look in the mirror. You're hot and sexy. A distraction."

She didn't know whether to be insulted or flattered. She wasn't sure she liked his answer. Most Nerakians were beautiful. She wasn't that concerned about her looks. "Do you have something against Nerakians?" She looked at him again, but he kept his gaze forward.

"I don't think they're anything special."

She bristled.

"But then, you're only half Nerakian," he said.

She sat straighter. "I'm proud of both sides of my ancestry."

Actually, she hadn't really thought about it that much. She was who she was, and that was all that mattered. Well, until lately. She found she was a little more curious about the Nerakian half of her heritage.

She knew very little about that side. Her mother had rarely spoken of the planet that had disowned her. Lyraka only knew that Nerakians had a heightened sexual awareness, and that chocolate could become an addiction.

She also knew Nerak was a planet populated only by women. After the elders had manipulated the DNA so only females would be born the wars stopped. Her mother, Aasera, had been an intergalactic traveler—until she'd gotten pregnant.

Aasera had been given the choice of aborting the pregnancy and returning to Nerak, or being exiled on Earth. Lyraka knew the decision had been difficult for her mother. She'd had to give up everything.

Aasera had protected Lyraka as best she could over the years so that Lyraka wouldn't make the same mistake. But the one night, well, almost a whole night, she had spent with a poet had awakened desires inside her that she was finding hard to keep under control.

She closed her eyes for a moment. It had been really good while it lasted. Lights had flashed around her. She'd in turn absorbed their color, her skin turning shades of deep purple, hot red, and cool blue.

The Jeep hit a bump in the road and she was thrown off balance. She quickly righted herself as she pulled her thoughts back to the present. She refused to relive that night. Poor Rick had been as white as a sheet of paper. She'd quickly realized he wasn't having nearly as much fun as she was having. What little she'd experienced though had been earth shattering.

If they'd have finished, she was pretty sure it would've been an awesome encounter. She had a feeling she was going to be doomed to a celibate life.

She glanced out the window at the trees on her side as they traveled higher into the mountains. For a moment, she longed to escape to the quiet serenity the woods would offer. They had always been as much a part of her as the colony. It was good to know they were close enough that she could lose herself in the fragrant scents and peace they had to offer if things became too chaotic.

Lyraka and Roan made the rest of the trip in silence, but

she couldn't help notice when Roan slid his hand along the curve of the steering wheel, absently stroking it with his thumb. She drew in a ragged breath and closed her eyes.

Why did Nerakians have to be such a passionate race? That was how her mother had ended up pregnant. A baby would be nice someday, but not at this time in her life.

"Home sweet home," Roan muttered as he pulled in front of the two-story building.

A cold shiver of foreboding swept over Lyraka as she stared at the stark, and very sterile, building. It was nothing like her mother's colony where there were bubbling fountains and fragrant flowers. This place looked institutional.

They got out of the Jeep and walked to the front door. It opened as they approached, and a man stepped outside. A very tall man, almost as tall as Roan, with broad shoulders. She wondered if he worked for the agency, too.

"We've been expecting you," the man said. "I'm Cole." An older woman joined him. "This is Frances."

Roan's eyes narrowed. "I was told we'd be working alone."

Cole smiled. "And so you will. We take care of the place. We'll be here but you won't really see us that much."

Roan took a phone out of his pocket and flipped it open. After he punched in some numbers he put it next to his ear.

"You said we'd be alone. Two of them. Yes, a man and a woman." He frowned. "Next time, tell me your plans before I blow off someone's head."

That's when Lyraka noticed Roan's hand was resting on the butt of a gun that was under his jacket. His stance had looked so casual that she hadn't noticed anything out of the ordinary.

"Joe should've told you about us." Cole shook his head. "I hate when he leaves out details."

"So you're what—a butler?" Roan asked as he replaced his phone.

Cole frowned. "Retired agent. I still like to help out, and I'm an extra pair of hands if needed."

"Sorry."

"I'll be preparing all the meals," Frances said. "I've been told I'm a good cook, and I do the housecleaning, too."

Lyraka thought the woman was a little abrupt. She had a feeling Frances might have a military background.

"Your rooms are across from each other," Frances continued as she started back inside.

Everyone followed.

"Second floor," she continued. "Roan's is the first room on the left, and Lyraka, I put you in the one across from him. I serve meals at nine, one and six. If you'd like the times changed, just let me know, otherwise we'll stay out of your way. We leave at seven in the evening, and return at eight the next morning. If you require something, you can leave a note here," she pointed to a desk in the hallway where there was a pad and pen.

"She runs a tight ship," Cole said with a twinkle in his eye.

Frances frowned. "I'm organized."

"The times to eat are fine," Roan said with little warmth.

Was he always this abrupt? He was going to be a lot of fun to be around. Yeah, right.

"If there's nothing you require, we'll leave you to get acquainted with your new home." They disappeared around a corner when Roan didn't say anything.

It wasn't exactly a homey atmosphere. There was nothing personal. Not even a picture on the wall. Lyraka had to remind herself that she'd wanted something different from what she'd known her whole life. It would just take a little adjusting on her part. She started up the stairs.

"Where are you going?" Roan asked.

"I thought I'd check out my room." He sounded awfully bossy, much like Frances, and she was getting a little tired of people telling her what to do.

"Wait."

"Why?"

"Your first lesson: treat everything as hostile."

She raised an eyebrow. "Like almost blowing away the help?"

His expression wasn't happy. "You can't be too cautious."

"I can take care of myself."

His gaze slowly roamed over her in a way that made her body go from hot to hotter. He really, really shouldn't look at her like that.

"That's my job from now on. Joe said your . . . abilities were different. That you needed more control and discipline."

"My abilities?"

"Joe told me your skills weren't the same as other Nerakians." His gaze moved over her again. "I can't see where you could be a national threat or anything. Most pure bred Nerakians don't have much power, if you ask me."

So Mr. Beacon hadn't mentioned that instead of lessening her abilities because she was half earthling, her skills were greater than anyone could imagine. It would be interesting to see his reaction.

She sauntered closer to him. "I think it goes deeper than you not wanting to be stuck training me. You really don't like me very much, do you?"

His gaze dropped to her lips and she could almost feel the warmth of his brushing across hers, but then he frowned again. He did that a lot.

"I don't have any feelings for you one way or another, lady."

She could actually accept him not liking her. She wasn't that crazy about him—only his body. It was time she got a little even, though.

"He was right you know," she told him.

"Who was right?"

"Mr. Beacon. My abilities are different."

"Whatever. I'll check the upstairs. Don't come up until I give the all clear."

"I don't take orders well."

"It's time you learned." He walked to the steps, stopping halfway and looking back at her. "I'm the boss while you're here." He turned and continued up the stairs.

Roan felt a brush of air and looked over his shoulder, his hand automatically reaching inside his jacket, resting on his gun, but the breeze hadn't come from an opened door. He turned back around and saw Lyraka at the top of the stairs. His gaze jerked back to where she'd been standing, then back to the top of the stairs.

"Like I said," Lyraka began, "I don't take orders very well." She sauntered toward her room.

How the hell had she made it past him! No one could move that fast. No one!

Crap! He should've made Joe explain more about Lyraka. Roan had assumed she'd be like all the others. He ran a hand through his hair. He had a feeling this assignment had just gotten a whole lot harder.

Chapter 3

"What the hell was that?" Roan asked as he burst inside Lyraka's room.

"What was what?" She stood at the window, looking at the dense trees.

"You know damn well what I mean."

Yeah, she did. She was stalling. He'd pissed her off, and she'd wanted to get even with him, with Mr. Beacon, with the fact she was being isolated again.

She turned, and for just a second, forgot what she was going to say. It wasn't fair that one man should look this devastatingly attractive, nor should her over active hormones be raging this much.

But he was, and they were.

"That was one of my abilities," she said. "I can move really fast. Want me to show you again?" She raised her eyebrows in question. "Maybe you didn't see it the first time."

Before he could answer, she moved to stand behind him. Now she was showing off and she knew it, but for a very long time she'd hidden most of her skills, not wanting to draw attention to herself. There was a sense of freedom that came with showing Roan exactly what she was capable of doing, and that she wasn't like every other Nerakian he'd trained.

"Did you see me that time?" she whispered, smirking, and not caring that she did.

He whirled around, grasping her shoulders so she couldn't move. Oops, she hadn't been expecting that.

"If you think you're being funny, you're not."

Even with him holding her, feeling the heat of his hands on her shoulders, she still couldn't help goading him just a little more. "But you're impressed, aren't you?"

It was rather interesting taunting him. She'd never felt this energy running through her before. She'd always been quiet and obedient and stayed in the background, as her mother had warned her to do. No one could discover they weren't quite normal.

But now, for the first time in her life, she felt alive. "Maybe you're thinking that you judged me too quickly? That I might be more than you bargained for?"

He let go of her as if to say he didn't give a damn if she left the room or not.

"You're fast."

He pulled his gun from under his jacket and held it up before she could think to move out of harm's way, not that he was actually pointing it at her.

"But I'd wager even you can't stop a bullet," he said.

Anger boiled inside her. He'd turned the tables on her, and she didn't like it. "Are you sure?" No, she couldn't stop a bullet but he didn't have to be so damned cocky about it.

His expression darkened. "Someone else might have been tempted to find out. This might be a game to you, but it isn't to me. If you're going to be on the elite force, you have to learn to follow the rules."

"We don't officially start until tomorrow, right?" she asked.

"Yeah."

"Then if you don't mind, leave." She stepped out of his way so he could walk past her and out the door.

He holstered his gun. "Anything you say, sweetheart."

He went around her, leaving her door open. She walked over, tempted to slam it. Instead, she very calmly closed it and reached inside her purse for her cell phone, then punched in Mr. Beacon's private number.

"Please tell me you haven't killed Roan," Mr. Beacon said before she could say a word.

She flopped down on the side of the bed. "If you knew what kind of a man he was, why did you pick him as my instructor?"

Silence.

She frowned.

"You didn't kill him, did you?"

"Why? Would he be such a great loss?" Mr. Beacon didn't know all her skills, but she couldn't just kill someone. What'd he think, that she'd vaporize people with one look? It was a tempting thought.

Silence.

"No, Mr. Beacon, I didn't kill Roan—yet."

His sigh of relief was audible. "I picked Roan because he's the best. He'll be able to train you in all areas of covert operations. And call me Joe. We're not so formal here."

She leaned back against the pillow and stared at the dull white ceiling. "Okay, Joe. Now tell me how Roan is going to complete my training in a few weeks?"

"It'll probably take longer," he hedged.

"But he thinks he'll be going back to field work pretty soon. Does he even know I'm not a warrior?"

"Not exactly."

She rolled her eyes. "He's not going to be happy."

"I don't think he'll mind too much once he witnesses some of your extraordinary abilities."

"Yeah, but I might."

"Just give it a little time. Roan has a tendency to grow on people."

"My mother once told me there's a species that grows on people. I'm not sure I want Roan to grow on me."

Joe chuckled. "That's what I like about you, Lyraka. You have a great sense of humor."

"Oh, yeah, I'm a regular comedian."

They talked a few more minutes and then said good-bye. She didn't feel the least bit reassured. Her gaze moved to the window. She didn't want to stay cooped up inside. Not when she was surrounded by woods just waiting for her to explore.

She opened the closet. Her clothes had been neatly put away. She changed out of her dark slacks and pulled on a pair of jeans and a dark green T-shirt. She traded her heels for socks and heavy, lace-up, hiking boots.

Lyraka made sure the coast was clear before she slipped out of her room and down the stairs. She needed space—air she could breathe without sharing it with another person. She needed the safety of the woods where she could feel at peace with the world, with herself. Roan had made her jittery and out of sync. It wasn't a feeling she liked.

Once outside, she began to calm down and breathe easier. The air was crisp with a hint of fall as summer began to fade away. The trees became thicker the farther she went. This was where she felt the most serenity. Deep in the woods where there was only the sound of animals and . . .

Her forehead puckered.

And the sound of someone following her. She stopped and listened. Not an animal, unless it was a bear. No, whoever it was walked too carefully to be a big, lumbering bear. But the tread was heavy. It had to be human. She hated that someone had taken it upon himself to disturb her tranquility, and she was pretty sure she knew who it was.

She moved past a tree, then stopped, leaning against it. For a moment, she stood still, eyes closed as she became one with the tree. She was getting faster at blending in. Like a chameleon, her body and her clothing transformed until she actually became part of the tree.

If someone had asked how she did this, she wouldn't know what to tell them, except that it just happened—when she had total concentration. It was the same with her speed and her hearing. She didn't know why she was so fast, or why she was sensitive to sound, she just was.

Whoever followed was getting closer. There was just the slightest noise of rustling in the fallen leaves. It really helped to have better than average hearing. She opened her eyes just enough to see who followed her.

Roan, of course. She'd already guessed as much.

He covertly crept past her.

"I'm sure you're not out for a nightly stroll. I'll just assume you're following me," she said.

Roan whirled around. His gaze quickly scanned the area. "Come out from whatever tree you're hiding behind."

She smiled. He was standing right in front of her. "You mean this one?" She stepped forward. There was barely a foot between them.

"Christ! How the hell did you do that?"

"Do what?" she innocently asked.

"Camouflage yourself with the tree."

"Practice."

"That's a good way to get yourself killed."

"I'm not scared of termites if that's what you're implying."

He closed the space between them. So close she could see flecks of gold in his green eyes. His presence dominated the space. It was all she could do not to step back.

"It's not termites I'm talking about. When I'm startled, sometimes I shoot first, and ask questions later."

"I doubt Joe would like it if you shot me."

"Don't come out here again. Not alone."

She raised her chin. "Like I said, I can take care of myself."

"Can you?" His eyes half closed and before she could stop him, his mouth lowered to hers.

At first, he only brushed his lips across hers. The chill she'd felt earlier quickly left her body as Roan ignited a fire inside her.

His hand moved to the back of her neck and began to massage. She couldn't stop the moan as she leaned in closer, wanting more, needing more. The familiar heat swelled inside her.

He didn't disappoint her as he deepened the kiss, moving his hand from the back of her neck to slide beneath her T-shirt and under her bra as he cupped her breast.

Shocked by his unexpected touch, she stepped back, but he followed her. The tree that had once meant safety now became her prison, but one she wasn't sure she wanted to escape as Roan rubbed his thumb over her hard nipple. Her body began to ache. She could feel the light, the colors.

Did he know what he was doing? Oh, God, yes, he knew exactly what he was doing, and he did it very well.

Rick had said she'd burned him. He had even cried out in pain. What if she did the same thing to Roan? Could she scar a man for life? Would she have an orgasm only to open her eyes afterwards and find a pile of ashes where a man had once been?

Bleh!

But she didn't want him to stop causing the sensations of pleasure that swarmed over her, and she couldn't think straight. Her arms automatically went around his neck.

He pressed closer, his erection pushing against the front of her pants. He nudged against her sex. Roan was making it difficult for her to breathe as the ache inside her grew.

Even Rick had never made her feel anything like this. Not this sudden burst of fire rushing through her. There was no awkward fumbling this time.

No, this wasn't Roan's first time, and she found herself wanting more, even though she wasn't sure she liked him. If this was what it felt like to be slutty, she didn't care, because it felt so damn good.

He abruptly pulled away from her. She grabbed his arms to keep from falling. Her breathing was ragged and filled the air around them.

"There's more than one kind of danger, and you just proved you can't protect yourself." Roan spoke softly, his words caressing her as much as his hands had a moment ago. That was probably why it took longer for the meaning of his words to sink in.

Lyraka shoved away from him, her back bumping the tree. He'd only been using her.

"Like I said," he continued. "Don't go into the woods alone again. And take a couple of aspirins, your skin felt hot. You might be coming down with something. Sick or not, we start your training tomorrow."

She used her speed to move away from him, and didn't stop until she was nearly back at the building. Before stepping from the trees, she dropped down to the ground.

He'd ruined the one place where she'd always been able to find solace. What was worse, he'd used her weakness against her. Of course he would know Nerakians were a passionate race. She hated him!

When she heard his heavier steps, she blended with her surroundings and glared at him. He stopped and looked around as if he sensed she watched him. She held her breath.

"As long as I'm your instructor, you'll follow my orders. If you don't, I'll tell Joe you're not working out. He might like you, but he'll go along with my recommendation. I guess it all comes down to how bad do you want this." He stepped from the woods and walked back toward the building.

She picked up a fistful of leaves and crumbled them in her hands. Roan was an ass. He probably wanted her to quit so he could be released to go back to active duty.

When Joe had told her about the elite force, she'd jumped at the chance. This was an opportunity to use her gifts. She didn't want to hide who she was any longer. She'd been doing that all her life. Growing up had been like living in a closed room where there was no light, no windows, but now the door was open, and she actually had the opportunity to do something she could be proud of.

At least, Lyraka hoped she could. Joe had already told her the training would be intense and that she would have a lot to learn in a short period of time. Only the best made it through his boot camp, and then there was more training. Maybe she wouldn't be good enough.

One thing she knew for sure, she wouldn't give Roan the satisfaction of knowing he'd made her quit.

Roan stomped back inside the building, but before he could close the door a breeze swept past him. He caught just a glimpse of short dark hair and the light fragrance Lyraka wore.

He'd had a feeling she was going to be some kind of pissed off at him for kissing her, then leaving her wanting more. He'd been right.

This wasn't the way to start off her training. Damn it, he shouldn't have kissed her. Now he'd be thinking about how she'd tasted, how her breast had felt cupped in his hand, the way her nipple had hardened when he'd brushed his thumb over it.

He stopped just inside and took a deep breath. He didn't need that image in his head, not when he was stuck in the middle of nowhere, with a woman he knew would join him in his bed with very little encouragement on his part. At least, in that respect, she was like all the other Nerakians he'd ever met. But he'd never taken one to his bed. None had ever tempted him, at least, until now.

He started up to his room, but changed his mind and went in the opposite direction. The building they were staying in was small and industrial looking. There certainly wasn't a feeling of home and hearth. But then, he had a job to do and he needed to make sure he remembered that. Getting cozy was not on his agenda, no matter how tempting Lyraka was. Better to get the lay of the building than to lay her.

The kitchen was to his right so he went to the left. There was a living room of sorts with a big fireplace, a couple of chairs, a coffee table, and a sofa just off the main entry. This room came closer to being comfortable.

The living room opened into the training area. It was about

half the size of a gym and was equipped with treadmills and weights—all the equipment anyone would need to stay in shape. He walked closer, then frowned. There were also machines to gauge one's performance. Joe could've forewarned him about Lyraka's abilities. His boss had a sick sense of humor.

Just off the gym was a classroom where he'd teach Lyraka the fundamentals of the force—bookwork. The one thing that every trainee detested, including the Nerakians.

Most of them were more like psychics. They could sense things others couldn't. There were a couple of warriors in the bunch—which was a joke. Their planet was at peace.

Warriors without a war. But they were trained, and some of them were pretty good fighters. He figured Lyraka was in that group since Joe said it should only take a few weeks to train her. It didn't mean he had to like doing it though.

Every last Nerakian was a female. Not a man among them.

That wasn't right. Not right at all.

The Nerakians knew about the universe and some of the other species that inhabited neighboring planets so the agency used the knowledge of the ones who'd left Nerak looking for something more.

Not that the Nerakians were getting much action on Earth. So far, the force hadn't had any trouble keeping the peace in the third zone, but it always paid to stay on one's toes. He didn't trust any aliens.

Especially Lyraka, now that he knew her skills went beyond the norm. No wonder Joe had practically been salivating when he talked about her. Her speed was phenomenal. But this camouflage thing she had was something else.

Excitement coursed through his veins at the thought of training someone like her. What other abilities did she have? His gaze moved upward, toward her room. He looked forward to finding out.

Except for the fact that she was probably put off by him right now. Not that he could really blame her. He hadn't acted like Mr. Charm.

He ran a hand through his hair. He wasn't even that irritated with her. Joe was the one who'd pissed him off. Roan could only take so much when it came to training people. He wanted to get back to actually working, rather than talking about it.

As long as the third zone was quiet, agents only had to make a couple of flybys to let other inhabitants know they were watching. The rest of the time he could do investigative work, maybe some undercover. With his clearance code, the possibilities were endless.

He walked out of the training area, glanced toward the stairs once more, and knew deep down inside himself that this assignment wasn't going to be as dreary as he'd first thought. His pulse sped up at the thought of working with Lyraka. He didn't think it was all because of her skills, either.

He'd pushed a button in her this afternoon, and she'd shown him what she could do. He wondered how many buttons he would need to push to find out all her secrets.

Chapter 4

Dinner that night was quiet. Lyraka sat at one end of a long table and Roan at the other. Frances had silently served them. As soon as they finished the meal, Lyraka moved to what she supposed could be called a living room.

The only thing that kept it from being cold and stark was the furniture and the fireplace. There were no pictures on the wall, no throws or pillows on the sofa or chair.

Shivers ran down her spine. There was a chill in the evening air that the crackling fire didn't quite remove, but she had a feeling that came more from Roan than the actual temperature. He'd spoken barely two words to her, but that was okay. After the incident in the woods, she wasn't sure she wanted to make idle conversation with him.

She walked closer to the fire and held out her hands in front of it, absorbing some of its warmth. She supposed Cole had started it. She had caught glimpses of him, but otherwise he and Frances had done exactly what they said they would do—stay in the background. It was nice to know she and Roan weren't the only two in the building.

Even at the colony, she hadn't felt this isolated from the outside world. She suddenly had a deep longing for home, and the comfortable silence that existed between her and her mother. Sometimes Aasera would read poetry, or they would walk beneath the night sky. As an explorer, her mother had told her all about the stars.

But Aasera was back on Nerak. She'd returned only once to Earth to make sure Lyraka was all right. Her mother had fairly glowed with happiness. Jealousy had flittered through Lyraka because her mother was training other Nerakians to explore. Once again, Aasera's world was exciting. Lyraka had never seen her mother so full of life.

It hurt, and she felt even more lonely, she wouldn't deny it. On the other hand, she couldn't take away her mother's joy. Not when the longing to return to Nerak had burned in Aasera's eyes the few times she'd mentioned her home planet. Lyraka was glad for her.

Although Lyraka missed her mother more than she thought she ever could, she'd told her everything was fine and that Mr. Beacon would take good care of her. He would, too. She wasn't so sure about Roan, though.

She glanced toward him and hoped she hadn't lied to her mother, albeit unknowingly. Lyraka wasn't so sure Roan would look out for her best interest. She glanced in his direction as he sat in one of the chairs in front of the fireplace, legs stretched out in front of him.

What was he thinking about? Was he remembering when he'd kissed her? Not likely. Roan had probably known many women, had made love to most of them. She was certain sharing one kiss with her wouldn't affect him one way or the other.

But it had her. More than she wanted to even think about. How could she enjoy when a man held her close, and hate him at the same time?

She moved away from the fireplace and stood in front of the window, staring at the blackness outside. She didn't need any more heat.

God, what was she doing here? If she was home, she'd take a walk to ease the restlessness growing inside her. She was even more restricted than before. Roan would probably get pissed if she even suggested going for a walk.

Anger flared inside her, but just as quickly was gone. She wanted to become a part of this elite force more than anything. If she went against Roan's demands, he would tell Joe about her non-compliance and it would all be over, then where would she be?

For a brief moment, headlights illuminated the trees. Cole and Frances were leaving for the evening. She was alone with Roan, and she was very aware of his presence. She might not like him that much but she couldn't stop the quickening of her pulse. There was just enough Nerakian blood flowing through her veins that her lust was strong, and enough Earth blood to be really pissed at him, all at the same time.

"We'll start early in the morning," he said, breaking the silence of the room.

She looked at him, then turned back to the window. "I always wake early." There was something peaceful about walking through the woods in the early morning when the dew kissed the earth. When the sun broke through the trees, the ground shimmered like diamonds.

Aasera had said there were lots of gems on Nerak. Diamonds as big as her thumb. Emeralds, rubies . . . stones that sparkled in the light of the bright sunshine. Someday she would like to go there.

Not that she thought that would ever really happen. She would probably be an outcast—not an earthling, not Nerakian. She wasn't quite sure exactly who she was.

Now she was getting maudlin. She knew who she was. She just wasn't sure exactly where she fit in. She was a square peg trying to fit into a round hole.

"Do you play chess?" Roan asked.

"No," she said without looking at him. They'd already played enough games for one day.

"Checkers?"

"No." She glanced at him.

He stood and again she marveled at just how tall he was. If he ever came to her mother's home he would have to duck just to get past the door. Not that she thought he'd ever visit.

"I noticed some board games when I was looking around earlier."

He went to a cabinet and opened it. There were stacks of boxed games. They seemed out of place here.

"I told you that I don't know how to play either of those games." What? Now he was trying to be Mr. Nice Guy?

"Then it's time you learned. I'll take it easy on you. We'll start off with checkers."

"Easy on me?" She was very smart and learned quickly. No one had to take it easy on her. But it still didn't mean she wanted to learn what would probably prove to be a very boring game.

He dragged his chair over to the coffee table and sat down, removing the board from the box. When he had it set up, he looked at her. "It's kind of hard to play from over there. Unless you have elastic arms or something."

"No, my arms don't stretch." Ass.

"Then let's play."

She frowned. It wasn't as though she had plans for tonight, unless she wanted to meditate in her room. She'd never enjoyed sitting in a corner with her legs crossed, thinking about absolutely nothing.

Okay, she'd play his stupid game. She dragged the other chair over, sitting across from him.

"You're black and I'm red," he said.

"Why do I have to be black?" Her favorite color was red, not black.

He turned the board so that the red disks faced her. "Okay, you're red. Better?"

She shrugged. It hadn't mattered that much, but since there was a choice, she'd rather be red. Roan probably thought she was spoiled and had to have her way. Not that she cared what he thought.

"The object of the game is to win my black pieces by moving around the board."

"How do I win them?" She stared at the board.

He quickly explained the rules which sounded simple enough.

"You move first," he said.

It was probably a trick. If she moved first, he would take her red game piece. "No, you move first."

"Whatever." He moved out. "Your turn."

He hadn't left himself unprotected so she couldn't steal his checker. She moved hers, he moved one of his, she moved hers, he moved his, then she moved again. He jumped two of her checkers and scooped them up. She frowned when she looked at him. "You took my checkers."

He raised his eyebrows. "That *is* the object of the game."

It might be the object of the game but she didn't have any of his. She was losing and it didn't sit very well with her.

She moved again, careful to protect her red pieces this time. He moved, leaving a checker vulnerable. She jumped him, gloating when she picked up his black chip. As she had first thought, this was a simple game and she did catch on fast. She made a production out of setting his chip on her side.

He jumped the piece that she'd used to take his, then had the nerve to gloat.

That hadn't been very nice.

"Your turn," he told her.

She glared at him. "I know." Leaning forward, she stared at the game board, calculating her next move. Five minutes later, she moved. He quickly followed her chip with his black one.

So, that was his strategy. He was trying to trap her. She studied the board, then moved a checker three rows over. He advanced another square. She moved in for the kill and jumped his. He jumped both hers.

"King me," he said.

Her frown deepened. That's exactly what she'd like to do!

But instead of turning violent, she placed one of her hard earned black chips on top of his. Then she studied the board again. She wanted a king. And why did they call it king, anyway. She'd call hers queens.

Roan watched Lyraka as she gazed intently at the board. Amazing how much you could learn from someone just playing a board game. She hated losing and didn't easily give up. No, she studied each one of his moves, weighed the risks, then moved her piece. She wouldn't win this game, but he had no doubt she would be winning before the night was over. He liked the way she thought out what she was going to do before she did it, rather than blindly rushing in.

She jumped three of his black pieces. He sat forward. How had she done that? He scanned the board. Did she maneuver him into position, or had it just been dumb luck? He looked at her. She smirked. For a moment, he forgot all about the game as he got lost in her eyes. When she turned her attention to taking his three checkers, the spell was broken.

"Good move," he told her.

"Yes, I know."

"Your modesty is admirable."

She laughed. The sound washed over him, touching him, caressing him. Was tempting men beyond reason another of her gifts?

"I won your pieces fair and square because I outthought you."

"You think so?"

"I know so."

He rested his elbows on his knees and studied every angle of the board. She would be a good opponent.

"Are you going to move or do you give up?" she said, breaking his concentration.

"What?"

"You've been studying the board for ten minutes."

He glanced at the clock on the wall. Actually, it had only

been nine. He looked back at the board again, then made his move.

She studied the board, then moved. He only took a few minutes this time. She was falling into his trap just as he planned. She moved. He moved. One more and he'd have her. She jumped the rest of his checkers and scooped them off the board.

How the hell had she done that? He looked at the board and immediately realized where he'd made a wrong move. Again he had to wonder if it had been skill or luck.

"You're not very good at checkers, are you?" she gloated.

"You got lucky."

"Sore loser?"

"You won't win the next one."

Five games later, and nearing eleven on the wall clock, Lyraka had won three out of five games. Maybe it hadn't been dumb luck. She was pretty good at figuring out her opponent's strategy.

She stood, stretching her arms above her head, revealing an expanse of creamy skin and a sexy little belly button. The only things going through his mind were how soft her skin actually felt, and how it was all he could do to restrain himself from pulling her into his lap and kissing her into submission.

"I'm beat," she said. "It's been a long day, and you did say we'd start at six."

He wouldn't tell her he'd already started his evaluation of her with the games of checkers they'd played. There were more ways to see how a person ticked than answering silly questions on a form some doctor made up when he was bored and didn't have anything better to do. No, Roan had his own way of doing things.

"Yes, six. I'll see you in the morning," he said.

She nodded as she headed for the stairs. Man, she had a nice walk. There was just enough sway in her hips to heat his blood. Her tight jeans hugged her ass in a way that made him almost jealous.

Damn, how the hell did Joe expect him to stay here in an isolated building, alone at night, with a woman who looked hot and sexy, and not touch her? Especially now that he knew she wasn't repulsed by him. The situation was almost impossible. If it wasn't for the fact that Joe had promised to let him return to active duty, Roan would have insisted someone else train Lyraka.

His problem wasn't that he wanted to make love to her, that was pretty much inevitable. No, his problem was not knowing how long he could survive until he did sleep with her.

Things were going to get complicated.

He put away the game board and the checkers, then went to the front door and stepped out. The night air was cool and crisp. So different from the city noises. A coyote howled, a deeply mournful sound. Roan took a couple of deep breaths, then went back inside and locked the door before going up to his room to get ready for bed.

He wore pajama bottoms, but that was all, and only because of Lyraka just in case something happened and he had to hurry from the room. He didn't want to send her into shock.

He picked up the manila envelope Joe had given him and dumped out the papers. There weren't that many. He began to read.

Joe mentioned her speed, but that was all. Apparently, he didn't know she could blend in with her surroundings. He flipped through the pages, skimming mostly, then replaced the papers and placed the envelope on his dresser.

Lyraka had lived at an artist colony all her life, been home schooled by an over protective mother—hell, Lyraka was probably a virgin. Oh, yeah, now he felt a hell of a lot better.

God, he was in such deep shit. A Nerakian virgin. If her powers were strengthened because she was of mixed blood, what happened when she made love? He'd heard all sorts of locker room tales. Some of the men had actually been leery of repeating the experience. He hadn't paid a lot of attention to their stories. Now, he kind of wished he'd listened a little more carefully.

Had he awakened Lyraka's sexual drive?

He dragged his fingers through his hair. Man, coming on to her in the woods had been low. Her Nerakian side had been hot and bothered in record time. Crap, not one day had passed and he'd already made a mess of things.

He sat on the side of his bed. Heat washed over him. He'd enjoyed kissing her, and it had been nice the way her breast had fit perfectly in the palm of his hand.

Go to sleep, Roan. Forget about her.

The little voice inside his head was right. He didn't want to get mixed up with a Nerakian, even if she was half earthling. They only spelled trouble as far as he was concerned.

He switched off the light, then lay back in the bed and closed his eyes, but sleep was a long time coming. When he did finally fall asleep, he dreamt of Lyraka and her naked body pressed against his, her hands roaming over his naked skin, drawing him closer before spreading her thighs in open invitation.

Sometime during the night Roan woke and reached for her, only to find that side of the bed empty. He cursed, flopped to his other side and closed his eyes as he prayed for peaceful sleep without visions of Lyraka.

Except it didn't happen.

Roan was in a foul mood when his alarm went off the next morning. He grabbed his clothes and headed toward the bathroom that was farther down the hall, knowing a shower might wake him up. He seriously doubted he would feel much better than he did now—which was pretty much like death warmed over.

He turned the knob. It was locked. He could hear faint humming on the other side.

Lyraka.

He rattled the doorknob.

"Just a minute."

He leaned against the door facing and waited. A few moments later, she opened it, looking like a breath of fresh air. His gaze slid lazily over her. She wore deep blue leggings that clung to her incredibly long limbs and a light blue T-shirt that reached the top of her thighs.

Had she not been tormented by dreams of them making love? He frowned. Apparently not.

"Roan, you look bad. What's the matter? Didn't sleep well?"

"You could say that," he grumbled as he went inside the bathroom and closed the door. Her expression said it didn't bother her a bit that he hadn't slept well. Hell, she probably relished his discomfort.

"I'll meet you downstairs," she called to him.

"Whatever." He untied the string to his pajamas and let them drop to the floor. As soon as the water was warm, he stepped under the spray and just stood there, letting the water sluice over him.

Thirty minutes later, he admitted to himself that he felt better after a shower and a shave, but he still needed his coffee. He glanced at his watch. A quarter till six. He'd have to make it fast.

But once he got to the kitchen, the coffee was already made. The tantalizing smell filled the room. Nectar of the gods. He went straight to the cabinet, got a cup, poured himself some, then savored the first drink.

"You really get into your coffee, don't you?" Lyraka commented.

He hadn't even noticed her. He'd been too intent on getting his first cup down before they started their day.

He raised his cup. "Thanks for putting a pot on."

"Don't thank me. It was on a timer. Frances probably started it."

"Then bless Frances." He finished his first cup and poured another, noticing she drank orange juice rather than coffee.

He could almost see the excitement oozing from her. Rookies. They'd be the death of him. Joe had told him all he needed to do was teach her the basics. She wouldn't be put in the field until he knew she was ready. Joe was like that. Most Nerakians were used for their brains and abilities, rather than fighting. That pretty much pissed off the warriors, except for one or two who showed exceptional fighting abilities and actually were chosen for field work.

Joe wanted Lyraka to sharpen her fighting tactics. That told Roan all he needed to know—Lyraka was going to be used for more than her brains. Roan could understand why, since witnessing her speed and ability to blend in with her surroundings.

"Ready?" he asked.

She nodded as she set her empty glass in the sink.

He watched her as they walked inside the training center—saw the excited expression on her face. Saw the way she tried to take all the equipment in at one glance.

"What are we going to do first?" she asked, the words practically bubbling out of her.

He knew what he'd like to do. He quickly cleared those kinds of thoughts from his mind.

"We're going to see what you can do." He set his coffee cup down on the desk. Top secret, Joe had said. Find out everything she can do. He had a feeling sex did not enter into the equation, though.

But Lyraka was definitely tempting.

It had only been a couple of nights since he'd been with a woman, but damn if it didn't seem longer than that. There was just something about Lyraka that made him think about making slow sweet love all day long.

Yeah, she was definitely going to be a temptation.

Chapter 5

Lyraka was not having fun. She glared at Roan. He'd had her running on the treadmill for nearly an hour. Oh, but first he'd stuck little tabs on her face, arms, wrists and ankles. Then he'd attached wires to the tabs and hooked her up to some stupid machine that beeped—a lot. So much it was starting to sound like fingernails on a chalkboard.

He jotted something down on a clipboard, then peered at the machine again. "Can you pick up the pace a little?"

Murder would be too good for him and this stupid elite force. She glared at him, even though he wasn't looking at her, and increased the speed of the treadmill—again.

She was a guinea pig to them. A stupid lab rat. What was she learning by running in one spot? This wasn't how it was supposed to be and she'd had enough!

Roan wanted faster? She jabbed the button three more times and her pace shot up. Oh, yeah, she'd give him speed that was off the charts. Her legs moved faster and faster. She jabbed the button again, then again for good measure.

"Slow down just a little," he said without looking at her.

She jabbed it again.

"That's good, Lyraka. Go ahead and slow down."

She gritted her teeth.

"Lyraka?" He finally turned his attention to her. "Is something the matter?"

Is something the matter? Her eyes narrowed on him.

His gaze dropped to her legs. "The machine is starting to smoke. I'd hate for it to break apart while you're running on it," he stated matter of factly before turning back to the gauges.

He only cared about the stupid machine, not her. She jabbed the decrease speed button several times. It wasn't her intention to splatter against the wall behind her. He was right, she could smell rubber burning.

The machine began to slow. She bumped the button a few more times. As soon as she came to a complete stop, she jerked the wires and pads from her body.

"Is something wrong?" he asked again.

"Yes, there's plenty wrong. I didn't join the elite force to be used as a guinea pig. I joined so I could do something useful with my abilities." Her voice rose with each word. When she finished, she was breathing hard. More so than when she'd been running.

"But first we need to see exactly what you can do," he explained in a calm voice.

"I'm tired of running." She clamped her lips together.

He glanced at his watch. "I have enough data on your speed anyway. Let's move to the weights."

She didn't move off the treadmill. It wasn't fair that she was isolated, then having a battery of tests run on her.

"You do want to join the force, right? If you've changed your mind let me know now, before you waste any more of my time." He waited for her to do something.

It all came back to that one question. She already knew the answer. "This isn't what I expected," she said, but moved to where weights were lined up on metal rods.

"It rarely is." He set the clipboard down. "Okay, let's start with a barbell." He loaded it with two weights on either end, then faced her. "Ready?"

"Whatever." She stood in front of him. He handed her the barbell. She took it, and was fine until he let go. She stumbled into him, her body crushed against his, which would've been sexy as hell if the barbell hadn't been between them.

"What are you trying to do—kill me?" she asked.

He frowned. "It's only a couple hundred pounds."

"Only a couple hundred pounds," she sputtered. "What? Do you think I'm an Amazon or something?"

He set the barbell on the floor, frowning. "You run fast."

"So throw a weight at me and I'll outrun it. Just because I can run fast doesn't mean I'm ready to enter a strongman tournament."

"I just thought . . ."

She raised an eyebrow.

He frowned. "Okay, then how much weight can you lift?"

She went to the dumbbells and lifted a five pound weight, then an eight. "Eight is about right. Can we get to some actual training?"

"First the weights, then I'll go over a few moves with you, if it'll make you happy."

She raised her chin. "Yes, it will." At least she was getting somewhere. She lifted the weight, then lowered it.

"You're not doing it right," he said.

"How would I know what's right or wrong? I don't normally lift weights."

"That's probably why you're not as tight as you could be."

"I beg your pardon." Now he was telling her she was flabby? There wasn't an ounce of flab on her.

"Don't get your nose out of joint. I didn't say you were fat or anything. I said you're not as toned as you could be."

She arched an eyebrow.

"The average woman would probably be envious of your body, but you won't be just an average woman, you'll be one of the elite force. They're toned from working all of their body."

"Well, excuse me that I didn't have access to a gym," she retorted.

"No problem. I'll get you in shape."

She just bet he would. She only hoped he didn't kill her in the process.

He proceeded to show her the proper way to raise and lower a weight. She couldn't help wondering what would happen if she dropped one of them on his foot. Would he buy her story that it was an accident? Probably not.

"Concentrate," he told her.

"Why?" It was a stupid weight. What was there to think about?

"You want to focus on the muscle group you're working. Concentrate on raising the weight, then slowly lowering it, not just letting it fall back into place."

He stepped closer and took her arm, then slowly raised and lowered it. His touch was gentle, almost like a caress. He stood close enough she could smell his aftershave—spicy, a heady scent that made her long to lean closer, and just inhale. Then he moved away, and the spell he'd momentarily cast over her was gone.

Not that she would have leaned closer. She had a feeling he had a major problem with his ego—as in over-inflated.

"Whatever," she said to cover the flurry of emotions that swirled inside her.

After twenty repetitions of raising and lowering the weight, she wished she'd chosen the lighter one. Maybe she did need to work on upper body strength training more.

He jotted something down on his clipboard again. She raised the weight five more times. What if he kept her doing this for an hour, like he'd done with the treadmill? She couldn't raise and lower the weight for an hour. Her arms were already starting to burn and ache.

"Getting tired already?" He frowned.

She gritted her teeth. "Of course not." She forced the weight over her head, then lowered it again.

"You look like you're getting tired."

"Well, I'm not. You made me lose my concentration." She wouldn't quit now if her arms fell off—which could happen any minute, judging from the way they burned all the way to the bone. She refused to quit and give him the satisfaction. He probably thought she'd give up because this wasn't one of her strengths. But then, he really didn't know her very well.

Roan jotted something on his clipboard, but watched Lyraka from the corner of his eye. Her arms had begun to tremble. She was pushing herself past her level of endurance, reaching beyond what she would normally do. It showed a lot of strength in her character. That, and stubbornness, but sometimes that worked well, too. She'd need that, and a whole lot more, if she wanted to meet the criteria to be an agent. They only took the best of the best.

"You can put the weights up now," he told her.

When she raised them one more time, he had to cough to cover his snort of laughter. She was probably the most stubborn female he'd ever met. He liked that about her. It reminded him a little of himself.

That was a scary thought. The world wasn't ready for two of him.

"Now can we do something where I can actually learn?"

Her look dared him to test her physical agility again. She was almost at the end of her rope, but he wasn't even close to the point where he was ready to stop pushing her.

Roan let his gaze slide over her, slowly, taking in everything from the moisture on her face, to the rise and fall of her chest . . . all the way down to her toes, before returning to her face.

"I'd thought you'd be in better shape than this. The way Joe hinted, I figured you were the answer to his idea of a dream agent."

Her back stiffened. "What do you mean—in better shape?"

He shrugged. "Sure, you have speed, and a few other minor abilities. Like most Nerakians, you're remarkable in a couple of areas. I'd rather be partnered with a cop who has had a little street experience. I doubt you can even fight very well. A warrior who's never been in a war."

"I'm not a warrior."

He opened his mouth, no words came out. Not a warrior? She was green? Just someone Joe had thought would work on a team because she had a few extraordinary abilities?

"You okay? You're turning red."

"Joe wouldn't send me someone who didn't have at least some training."

"I told him you wouldn't be happy."

He dropped the clipboard to the floor. There was no way this was only going to take two weeks. More like months. "He lied to me." When she started to say something, he glared at her. She snapped her mouth shut. "He lied by omission, same thing as an outright lie."

He reached in his pocket and opened his phone, then punched in a speed-dial number.

"Mr. Beacon's office," Sally said.

"Let me talk to Joe. This is Roan."

"Hello, Roan. Joe is in meetings all day."

"No, he isn't."

Silence.

Roan closed his eyes for a second and silently counted to five. He'd bet his last dollar Joe was in his office. "Tell him I know Lyraka isn't a warrior, doesn't have any training whatsoever, and that I think he's a crazy son of a bitch!"

". . . and that he's a crazy . . . Do you really want me to tell him all of that, Roan?"

"Yes," he growled then snapped his phone closed.

"I am very good, you know," Lyraka told him.

"Yeah, right. You've lived a sheltered life at an artist colony. I read your file. How good can you be? I thought maybe you'd been trained along the way in combat maneuvers or something." He eyed her. "You haven't been trained in anything, have you?"

She raised her chin. "I learn fast. That is, if someone has the—" She let her gaze slide down him, stopping just below his waist. "—that is if someone has the *skill* to train me."

"You can't even fight, for Christ's sake!"

"I can, too."

He snorted. "Come on. Show me what you've got." He watched, saw the anger building inside her.

"You want me to hit you?" she asked, pursing her lips.

"Yeah, come at me. Give me your best swing. Unless you're afraid you'll hurt yourself."

She reared back and swung. He stepped out of the way just in time. Damn, she threw a punch better than he'd thought she would, but rather than tell her that, he laughed. "Is that all you've got?"

She growled and lunged again. He dodged and she slipped, going to the floor. Instinct had him moving toward her to help her up, but he quickly tamped down the urge.

"Not very good, are you?"

She got to her feet, anger practically oozing from her pores. She growled and came off the floor, hurling her body at him, but he was ready for her. He caught her to him, pinning her back against his body.

Her sensual scent invaded his space, her soft feminine curves pressed against him and for a moment, all he could think about was the way she felt.

"Let go of me!" she ground out.

"Here's a lesson for you," he said close to her ear as he forced himself to concentrate on anything other than the way she felt, the sexy way she smelled. Not easy when all he thought about right now was the way she would feel if she were naked, and they were in bed together. "Think with your head and not your emotions."

Her body relaxed against him, the tension leaving her. "Are you going to train me?"

His thoughts warred with what he should do, and what he wanted to do. If he walked away, Joe would only send someone else to train her. Roan knew he was the best. He wouldn't let her get herself killed.

"Yeah, I'll train you," he finally said.

"I screwed up when I came at you, didn't I?" she asked.

He swallowed, forcing himself to rein in what he felt. Man, she was so damned addictive and like an addict, he wanted more. He forced himself to let go of her and step away from temptation.

"Most people do fail in the beginning," he said as she turned to face him. She looked genuinely worried, and for a moment he felt a little sorry he'd been so rough on her. "Sometimes it's better to walk away from taunts and jabs that people throw your way. Your goal shouldn't be to get even, but to get away if you're ever caught between a rock and a hard place."

She frowned. "What do you mean?"

"You could've agreed with me and diffused the anger, but you chose to respond to it."

"You think it's better to wimp out?"

"If your life is threatened, yes. Control the situation to your advantage, and you still come out the victor.

"Say you're coming out of a mall and it's later than you'd planned on leaving. You have packages in one hand and your keys in your other. Imagine a man comes at you. The parking lot is dark and no one else is around. Are you going to use the keys as a weapon and charge him like an angry bull? You're better off dropping your packages and running. He's probably bigger and stronger. All you're going to do is piss him off if you try to gouge his eyes out or jab him in the arm."

"You goaded me into fighting back."

"And I overpowered you."

She raised a haughty eyebrow. "This time."

Had she not understood a word he'd said?

"It was a good lesson, though. I'll make sure I think before I act next time."

A slow grin curved his lips. "You think you'll get good enough to beat me?"

"Yes, I do."

He shook his head. "You'll never be strong enough, sweetheart."

"I won't use muscle, I'll use my brain."

"Think you can ever win?"

"Yes."

Damn, he loved her defiance. Not that defiance would get her very far when it came to beating him. He'd been a cop, then an agent, too long. He knew the ropes. But he liked that she might try.

Damn it, this wasn't a sport to win or lose. He had to remember that. What was he thinking? Hell, what was Joe thinking? Lyraka wasn't agent material. She might be able to do more than some, but when it came down to the wire, her extra abilities might not be enough to keep her from getting killed. He didn't want her death on his conscience.

"This isn't a game of checkers, little girl. Losing might cost you your life."

She cocked an eyebrow. "I know exactly why Joe recruited me and the dangers involved. I'm willing to take that risk. And in case you haven't noticed, I'm not a little girl."

His gaze slid seductively down her body before slowly returning to her face. "You're right. I have noticed you're not a little girl." Her cheeks took on a rosy hue. He'd pushed another one of her buttons, but in a different way. He kind of liked the idea that he flustered her.

You're wading off in deep water, Roan. It was a good thing he knew how to swim.

He glanced at his watch. "Let's take a break and eat." Without waiting for her, he walked out of the training area.

Lyraka had done better than he thought she would, and then some. She must want this pretty badly. But there was no way he could have her ready in a few weeks. She'd never had any training. Unless Joe only planned to use her where she wouldn't be in any danger. But with her skills, and one-on-one training, why wouldn't Joe expect Lyraka to go straight into field work?

Damn, with her stubbornness, she'd probably get killed the first day, and Roan would be partially responsible. He didn't want to live with that kind of guilt for the rest of his life.

That had happened to his instructor, John Williams. Man, he'd been good. The best of the best. There'd been a kid in John's class who was one cocky bastard. No one cared that much for him. Hell, Roan hadn't thought he'd make it through training. He was one of those rich kids who wanted to play at being a cop because he was bored, a real jerk-off.

His money was probably what got him through the training. John let the powers that be send the boy out too soon, even though John had argued against it.

The kid had been killed his first day. John had never been the same since. He'd started drinking and ended up taking an early retirement.

Roan stepped into the dining room. The buffet was set up with covered serving dishes, plates and silverware at one end.

Lyraka walked in behind him. "It smells good. I'm starved. I think I'll just wash up first."

He looked at Lyraka, really looked at her. God, she was so young and innocent. Life hadn't left its mark on her yet. As she walked out of the room, he knew he couldn't let Joe send her into the field. Roan wouldn't have her death on his conscience.

It was time to push her training up a few notches, and it was time to take the gloves off. He had to make her see this wasn't the life for her.

If she could take what he dished out, then she might become an agent someday. He could at least make sure she didn't get herself killed. That is, if she lasted long enough.

Chapter 6

Paperwork! Lyraka would rather go back to running on the treadmill than fill out another piece of paperwork. All week it had been paperwork and testing and she was sick of it. She might as well have stayed at the colony. At least she'd have been able to walk in the woods there. She'd been outside the first day she'd arrived for training and that was it. Roan had made sure she was busy the rest of the time.

Enough was enough! She pushed the sheets of paper away from her and scooted her chair back from the desk before coming to her feet.

"Finished?" Roan asked.

"No." She glanced at the clock. "I've been doing paperwork, and exercising, and tests all week and I'm sick of it. The questions on the tests are stupid."

"They are."

Was this another game he was playing? She eyed him with more than a little trepidation. "You're agreeing with me?"

He laid down the book he was reading. She'd seen the cover on the paperback. It was a suspense novel. *He* got to enjoy himself while *she* had to wade through mountains of paperwork. That figured.

"Everyone in the elite force has had to do the same amount of paperwork, take the same stupid tests, and do all the physical agility crap that you're having to do. The only difference is you're getting preferential treatment, one-on-one training. The others, including me, weren't that lucky. Do you think I wanted to be stuck in here every day this week?"

That didn't make her feel better. Now she felt like a whiner, and she wasn't, not really. At least, not until she'd gotten around Roan.

She sat back down. "I'm sorry," she muttered. "It's just that I was expecting more. I've been cooped up all my life. I didn't even get to go to public school. I was home schooled." She shrugged as she leaned back in the chair. "I was hoping for more."

"You want to go out and kill bad guys?"

It took her a second to realize he was teasing her. A teasing Roan could be just as dangerous as one who didn't give an inch, maybe more so because there was just a bit of a twinkle in his eyes, and a slight upward curve to his lips. She couldn't stop her own smile from forming.

"No, I don't want to go out and kill bad guys. At least, not in the next few days. But I hate being cooped up all the time."

"I do, too. Let's hit the obstacle course."

Her shoulders slumped. "More physical agility?"

His grin widened. "I think you'll like this."

She wasn't sure she trusted him.

"But you'll need to change your clothes. Wear something a little more rugged."

Now she knew she didn't trust him.

Roan almost felt sorry for her. The obstacle course was tough. Even he could barely get through it. Of course, his injury had slowed him down somewhat. He'd gone out a few days ago just to see how his endurance was and knew he was fit to go back on active duty. It was a tough course, though. This might be the last straw for Lyraka.

"I'll meet you back downstairs in fifteen minutes," he told her.

She didn't wait on him as she hurried from the room. Damn, he'd hate to see her leave. She was definitely a temptation, had been all week. But it was for her own good.

While she was changing, he went to the kitchen and had Frances fix them a sack lunch. While she was doing that, he grabbed some bottled water out of the refrigerator, then took everything to the Jeep.

There was a crisp bite in the air. A good day to go up the mountain. He just wondered how long Lyraka would last. She might have speed, and could blend in with her surroundings, but the course would test her mettle. That would tell her true worth, and he didn't plan to take it easy on her. He set everything in the Jeep and went back inside.

Twenty minutes after she'd first gone upstairs, Lyraka joined him back downstairs. She wore pretty much the same thing she'd worn that first night in the woods. He wondered if her bra was like the lacy one she'd been wearing that night.

"Is this okay?" she asked when she got to the bottom of the stairs.

He realized he'd been staring, but who could blame him. She was hot and sexy and it was hard not to let his gaze linger or to remember how it had felt to hold her in his arms. Keeping his distance all week had not been easy.

"It'll do," he told her, then turned and headed toward the front door. "You're late, by the way."

"Only five minutes or so."

"Five minutes could mean whether your partner lives or dies. Five minutes could make or break a mission. Five minutes—"

"Okay, okay. I won't let it happen again."

"Good, then let's go." He didn't wait to see if she followed. She did, and as he climbed into the driver's side, she opened the door and got in on the passenger side.

He noticed she didn't press herself against the door like she had on the drive up. Good, if she did survive training, she had to learn to trust him in all things. He would be her team leader. He couldn't have her balking when he gave an order, and getting someone killed. Today, he would start her lesson in trust.

They traveled a few miles, going higher up the mountain. The road they traveled wasn't much more than a dirt path cleared between the trees—tall pines and oaks almost as old as time itself.

"You'd think the government could build a decent road up here," she yelled over the bouncing of the Jeep as she hung on to the door with one hand and the dash with the other.

"You'd think." He agreed with her on that. Hell, it was almost an obstacle course just getting up the mountain. He always felt as though a few of his teeth had been jarred loose. "We're almost there," he said.

He gave the Jeep a little more gas as he topped a small rise. There was a clearing on the right. He pulled head-in and parked, setting the emergency break before he killed the engine.

She wore a look of disappointment. "This is it?" She slowly climbed out of the Jeep, looking around. "I guess I expected it to look different.

He followed her gaze. "You can't see it from here. This is as far as we go by Jeep."

She'd wish she'd never heard the word obstacle course by the end of the day. There were ditches to leap over, hills to climb. Trees to dodge, knotted ropes to swing from. Farther into the woods there was a thirty foot A-frame outfitted with a cargo net to climb up and over. And if all that didn't get her, there were pipes and beams to test her balance.

Those were just a few of the things he would have her doing. It usually took longer than a couple of days to go through the whole thing. Lyraka might run fast, but he had a feeling she wouldn't make it through half the course without calling a stop to the exercise.

"Where do we start?" she asked, breaking into his thoughts.

"Are you scared of heights?"

"I can climb a tree." She shrugged. "It's never bothered me before."

"Good."

"We're going to climb a tree?"

"Yeah. Then we'll fall out of it." He strolled over to one of the tallest trees around. "See that metal cable?" He pointed up.

"The one way up there?" Some of her bravado slipped.

"That's the one. We're going to climb the tree. Once we get to the cable, we'll clip on to it and glide through the trees for about a quarter mile."

"You're sure about that?" She placed a hand above her eyes to shield the sunlight and narrowed them as she tried to follow the path of the cable.

"I'm positive." It would be the last time she had fun today. He had to admit that he loved the metal cable. When he'd gone through the academy, his instructor had brought a group of them to the course. They'd all had their turn on it. Roan had felt like a bird gliding past the trees.

When his flight ended, he knew this was exactly what he wanted to do. By the end of that first day, he hadn't been so sure. Every muscle in his body had not only ached, they'd screamed in protest.

"So how do we climb the tree?" she asked.

Roan walked to the other side and knelt down in front of a metal box. "Everything we need is right here." He opened it and brought out two sets of metal spikes, and the leather straps that would fit around the tree as they climbed.

"It doesn't look very safe."

He caught the worried expression on her face when he glanced up. "It's the same gear a lineman would use to check the telephone lines. If you don't think you can handle this, we can always go back."

She arched an eyebrow. "I bet you'd like that."

He slowly stood. "Like I said, this isn't a game of checkers."

She picked up one of the spikes. "How does this work?"

Yeah, he liked that she acted tough. Not that acting would

do her any good. This was a dangerous line of work and she had no business being here, but yeah, he had to admire her tenacity.

He knelt in front of her again. "It straps to your leg, the sharp prong goes on the inside so you can jab it into the tree." He looked at her once more, silently asking her if she was ready to do this.

She took a deep breath, then nodded. "I'm ready."

Yeah, she was like a puppy with a sock and she wasn't about to let go. He fastened the lower strap, then took his time moving his hands up her jean clad leg to fasten the other one. He felt her flinch, then tremble. It was nice to know she wasn't immune to his touch.

It amazed Roan to know that with very little effort he could probably get Lyraka into his bed, and could be making sweet love to her, but instead, he was strapping metal spikes to her legs, and they were about to climb a really tall tree. He needed his head examined. Sometimes he wondered if this job was worth it. He strapped the other spike on, then straightened.

"Now what?" Her words came out kind of husky, breathless.

That was almost enough to do him in. He had a blanket in his Jeep and . . .

Joe would kill him. Probably wouldn't give him his release, either. Damned if he wasn't tempted to keep teaching a bunch of over-eager, trigger-happy rookies for just one day spent in Lyraka's arms.

But she was wearing metal spikes and her feet were really fast. Now might not be the time to push his luck by asking her if she wanted to have a quickie instead of flying through the trees, even if he did think he might talk her into it. There was still that little percentage that he might make her mad instead. He'd rather not become shish kabob today.

Okay, she wanted to know what was next. Maybe it was better to concentrate on that. "We'll put on the harnesses, then I'll put on my spikes and we climb the tree." But man was he tempted.

The harnesses went over the shoulder, like a vest. They'd use them when they went down the cable. He put his on. Before he could help Lyraka with hers, she already had it fastened. A shame. He'd have liked to tighten her straps.

It only took him a few minutes to finish putting all the gear on. "I'll show you first, then I'll let you go in front of me. If you fall, you'll land on me."

"What if you fall?"

"Then we're both screwed, so try not to fall." He stood next to the tree, then hooked the strap on the belt. "The strap goes around the tree and buckles to the other side of the belt. Next you jab the spike into the tree, then you jab the other spike in, let the waist strap help hold your weight." He demonstrated how to climb the tree by moving the strap up and continuing to climb using the spikes. He went up a few feet, then came back down. "Do you think you can do that?"

"Of course. It doesn't look that hard."

He could almost hear her adding, if you can do it, so can I. He liked the competitive streak in her. It made his life more interesting. He was curious to see how long it would last as the day progressed.

She positioned herself in front of the tree and leaned forward so she could swing her strap around it.

"Be careful you don't get a splinter."

She frowned at him. He smiled.

She started up the tree just as he'd shown her, with only a wobble or two. She was a fast learner. He got his footing and started up after her. Nice view. He liked the way the material cupped her ass and . . .

Her spike dug into the tree an inch from his fingers.

"Jesus!" He jerked his hand away, lost his footing and hugged the tree, sliding down a couple of inches before he got another foothold.

She looked down at him. "Be careful you don't get a splinter," she said before continuing up the tree as though she'd been climbing with spikes all her life.

"You sure you haven't done this before?"

"Positive. Like I said, I'm a fast learner."

They made it up the rest of the tree without incident. At the top was a small platform barely big enough for two people to stand on. As he squeezed in next to her, Roan realized this was a hell of a lot nicer than when he'd been up here with his burly instructor. Lyraka smelled a lot better, and he liked being up close and personal with her curves.

"This is really high. I didn't realize we'd climbed up this far."

"Scared?" he asked.

She shook her head. "No, I like being able to see this far. I feel as though I'm on top of the world. I almost don't want to leave."

She looked at him and he became lost in her eyes, her scent. If he wasn't afraid of falling out of the tree, he'd kiss her.

Instead, he grabbed the metal loop and strapped it to her harness, then removed her spikes, letting them fall to the ground below. "Ready?"

"Not exactly."

Roan hadn't thought she'd last very long, but he hadn't expected her to give up this soon. He couldn't stop the flash of disappointment that swept through him.

"Hey, it's okay. Some people are just not cut out for this kind of life."

"No, it's not that. I know this is where we start, but exactly where and how do we finish?"

He'd forgotten that detail. Man, Lyraka could make a man forget his own name when she stood this close, smelled this sweet, and looked so incredibly hot.

He cleared his throat, then reached up and tugged on the cable. "It's not that tight. Your weight will slacken it some more. Because it's a more gradual drop, rather than a sharper angle, you won't actually be going that fast. At the end of the cable, there's a big inflated mattress to land on. Just keep your feet straight out in front of you."

"You know it's inflated? I mean, someone could forget to take off their spikes or something."

"Everything on the course is checked twice a day. Trust me."

She didn't. He could tell by the look in her eyes, but if she lasted the next few days, he would make sure she didn't hesitate to put her complete faith in him.

"Ready?"

She nodded and grabbed hold of the sides of the harness. "Geronimo," she said as she raised her feet.

Roan gave her a little shove and off she went with a squeal. He knew exactly what she felt—the exhilaration, the adrenaline rush, and the thrill.

He undid his spikes and let them drop to the ground, then strapped in and pushed off. There was a little bounce, then he was gliding through the trees, feeling the rush of air on his face. This was living.

When he got to the end, Lyraka was sitting in the middle of the inflated mattress. Now that was temptation. The cable dipped lower and lower. He landed with the ease of a hawk honing in on its prey. Careful not to ram his legs into her, he spread his, coming to a stop against her backside.

"Oh, I guess I should have unhooked and moved out of the way."

"I don't know. This is kind of nice." He reached around her waist and pulled her back against him. God, she felt good snuggled next to him. Her curves melted against his harder muscles.

He turned her just a bit so he had easy access to her mouth. When he lowered his lips to hers, he couldn't stop the groan that escaped. The dreams he'd had of her all week, her naked body pressed against his, her breasts crushed against his chest, her nipples hard little nubs—all of it came back to him in a flood of memories and created a burning ache deep inside him.

And she was kissing him back, pulling his head closer. He tasted her need for more.

"No," she said, suddenly pulling away.

Roan immediately let go. She was breathing hard as she lay in his arms. Her eyes were wide as she fought her own battle to control her natural instincts to lie back and let nature run its course.

He should apologize, but the words wouldn't come. Instead, he said, "I want you. I think you want me, too."

"No, I don't. I'm here to . . . to . . ."

"Become an agent?"

She frowned. "I know exactly what I'm here for and it isn't to have sex with you."

She was killing him. "We'd both enjoy it."

She visibly swallowed, her pupils dilating.

"I want to remove each article of your clothing until you're completely naked in front of me, then I'll stroke you, run my finger down your clit and slip a finger inside the moist heat of your body." Damn it, he was being a jerk, but there was something about her that pushed him past rational thought.

"I'm . . . Oh, God . . . I can't."

He looked around. "There's no one here to stop us."

"I just . . . can't. It wouldn't be safe."

"I have protection."

She grimaced. "Not that kind of safe."

Roan had no idea what the hell she was talking about. Maybe she was afraid someone would stumble on them while they were making love. It wouldn't happen. At least, he didn't think so.

He sighed when she unhooked from the cable and scrambled to her feet. It had been nice while it lasted.

"I don't want to even talk about it. What's next?"

A dip in the lake to cool him off? Clothes optional. He really needed to get control of his thoughts. He unhooked and came to his feet.

"Please," she said.

How could he resist when she put it that way?

"Okay, we'll see if you have what it takes to become an agent." He'd let the matter drop, for now. But he was definitely curious to know exactly what she'd meant about it not being safe.

She squared her shoulders. "Bring it on. I can take everything you want to dish out."

They would soon see.

Chapter 7

The only thing fun about the obstacle course had been when she'd glided through the trees. It had gone downhill from there.

Had Roan really held her in his arms, kissed her? Awakened desires that she'd been trying desperately to keep under control? Lyraka glanced his way, then had to bite back a moan. Oh, yeah, he'd awakened *everything* inside her.

All her adult life, she'd tried to control that side of her emotions. She knew that Nerakians could be consumed by their need for sex. But with her, the need was stronger because of her mixed blood. She didn't know why, it just was. She felt everything more intensely than earthlings or Nerakians. She was cursed.

Rick, her one and only experience, had given her sexual side a little nudge. She would've gladly continued to meet him in the woods if he hadn't been frightened and run away before they'd finished what he'd started.

He'd said she'd burned him. It wasn't as if he'd been on fire, or even smoking, for that matter. As far as she could tell, he hadn't been scarred.

All the excuses in the world wouldn't change the fact that *something* had happened. If they had finished the act, poor Rick might have disintegrated. Now, she was afraid to have sex. She gave new meaning to the phrase "hot babe."

If they'd continued, would he have incinerated? She wasn't sure. The only thing she knew for certain was that her frustratingly short experience with a man had only made her want more. And now Roan was fueling the fire of her passion.

The sex would be good, a little voice inside her head told her.

No, she wouldn't give in to temptation. She was here to learn, and learn she would. She wouldn't disintegrate the teacher.

Maybe there was more to his advances than met the eye. Maybe this was Roan's way of breaking her. She already knew he didn't want to train her. If she quit, he'd be off the hook. That had to be why he was toying with her, setting the trap for the unsuspecting mouse. She could almost feel the snap of the metal bar crushing her neck if she got too close. There was more to her than that. She wouldn't give up. She wouldn't give Roan the satisfaction.

"This obstacle is about balance," Roan said, breaking into her thoughts as they approached the next torture device, which was what she'd begun to think of each obstacle. She focused on what he was telling her, determined to conquer this one, too.

"Balance and strength," he said.

They stood in front of an oversized net. She looked up. It was only as tall as a single story house. The cargo net didn't look that difficult to master. In fact, Lyraka had a feeling she'd surprised Roan with her abilities. She hadn't mastered anything, but she hadn't let any of the obstacles beat her. She'd finished each and every one of them.

She grabbed the rope and put her foot into one of the slots, then began pulling herself up, one rung at a time. They were farther apart than they looked so she had to stretch out her body to move up.

"Keep your body close to the ropes. If you lean out, you'll lose your balance."

"Easier said than done," she muttered as she reached for

another cross rope. It didn't help that the ropes were as big around as her wrist and hard to grip. By the time she got to the top, she was sweating. There were more wet patches on her shirt than there were dry ones. But this obstacle hadn't beaten her, either. She straddled the top bar and smiled triumphantly down at him.

Roan smiled back as if he knew something she didn't, then he flipped a switch. There was a deep, throbbing noise as a motor started up.

What the hell was he up to? She looked around.

"Hold on tight, princess."

He flipped another switch. The frame began to move.

"I don't think that's the safest place for you right now," he said. "How fast can you get down before it collapses?"

He was going to kill her! That had been his plan all along. Kill her, then Joe would let him go back on active duty. Everyone would think she hadn't been cut out to be an agent, but they wouldn't dream of blaming him.

"Are you sure you want to stay up there? The whole structure is about to collapse."

He was right. The frame was teetering back and forth. She flung her leg over the side, grasping the top rail. It shifted and she was left grabbing air. Panic squeezed her chest.

"Grab the rope!"

She blindly obeyed and caught one of the rungs, clinging to it.

"The whole thing is going to come down, Lyraka. You have to get off now!"

There was no taking her time this go-round. She blindly found her footing, falling and grabbing as she went. The ropes burned her arms, chafing her skin until she finally felt solid ground beneath her feet. She untangled from the ropes and scrambled back, out of harm's way, plopping down hard on the ground when she stumbled over a branch, her chest barely expanding as she gasped for air.

She watched as Roan calmly hit the switch. The A-frame stopped moving. She looked from him, back to the A-frame, then back to him.

"Good job," he said and calmly began to walk away.

She came to her feet and hurried after him. When she caught up to him, she grabbed his arm, and forced him to stop and look at her.

"It wasn't going to fall, was it?"

"No."

She shoved against his chest as hard as she could. It frustrated her when he didn't move. His feet stayed firmly planted on the ground.

"I hate you!"

"No you don't."

"Yes, I do! You can't tell me that I don't hate you when I do," she ground out.

He pulled her against him and lowered his mouth to hers. For a second, she resisted, but the heat of his mouth, the way his tongue stabbed hers, then lightly stroked, sent flames licking over her body. She returned his kiss with all the pain and anger she felt and all the terror that had gone through her when she thought the A-frame was falling. She kissed him back with all the pent-up sexual deprivation she was feeling right now.

But he pulled away, leaving her wanting more, needing more, her body aching for more.

"See, I told you that you didn't hate me. You wouldn't kiss me like that if you hated me."

"Ugh!" She stomped her foot and pursed her lips.

"You had to think the frame would fall. Sure, you made it up with little effort. No biggie. Sometimes when we go on what looks like an easy mission things will happen and all of a sudden, what should've been easy becomes difficult without notice. You have to be prepared for the unexpected."

Okay, he'd made a point, and it was a valid one. "You still didn't have to kiss me."

"You're sexy as hell when you're angry. I couldn't resist."

"Well make an effort next time."

"Ready for another obstacle?"

"I'm hungry." And sweaty, and tired, and she probably smelled to high heaven and had no idea why any man would think she was sexy right now.

"One more, and then we'll eat."

Her stomach rumbled and she knew she was heading toward a foul mood. She could do one more even if it was to prove she could. He hadn't beaten her yet. "One more then."

He reached into his pocket and brought out a piece of black silk. She warily eyed the scrap of material.

"What are you going to do with that?"

"Blindfold you." He walked behind her.

"I'm not so sure about this."

"You have to learn to trust everyone on the elite force."

"Do I have to kiss them, too?"

He laughed lightly as he placed the blindfold over her eyes. "No. Just trust them. It's a two way street. They'll be trusting you with their lives as well."

As the light went out and she was in the dark, uneasiness trickled down her spine. She wasn't so sure this was a good idea. "What are we going to do?" She felt Roan knot the scarf at the back of her head.

"You'll just have to trust me."

She didn't want to trust him. She'd never trusted in anyone except herself. She'd known coming into this that she would have to work with a team, at the very least, a partner. There was always a certain amount of trust that went along with that, but Roan wanted her to give one hundred percent and for the first time since coming here, she wasn't sure she could complete the training. Asking her to give one hundred percent was asking too much.

"Ready?"

The other alternative would be to go back to her mother's artist colony and help Anna run it. Anna was a friend of her mother's. A little scatter-brained at times, but nice enough and her mother had known her a long time. Was she ready to go back to being alone even though she was surrounded by people? She'd hated being alone.

"Lyraka?"

"I'm ready," she said, quickly making up her mind.

"Trust me to be your eyes."

He took her hand in his. Maybe it was because she had the blindfold on, but she was more aware of how his hand felt, the calluses, but also the strength. And the heat. The heat was good.

They walked for what seemed forever. She could feel the trees getting denser, the breeze not as strong. She began to worry. Really, what did she know about Roan. She only had Joe's word that he was a good man, an excellent trainer.

For that matter, how well did she really know Joe? He'd come to the artist colony a few times a year. He'd lied about why he was there. He wasn't artistic. He'd only wanted to observe Aasera. Roan could be a mass murderer for all she knew.

Her heart began to pound. She drew in a deep breath, forcing herself to calm down. If it came down to it, she could outrun Roan, and she could always blend in to her surrounding if she had to take cover. But she couldn't do any of that with this stupid blindfold on. But when she reached up, he caught her hand.

"We're almost there."

"Almost where?"

"To where we're going."

"Do you really expect me to blindly trust you?"

"Well, you are blindfolded so, yeah, I guess I do."

"I barely know you."

"You don't have to know me that well, or anyone on the team for that matter. You only need to trust us." He tugged on her hand to stop her forward movement.

"Are we here?" she asked.

"We're here."

She reached up to remove the blindfold, but again, he stilled her hand.

"No, not yet."

"This is ridiculous. I don't think it's a part of the training at all."

"Scared?"

"No."

"Liar," he whispered close to her ear. His warm breath tickled her ear.

Oh, God, what if he planned to tie her up and strip away her clothes. Her nipples tightened in anticipation. When had she gotten so pathetic?

"Step up," he told her.

She took a deep breath and raised her foot, setting it down on what felt like a wooden step. She brought her other foot up. "What is this?"

"Trust me."

She didn't want to trust him. He'd probably get her killed.

They climbed up and up. Her hands began to sweat. How high were they?

"This is as far as we go," he said.

They were on some kind of platform. He turned her in the direction they'd come up. Were they going down now? He kept his hands on her shoulders, nudging her backward.

"Right there. Don't move anymore. All I want you to do is open your arms wide."

"Why?"

"Just do it."

Whatever. She opened her arms wide.

"Now fall backwards."

Her breath caught in her throat. Was he serious? "I'm not going to fall backwards. That's crazy!"

"Trust me."

"No!" She jerked the blindfold off at the same time he pushed. She was falling! She was going to die!

She landed on what felt like a bed of the softest feathers. The blindfold still covered one of her eyes. She tugged it the rest of the way off and looked up at him. He was only two feet above her. But how?

She looked at what she'd just climbed and saw that it had all been an illusion to make her think they were climbing higher than what they had.

"That wasn't funny." She glared at him.

"It wasn't supposed to be. This was a lesson in trust. You failed. Before you can pass my training, you have to learn to trust me."

She wasn't sure she could.

He jumped down, landing just to the side of the air bag, then reached out his hand toward her. "Come on, let's go eat."

She hesitated, then took his hand and let him help her to her feet before they started the trek back to the Jeep.

He'd cheated with this obstacle. It hadn't even been a real challenge. Something he'd probably created in his own mind to torture his students. It hadn't been fair to make her think she was falling to her death.

It wasn't as though she didn't get the concept of trusting her team. She did. She just didn't think it had to be carried to this extreme.

She glanced up the side of the mountain, saw the cable they'd come down on, but nothing else. Good Lord, how far away was the Jeep? Her legs were burning from everything Roan had put her through today. He traipsed up the side of the mountain with little effort, but then, he hadn't run any of the course. She was the one who'd been working her ass off most of the day.

He looked over his shoulder and she quickly made her expression neutral. She wasn't about to let him know just how exhausted she really was.

"What?" she asked.

He shook his head. "Nothing. Just making sure you were keeping up. I imagine you're pretty tired right now."

"Nope, not a bit."

"Good. After we eat and let our food settle, we still have more obstacles."

"You've got to be kidding."

"Did you say something?" he asked.

"I said that I felt like a kid again. I'm looking forward to it," she lied. Oh, God, she was so *not* looking forward to it. She longed for the days when she could slip into the woods that bordered her mother's colony and blend in with her surroundings. She even missed the lazy days of meditating. Not that she was very good at it. Her mother had tried to teach her but she could never sit still long enough, could never completely empty her mind.

Especially now that she knew about sex. She really needed to get laid.

She glared at Roan's back. He certainly wasn't making things easier. She wouldn't give Roan the satisfaction of letting him see she was tired, or that her muscles screamed in pain. Not even if it killed her.

Well, maybe she wouldn't go that far. She'd only hope he stopped before she got to the point of keeling over dead.

They finally made it back to where they'd started. She stopped and looked behind her. It really was fantastic scenery. She inhaled the scent of pine that clung to the air.

"Beautiful, isn't it?"

She looked at him. In this, they totally agreed. "I love the woods. The trees, the animals . . . everything."

"I have a cabin up in the mountains where I stay when I want to get away from everything. When it snows, and there's a fire in the hearth, it feels as though I'm the only one on Earth."

She knew the feeling. That's how she felt when she walked in the woods. Somehow, that made her feel as though they shared a secret.

That wasn't good.

Before she could let herself dwell on her thoughts for very

long, Roan broke the spell. He turned and walked the short distance to the Jeep, then pulled out a picnic basket.

For some strange reason she had never pictured him as someone who would carry a picnic basket. He was rugged, with hard muscles. He was strong and . . . and . . . manly.

"What? Does the picnic basket not fit in with your image of me?" he asked, correctly reading her thoughts.

"I haven't formed any kind of image of you." She shrugged.

He stopped next to her, a pained expression on his face. "You mean you haven't pictured me naked? Or us together, lying in bed naked, my hands caressing your curves, my lips teasing one of your tight nipples? I had hoped for more fantasies from you." He turned and walked to a picnic table and set the basket on top.

"I picture it now," she angrily muttered as a burning need turned her belly into knots. "No, I didn't picture any of that," she called out in a louder voice.

She stomped over to the basket, jerked out the tablecloth that Frances had packed, and spread it out. Lyraka had a feeling this was going to be a long day if he kept talking about sex.

But damned if she didn't feel giddy with excitement. She didn't feel so alone anymore. Yeah, she felt alive. Really alive and it felt damned good.

She sat down on the bench opposite him. He looked up and grinned. She didn't care what he thought. She wasn't about to sit next to him.

He reached inside the basket and brought out two sandwiches, then studied them. "Looks like they're both ham." When he handed one to her, she noticed the ring on his finger. He'd been wearing it every day since she'd first met him. Joe wore one just like it. It was silver with a red lightning rod on the side and a diamond stone in the center. The diamond wasn't large, but slightly raised.

"What's with the ring? Some kind of fraternity?" she asked.

He removed the plastic wrap from his sandwich. She noticed his face was a little red.

He shrugged. "It's kind of like a Super Bowl ring, but for agents. No biggie."

"But not all the agents have one."

"You get it if you go above and beyond the call of duty."

"And you did." He didn't look as though he wanted to talk about it, but she was curious.

"Yeah."

She took a bite of her sandwich, chewed slowly, then swallowed. "What exactly did you do?"

"You're not going to let this drop, are you?"

She shook her head.

He sighed. "The team was in trouble. We were on a mission."

"On another planet?"

"Might as well have been. No, it was in L.A. We go anywhere we're needed. A gang had us pinned down. I unpinned us."

"Is that how you hurt your leg?"

"Yeah. I lived. So did everyone else."

"Can I see the ring?"

He slipped it off his finger and handed it to her. The workmanship was beautiful. She ran her finger over the tip of the diamond. "It looks smooth, but the edges on top are rough."

"If you think that's rough, you should see the mark it leaves on someone's face. Not that I go around hitting people. Unless of course they need hitting."

She looked at him. "You are the best of the best, aren't you? I mean, that's why Joe has you training me."

"I'm good at what I do." He cleared his throat. "Here, drink some water."

And quit asking questions, is what he left unsaid. She probably should, too. He was starting to become a hero in her eyes and that wasn't good. Not one little bit.

Chapter 8

Lyraka had died and gone straight to hell. It was her penance for wanting sex. Someone from above had heard her thoughts and decided to give her something else to think about.

It had worked, too. She no longer thought about jumping Roan's bones. Nope, that was probably the furthest thing from her mind right now.

Oh, Lord, even her toenails ached. Her eyeballs ached. She closed her eyes and leaned back in the tub of bubbles. Her fingernails ached. The small mole on her right shoulder blade ached. Her knees ached.

She sniffed.

Oh, no, she wasn't even going there. She was so not going to cry like a little baby. Yes, she hurt, but she'd made it through the day. She had conquered every obstacle that Roan had thrown her way.

Well, except for the trust issue. She hadn't managed that one. One out of a dozen or more wasn't bad.

She sank down a little more into the tub. God, she hurt so much. She sniffed again, and a tear slipped from her eye, making a trail down her cheek. She didn't bother to raise her hand and brush it away. She couldn't. She hurt too much.

There was a light tapping on the bathroom door. She opened one eye, and peered at the door. "Go away."

"I brought you a hot, soothing, cup of tea," Roan said. "I thought it might relax you. At supper, you were moving around like you were sore."

"I'm not sore. Go away," she called out. Even her jaw hurt. She closed her eyes again and tried to reach that point of utter relaxation.

The knob jiggled. She tensed. The door opened and Roan walked in.

"I locked the door!"

He grinned and her toes curled. Just cramps, she told herself. Her toes were not curling because he looked devastatingly handsome in a deep blue turtleneck and a pair of jeans. A painter at the colony once told her that only a Texan could look good in a pair of jeans. The painter had never seen Roan because he was looking pretty fine right now.

"I'm good at picking locks," he said.

"Next time I'll put a chair in front of it. Now go away."

"Don't you want the tea? It's chai."

She sniffed. The wonderful smell of spices drifted over to her. "Okay, you can leave the cup of tea." She glanced down at the water to make sure the bubbles still covered her nakedness. They did, although they were starting to dissipate.

He walked closer and handed her the cup.

The tea invoked memories of winter months when Aasera would brew a pot of tea, and they would sit on the plush sofa in front of a roaring fire. She took a drink, savoring the taste. This was nice.

Except Roan was still standing there as if he didn't plan on leaving. "Thanks. You can go now," she told him again.

Instead, he began rolling up his sleeves.

"What are you doing?"

"If you don't get the stiffness out, you'll end up in the emergency room with muscle cramps." He knelt behind her.

The first touch of his hands on her shoulders made her jump.

"Easy now. Just drink the tea. I won't ever do anything you don't want me to."

Yeah, that was what she was afraid of, but the gentle massage of his fingers on her taut shoulders was too much of a temptation to let pass. She began to relax as he massaged away the tightness.

It wouldn't be hard to get used to a personal masseur. She took another drink of the tea, then closed her eyes, sighing deeply. Maybe it was the long day, or the tea, or even the bubble bath, but after a few minutes, his gentle touch began to stir more inside her. Her nipples hardened and began to ache.

This wasn't supposed to happen. Instructors were not supposed to make out with their students. God, she hoped he didn't stop.

She held her breath when his hands massaged down a little farther, but not far enough to give satisfaction. No, he was only stoking the fire that was steadily growing hotter deep inside her.

She took another drink of tea, noting the slight tremble in her hand. Had he noticed? Probably, he seemed to notice a lot of things.

He suddenly stopped, and kissed her on top of her head. "I hope that helped," he said as he stood and started to leave the room.

She opened her mouth, then snapped it closed. What could she say? Or do? She wasn't ready to ask him to stay.

"Uh . . . thanks." How lame was that?

He looked over his shoulder, hand on the doorknob. "By the way, you might want to add more bubbles to your bath." He opened the door and walked out, closing it behind him.

She looked at the water. He was right. The bubbles were gone. There was zilch left to the imagination and her nipples were hard as pebbles. He knew exactly what he'd made her feel.

Ass.

At least she didn't need to add more hot water. No, her body temperature had pretty well taken care of that. She set the cup of tea on the tub edge and poured in more bubble bath and stirred it around until she had frothy bubbles. She reached for the cup again. The tea was good. The massage had been better. She slipped lower into the tub as hot water covered her like an electric blanket.

Nice.

How long would she be able to tamp down the Nerakian need for sex that warred within her? It wasn't as if she even liked Roan. He'd pushed her to the limits all week, especially today.

On top of all that, he'd made sexual advances toward her. For a moment, she closed her eyes and could almost taste his lips on hers. He was a fantastic kisser. But that still didn't mean she liked him.

She frowned. She was pretty sure liking someone wasn't a requisite for having sex. If he did burn to a crisp, she wouldn't feel quite as guilty—especially after the day he'd put her through.

She finished off the last drop of tea and set her cup to the side. Six o'clock would be here before she knew it. If she was smart, she would get out of the tub and crawl into bed.

Roan had picked this lock, would he pick the one to her bedroom as well? Her thighs trembled at the thought. Muscle spasms. Yeah, right. More like *coming-in-heat* spasms.

She climbed out of the tub and dried off, slipping her arms into a terrycloth robe. She glanced toward his room as she walked down the hall. There was no light beneath the door that she could tell. Maybe he waited in her room.

She cautiously opened the door and flipped on the light switch. Disappointment filled her. Okay, so she wouldn't mind having sex with him. He was making her horny. She was pretty sure that wasn't part of her training.

She shut her door and tossed the robe across a chair, then pulled out a silky red gown from the dresser drawer. As the whisper-soft material cascaded over her naked skin, rippling across her sensitive breasts, she closed her eyes and arched her back.

The man was making her utterly crazy!

She grabbed the chair, sending the robe to the floor, then crammed the back under the doorknob to secure it. *See if you can get past that!* She turned off the light, then went to the bed, and flung the covers back.

There was no way he'd get into her room tonight. He wouldn't sneak into her bed, and caress her breasts and slide his hand between her legs, and rub her until she felt as if she would explode if he didn't bury himself deep inside her and put her out of her misery. No way was he getting past the chair.

She lay in bed listening to the quiet, hearing her own breathing.

Life really sucked.

She flung the cover to the side, went to the door, and quietly moved the chair back where it had been before she'd propped it beneath the knob. She was so pathetic. She crawled beneath the covers once again and let the fantasy envelop her.

If he was that good of a kisser, how would he be at making love? Would he be a tender lover? Or demanding? Maybe forcing her to do things she might never have thought to try on her own? A delicious tingle ran down her spine. She rather liked the idea that he would be the dominant partner.

She rolled to her back, snaking her hand beneath the covers, touching her breasts, biting her bottom lip as her fingers grazed across her tender, aching nipples. She squeezed them between her thumb and forefinger, gasping when pleasure shot through her. Would his touch feel like this? If he were lying beside her, she would throw her leg over his hip and press herself closer to him.

A door closed.

The front door? She stopped and listened. Her super-sensitive hearing detected footsteps walking away from the building. She got out of bed and went to the window, pulling back the curtain. Roan walked up the road, and then disappeared into the dark of night.

Where was he going? What was he doing?

She was thoughtful as she went back to bed, turning on her side and scrunching the extra pillow against her chest much like a lover would hold her close. It didn't matter where he was going. Only where he wasn't, and that was not in her bed.

Ass.

Roan had to get out of the building. Damn it, he knew he'd gone way past the boundaries of where an instructor should go. Lyraka knew how to push his buttons, and she'd pushed.

He took off at a jog up the hill. Even though it was dark, he knew the path well, and there was enough light from the full moon that he could see a few feet in front of him.

Hell, he should know every bump in the road. He'd been running it for the last few weeks, coming up here when he knew no one would be around. He knew he was pushing himself to get back into shape. Sometimes a person had to do what they had to do. He was stifled here at the training center. It hadn't taken him long to get his fill of training rookies, especially Nerakians.

The familiar ache in his left leg began to throb. He gritted his teeth and pushed past the pain. Instead, he focused on the beat of his heart, on his lungs as he inhaled and exhaled.

Besides, it would get his mind off Lyraka. He stumbled. Damn, why did she intrude on his thoughts? Probably because he knew what she looked like naked. Man, it had been better than anything he could've imagined—high pointed breasts with dark rosy nipples, small waist, and hips that gently curved. He shouldn't have stayed, but the bubbles had begun to disappear and he couldn't make himself leave.

He drew in a deep breath as sweat broke out on his forehead.

Ah, hell, he had to quit thinking about her. He hurt so bad right now that he could barely stand it. He picked up the pace.

When his leg throbbed to the point that he finally cried out, he knew he had to stop. He began the journey back to the building, limping. It served him right for coming on to her like he had today. But man, what he wouldn't give for just one night curled up next to her.

Chapter 9

"We have to strike soon!" Chief advisor Kragen warned as he paced across the royal bed chamber.

Prince Banyon, only child of the ruler of the Rovert nation, narrowed his eyes on the other man. "You forget your place." Did no one respect their leaders anymore? Technically, he wasn't a leader yet, but any moment his father would die, and he, Banyon, would be the supreme ruler.

Kragen visibly swallowed before lowering his gaze to the floor. "Of course, Prince. I only worry for your safety and the safety of our planet."

"And no doubt, your own neck." Banyon let his gaze trail over Kragen. He was getting fat and lazy as he wallowed in his wealth. Perfection was beauty, and right now, Kragen was ugly. The prince hated ugly people.

He caught a glimpse of himself in the full-length mirror and knew he looked perfect. He preened as he studied his reflection—hair as dark as his planet, creamy pale skin, lazy brown eyes. He was more than handsome. Women fell at his feet, begging him to mate with them. Rovert men were known for their good looks, and the royals more so. Even his father, as he lay dying in his bed, was still a handsome man.

His gaze went to the small scar above his right eye. His only imperfection. Anger filled him. He regretted not being able to get revenge even after all these years.

A bug crawled across the floor. A big, fat, juicy croacher. Banyon's tongue shot out of his mouth like a lizard, wrapped around the insect, and snapped back into his mouth. He closed his eyes and savored the sweet juices.

When he opened his eyes, he caught Kragen's reflection in the mirror. He knew Kragen well. The man would have taken the bug for himself if Banyon hadn't been paying attention. The man ate too much as it was.

Banyon's gaze swept over Kragen. His chief advisor had no cares for his own appearance. It was disgusting, but he was still useful, even though he sometimes overstepped his boundaries. Of course, if the day ever came when Kragen proved to be too much of a bother, Banyon would have him disposed of.

"What I meant to say was that Nerak is allowing earthlings to land, male earthlings. You remember what's been passed down from ancient times. What if they breed? The Nerakian men were fierce warriors. They invaded our planet, killed our people."

"Because we invaded them first and killed their people," Banyon said. "They retaliated. No one can blame them for that. It's the way of the universe."

He brushed a white speck off his dark coat, doubting there were more than ten people on the whole Nerakian planet who could even fight. They'd grown lazy since there weren't any more wars.

"What if they start breeding and someday invade us again? What if they bring more men and train them to fight? Will there be threats against us again?"

"That won't happen."

"How can you be so sure?"

"We are at peace with Nerak," he spat. "My father signed the peace treaty ages ago." And ruined all their lives.

"But your father is dying."

Kragen was right. Even now his father gasped for each

breath. When that last breath ceased, Banyon would be given the power to make decisions. He would restore their people to what they once were—fierce fighters who brought all the spoils of war to their king.

"It's almost a shame that he has to suffer so," Kragen spoke softly. "He would be better off if he were to . . . die quietly."

Anger rushed through Banyon. "You dare to speak treason against the Supreme Ruler? Would you do the same if it was I lying in the royal chambers? Would you talk of ending my life?"

"Of course not, Prince." Sweat ran down Kragen's fat jowls. He pulled a cloth from his pocket and mopped his face. "I don't want the Nerakians to gain in strength and our planet caught unaware."

"That would never happen." But Banyon wasn't so sure. His warriors had gotten lax from years with only an occasional raid. They were fat and lazy. Captives were brought in by the slave traders, rather than the men going out and hunting for themselves.

"My spies have told me some familiar faces have returned to Nerak."

Banyon was bored with their conversation. He wanted to hear no more talk about what could happen. His father's men guarded their king well, protecting him from crossing over until it was his time. Until he died, Banyon could do nothing. He turned away from Kragen, dismissing him with a supercilious wave of his hand.

"As you wish, Prince. I only thought you might want to know Aasera lives."

Banyon whipped around. "What is this you speak? She's dead. Her country celebrated her life." He reached up and ran a finger down the scar above his right eye. Cold fear was quickly replaced with burning anger.

Kragen shook his head. "No, she lives. My informant tells me she's training new explorers for travel."

Frustration filled Banyon. It wasn't fair that she'd been alive all this time while he'd had to suffer unmercifully every time he looked in the mirror and saw the two inch scar.

"It makes no difference. No one has ever been able to capture a Nerakian female off Nerak. Do you propose we land on their planet undetected? It's never been done. Again, you give me information without solutions. I'm beginning to wonder what use you are to me."

"There are other ways to get revenge." Kragen looked pointedly at Banyon's scar, something few men were brave enough to do.

"What, snap my fingers and she appears before me?"

"Aasera was banished from Nerak when she became pregnant. She made the decision to keep the child and live on Earth." Kragen examined his fingers. "The child must mean a lot to her. I mean, she gave up everything for it. The girl is still on Earth."

Excitement coursed through Banyon. "This is good." Aasera would be destroyed if her child was harmed. Finally, after all this time, he would take his revenge.

"I'll never be able to leave until my father dies. The ships are closely guarded."

"Like I said, there is a way that will . . . ease your father's passing. It could be costly, though."

This was where Kragen had been leading him all along. His advisor thought he was being crafty. He didn't know that nothing mattered as long as the end result was the same.

"Make it happen. The gems will be waiting when it's done."

"I will also send men to Earth as soon as it is safe."

"No, I'll go myself."

"It's dangerous, Prince."

"The stupid earthlings won't suspect me of landing on their planet. Besides, I want to see this place I've only heard about."

"But . . . but . . . we aren't travelers."

"We are now."

"When do you plan to leave, Your Highness?"

"Soon." He smiled, his pupils turning to gray shards of glass. "Leave me. On your way out, tell them to send in the new female."

Kragen started to say something, apparently thought better of it, and bowed instead. The door closed silently behind him.

Banyon began to laugh. Oh how he would make Aasera pay for disfiguring him. A Rovert's skin did not heal like other species. They had to carry scars around until they crossed over. The mark Aasera had left on him was a testament to the fact he'd been beaten. He'd make Aasera's child pay, and she'd pay dearly.

There was a light knock on his chamber door.

Banyon hadn't seen the new female. One of the traders had brought her. He'd been told she was quite beautiful. Anticipation rose to the surface. He was more than ready to conquer her.

"Enter."

The female was in chains, bound at her wrists, a longer chain dropped down to her bound feet. Ah, he did like a chained female. This one trembled. He would've liked one with a little more spirit, more fight. His pulse raced. He needed an outlet for his anger. He nodded at the guard. The man bowed, then left.

Banyon walked around the female. She trembled more, her chains rattling. She was easy to look upon. The trader hadn't lied about her beauty. Her pale green hair flowed past her shoulders.

When he faced her again, she raised her eyes, then quickly lowered them.

They were deep crimson. He didn't have a fondness for that shade. He stepped closer and removed the clasp at her shoulder, tossing it to the side. She gasped and tried to hold her robe in place.

"Let it fall," he told her in a voice that was soft to the ears.

The trembles that plagued her body became more fierce. No, she wouldn't be any sport at all. Her robe fell to the floor.

"Ah, I see the trader was right. You are quite magnificent."

The girl cowered before him as she tried to shield her nakedness. It would do her no good, of course. Tears formed in her eyes as she began to cry and beg. It always amazed him when he saw species who cried. Roverts didn't have tear ducts so couldn't produce any moisture.

"Please . . ." she pleaded. "I beg you . . ."

"Yes, you usually all do, but of course, it never does any good. I will still look upon your nakedness."

"I will be shamed if you take me," she cried, turning her head away.

"Even if I shower you in magnificent jewels? The finest furs?"

Her eyes widened. "Furs? Jewels?"

When she looked at him, he saw the speculative gleam in her eyes. It was just as he'd thought, she would be no sport.

"Will you remove the chains, my Prince," she whispered. "I want to hold you close."

He laughed. Her smile wavered when he looked at her, and the look of fear reentered her eyes. She tried to wiggle away when his mouth opened over hers, then connected to her lips with an unbreakable suction. He held her head in place while she squirmed beneath him. She was sweet, like the fruit the traders brought to him, but there was a bitter aftertaste.

When he finished with her, he moved away, and she crumpled to the floor. He hadn't really meant to steal all her essence. Not right now, anyway. She'd been rather fun to toy with, and he'd wanted to mate. Oh, well. It would be at least a week before she had any fight inside her, and he was well satiated for the time being.

He called for the guards. "Take her away. And the next time that trader lands here, bring him to me. I don't like the lower classes. He needs to be taught a lesson."

He barely gave the female another glance. Were there none left that had any fight in them? He flung himself down on the lounging sofa, and placed the back of his hand on his forehead. Life could be so dreary at times.

Yes, it was time he went to Earth.

Chapter 10

Lyraka slapped her hand down on the alarm so it would shut up. When she rolled over, she gasped with pain. She'd only thought she was sore last night. Her whole body was one big ball of ache. It was a good thing Roan hadn't come to her room during the night.

Anyone would have thought all the exercising she'd been doing for the last week would have prepared her for the obstacle course.

Not.

She slowly sat up, easing her legs over the side of the bed, then just sat there. How was she going to make it through the day? She glanced at the clock again, hoping time would slow down—or stop. That's when she noticed the jar. It hadn't been there last night. She grimaced as she reached for it.

Mentholated cream, she read. *Eases sore muscles.*

So, Roan had come into her room during the night. Had he looked down at her? Had he wanted to crawl beneath the covers? Make love to her? Apparently not, since the other side of the bed was empty. Had she been drooling in her sleep? Ugh, she hoped not. Major turn-off.

No, she had a feeling he only played her like a cat with a mouse. She wasn't giving up and going home.

But she would use the cream.

She unscrewed the lid and sniffed, then quickly moved it

away from her nose. This would certainly keep him at arm's length.

With ten minutes to spare, she walked into the kitchen. Roan was already there, sitting at the table drinking coffee. She didn't speak as she walked past him to the refrigerator and opened the door.

"I see you found the cream on your night table."

Her lip curled. Yeah, she stunk and she knew it. She'd practically bathed in the stuff, and smelled to high heaven now, but she had to admit, the heat from the cream eased the tightness in her muscles.

Roan didn't have to leave the jar in her room. He could've let her suffer all day. So maybe he wasn't all bad.

She grabbed the carton of juice and shut the refrigerator door. "It's helping. Thanks."

"You'll feel better the more you work out."

"I can't wait," she said, sarcasm dripping from her words.

He chuckled. She paused pouring her juice. He didn't laugh that often. She sort of wished he'd do it more. It had a nice sound, and for some reason, she didn't feel quite so alone. Alone wasn't good.

"The obstacle course is everyone's worst nightmare." He leaned back in his chair. "You did good. I was impressed and I'm not impressed very often."

Shock was a mild word for what she was feeling right now. Shock and pleasure. Just when she wanted to dislike the man, he surprised her. Maybe dislike wasn't the right word. He'd taught her a lot this week. The basics were a necessary evil, they were boring, and they frustrated her. Rather than dislike, maybe he just aggravated her—a lot.

Roan drained his cup and went back to the pot to pour another. The man was a serious caffeine addict. So was her mom. Aasera had adopted quite a few of Earth's customs. Lyraka wondered if her mother was able to get coffee on Nerak.

Once, Aasera had told her that they had smoothies and

food capsules on Nerak, but no real food. It didn't sound like such a great planet to her. She suddenly realized just how much she missed her mother.

Roan wasn't a bad sub for company. He still made her pulse speed up and not just because he had her running on the treadmill every day.

He looked up and caught her gaze before she had a chance to look away.

"Uh . . ." She cleared her throat. "What exactly are we going to be doing today?"

"Have you ever fired a weapon?"

"No."

His grin was slow. "How did you expect to kill the bad guys without a gun?"

"I guess I never really thought about it." And now that she had, she wasn't sure she wanted to. "Do we really kill people?" Could she kill someone? How did anyone know these things unless they were actually in that sort of situation?

"Sometimes. Not as often as people think. And only the really nasty bad guys."

She nodded, but wondered if the time ever came, could she kill someone?

"Killing isn't easy. You can't hesitate. If you do, it could cost you your life."

She took a deep breath. Coming into this, she'd known there would be things she wouldn't like doing. But taking a life?

"If someone had a gun pointed at your mother, and you knew in your heart he was going to pull the trigger, and you had a gun and could take him out, what would you do?"

"I think I could pull the trigger to save someone." She downed her juice, then set the glass in the sink. "So, we're going to a target range?"

He set his cup in the sink beside her glass. "It's inside, but grab a jacket. It's still a little cool out."

She was actually getting to do something. Target practice—firing a real gun.The only gun she'd ever held was on a video game an artist's kid had left behind. Her mother had confiscated it when she'd seen Lyraka firing at bad guys. Aasera said it was too violent.

She hurried to her room and opened her closet door, excitement building inside her. The rush of adrenaline running through her right now made her giddy. She reached for her jacket, but it flew toward her, the hanger slapping her in the face.

"Ow!" She jumped back a step.

What just happened? She looked at the jacket still on the hanger, then back at the closet. Whoa! This had never happened before. She put the jacket back, then reached for it again. Nothing happened.

But it had flown to her before she even had a chance to touch it. Now it just hung on the hanger. She backed up a few steps, and raised her hand.

"Come to me!"

Nothing happened. She moved a step closer.

"Come to me!" She lowered her voice.

"Usually, people just reach in and take it off the hanger," Roan said from behind her.

She jumped, whirling around to face him. He stood in the doorway, hands crossed in front of him. Heat traveled over her. This was so embarrassing.

"You did want to try some target practice . . . today, that is?"

She gave him her best glare. "I reached in to grab my jacket, but before I could touch it, it flew out to me."

"Maybe it really likes you."

"Not funny, and it did happen."

He sighed. "After what I've seen you do, I wouldn't doubt it." He walked farther into the room. "What were you feeling when you opened the closet door?"

He was right. Her emotions usually caused most of her abilities. When she was calm, she could blend in. When she was emotionally charged up, she ran faster.

"I was excited about going to the firing range."

"Then try being excited again."

She faced the closet and held out her hand.

Nothing.

"Concentrate."

"I am."

She closed her eyes. Yea, she was going to the firing range.

Nothing happened.

She took a deep breath. Wow! She was going to the firing range.

"Are you sure it flew out to you?" Roan said.

"Yes, I'm sure. I can't do it with you watching me. Besides, I think it was my initial reaction. I don't feel that same thrill."

He stepped closer, running the back of his hand down the side of her cheek. Her nipples immediately hardened and there was a tightness in her belly.

"Maybe I can get you excited," he murmured.

Her jacket didn't jump out at her, but she could feel the pounding of her heart. She closed her eyes, surrendering to his touch.

"I can feel the heat coming off your body," he whispered close to her ear.

Heat. Burn. Incinerate into a pile of ashes.

She stepped away, reaching into the closet to get her jacket. "I thought we were going to the firing range."

"I'd rather make love to you."

"Are all instructors this . . . this intent on taking their students to bed?"

He casually leaned against the chest of drawers. "Only when they're as sexy as you."

"I think you're trying to scare me away from being an agent."

"That too, but I wouldn't mind taking you to bed, either. In fact, I think I'd enjoy it."

"You admit you're trying to run me off?" She couldn't believe he was actually admitting it. "Less than ten minutes ago, you said I'd impressed you."

"Just because you can make it through a portion of an obstacle course doesn't mean you're cut out for this line of work. You and I both know you're not agent material. You've practically lived the life of a nun. You wouldn't know a bad guy if he stepped out in front of you. All you'll accomplish is getting yourself killed, and that would be a damn shame."

"Oh!" She stomped her foot, anger rushing through her.

The hangers inside the closet trembled, then clothes and all, flew out, landing on Roan's head. He didn't move, just stood there with her clothes draped over him. Her hand flew to her mouth.

"It would seem you've discovered another talent, but I don't really think throwing clothes at the bad guy will be a sufficient deterrent." He pushed the clothes off. They landed with a plop on the floor.

She raised an eyebrow. "No, but then, I can always shoot them." She turned and walked out of the room.

Roan watched the swing in her hips. She had a sense of humor. He liked that in a woman, but he still wasn't so sure about her making a good agent. Agents were supposed to be ultimate fighting machines. So far, Lyraka could hide from them, outrun them, and throw clothes at them.

She had yet to prove her worth as one of the best. Sure, there had been a few people who came in off the streets without a bit of experience and they'd made it. They'd had to work harder, though. It all came down to how bad she wanted to be an agent.

He left her room and started down the stairs. She waited for him at the bottom.

"I will make a damn good agent. Just watch and see." She turned on her heel and walked to the door.

Agents didn't walk like she did, either. Even the female agents. And it was getting harder and harder to keep his hands to himself. Maybe she was putting off some kind of pheromones that made him attracted to her. Now that would be a good weapon to have. An agent that could bring men to their knees—Lethal Lyraka.

He closed the front door and walked to the Jeep. Maybe that was another reason why Joe had wanted the one-on-one training—to keep her away from other men.

She was already sitting in the passenger seat when he climbed in. Very prim and proper. But he knew different. She wanted him as much as he wanted her. So why did she hold back? It wasn't as though it was against the rules. In their line of work, death could be right around the corner. You lived hard, you played harder. As long as it didn't interfere with a mission.

Man, what was that scent she wore? It was driving him crazy. He'd never smelled anything like it. It was a little musky, and sexy as hell.

They were silent on the way to the firing range, each lost in their own thoughts, and he lost in inhaling the fragrance she wore. When he pulled up and parked, she turned to him.

"I have some allergy pills back at the building," she reluctantly told him.

"And?"

Her forehead puckered. "And what?"

"And why would I need allergy pills?"

"Because you've been sniffing since we got inside the Jeep. I thought maybe you were having allergy problems."

He started to laugh. Her frown deepened.

"I don't see a thing funny about me offering you some relief."

"Oh, baby, it's not allergy relief that I need."

She opened her door, slamming it closed after she got out, except it had almost looked as if her hand hadn't touched the door. It might pay to not make her angry when he gave her a gun with real bullets.

Sometimes the Nerakians discovered they could do more the longer they were training. They were pushed past the normal point of their endurance level and that had a way of bringing more of their abilities to the surface. It would be interesting to see just how much Lyraka could do.

He caught up to her before she could open the door to the firing range. "Don't wear that perfume again. Too distracting."

"I'm not wearing perfume. It must be the soap."

He doubted it since he'd used the same soap. They went inside. Mike Avery sat behind the desk, but looked up when they walked in. Mike was older, an ex-cop adding a little to his retirement by manning the firing range.

"Hiya, Roan. Haven't seen you in a few days."

"Been busy."

Mike let his gaze wander over Lyraka. "Yeah, don't blame you."

"Lyraka is an agent-in-training. Lyraka, this is Mike. I heard he's a ladies man so watch yourself around him."

Mike shook his head. "I never got so lucky as to have a partner who looked quite as pretty as Lyraka. Nice meeting you ma'am."

Lyraka focused her smile on the older man. "Hello, Mike. It's nice to meet you."

Mike leaned his elbows on the counter and grinned like a fool. "If you ever want someone with more experience, then I'm your man." His face immediately turned a dark shade of red. "I mean to train you . . . uh . . . to be an agent."

Roan had never seen Mike this flustered. It was like he'd thought. Lyraka was going to be more trouble than any of her abilities were worth.

"Want me to get you both a gun?" Mike asked as he cleared his throat.

"Sure, Mike. How about a three-fifty-seven mag and a nine mil."

"Coming up."

Roan walked to a door on the right. Lyraka followed. One side was lined with stalls. He flipped on the lights and walked to the end stall. In case someone else came in, it would give them a little privacy from prying eyes, although, at some time or other, Lyraka was going to need to be integrated with a team.

Mike brought the guns, laying them out on the waist-high shelf of the stall. Roan watched as Lyraka warily eyed them. If she couldn't fire a weapon, she'd never make it as an agent. She met his gaze after Mike left, then took a deep breath, and picked up one of the guns.

Good girl. He had expected her to do no less. Hell, maybe she would make an agent after all.

He pushed a button. A light came on at the end of the stall away from where they stood. He pushed another button and a paper target appeared.

Sweat beaded Lyraka's upper lip. "I'm ready. What do I do?"

"Point and shoot. Try to hit the target."

She nodded, pointed, and pulled the trigger. Nothing happened. She looked at the gun, then at him.

"It's broken."

"The safety is on."

"Oh, what's the safety?"

This was going to be a very long day. "The little switch on the side. If it's on, the gun won't fire."

She slid the switch to the other side, then pointed. He stepped behind her. She pulled the trigger. The gun fired, her arm jerked up, and she slammed into him—just as he'd known she would.

"I didn't expect that," she said in a breathless whisper, then looked up at him.

All he could think about was how much he wanted to kiss her, but she moved away from him.

"What did I do wrong?"

He proceeded to show her. After an hour of practice, Roan had to admit she impressed him. She hit her target more often than not, and she even seemed more comfortable holding the gun.

She fired, hitting the heart on the paper target dead center, then looked over her shoulder and grinned. "I bet you didn't think I'd be this good."

"I thought you'd never fired a gun before."

She shrugged. "I haven't, but there was a woman who came to the colony and sometimes she brought her daughter. The daughter was more into video games than painting. One of the games had a gun. This is way more cool, though."

He started to say something, but stopped when the door partially opened and he heard someone talking to Mike. Damn, Roan had hoped they'd be out of there before anyone else arrived. Maybe they could slip out in a few minutes when the agent was busy.

The door opened the rest of the way and Roan immediately knew they wouldn't be sneaking out. Damn, of all the people to stop by the firing range today, it had to be him.

Chapter 11

Lyraka fired the gun, hitting the silhouette of a head that was on the paper target. Ha! She'd nailed it.

"Roan, I'd wondered where you were hiding."

Lyraka looked up. She'd been so absorbed in hitting the target that she hadn't even heard the door open.

Good Lord, where did they get these men? Hotties R Us? The man was delicious—thick, light brown hair, beautiful caramel-colored eyes, and shoulders almost as wide as the door. And he was looking at her as if she was the only woman in the room. Which technically, she was, but he was giving her a slow, sexy appraisal that was a huge boost to her ego.

She felt Roan tense beside her and wondered what was up with him. She looked back at the new guy, who was smiling from ear to ear. He had pretty white teeth. She smiled back.

"Aren't you going to introduce us?" he asked.

"No. We were just leaving," Roan said.

She met Roan's gaze. He gave an almost imperceptible nod of his head for her to walk in front of him. Well, he might like the personal trainer stuff, but she was tired of the isolation. She turned back to the newcomer.

"Hi, I'm Lyraka, and we weren't just about to leave." She held out her hand and he took it in his. His hand was large and warm.

"Since Roan doesn't want to introduce us, I'll do it for him. I'm Gavin Chambers."

"It's nice to meet you, Gavin."

"So, what's a pretty girl like you doing in a place like this?"

She laughed. It was a corny line, but the way he said it made it sound funny. "I'm shooting bad guys, at least on paper."

"Why would you want to shoot bad guys when you have me around? I'll do it for you, cross my heart." He made a motion of crossing his heart.

"But if I let you do it, then how will I ever become an agent?"

Gavin straightened from his relaxed pose, looking at Roan as if for confirmation.

"She's in training," Roan finally admitted.

Really, he acted as though she were top secret. Sooner or later people were bound to find out about her. It wasn't as though they didn't know what aliens were. Nerakians trained side by side with earthlings all the time.

Gavin studied her a little closer. "Nerakian?" he asked.

"Yes," Roan said.

"No," Lyraka said at the same time.

Gavin raised his eyebrows. "Okay, is it yes or no?"

Roan's jaw had started to twitch. She'd already figured out that wasn't a good sign. Why was he getting so irritated?

"I'm half earthling, half Nerakian," she said.

"That's a first." Gavin looked from Lyraka to Roan. "She must be special."

"Joe wants her kept under wraps."

"I've been under wraps all my life. It's boring. I want to experience life. I feel as though I've traded one prison for another and I don't like it. And you're both talking as if I'm not even here . . . excuse me!"

Gavin suddenly grinned, then looked at Roan. "Keeping you busy, huh?"

"You can't imagine."

Men, they were all alike. No wonder her mother had advised her to stay away from them.

"You're right. Maybe it *is* time for us to leave." She started to walk toward the door, but decided to give them something they could really talk about and hit her internal speed button, zipping past Gavin in a blur.

"What the hell?" Gavin whirled around.

She stopped at the door. "I'm not just special, I'm their secret weapon." She let the door slam behind her and headed for the Jeep.

Maybe this wasn't what she was meant to do in life. She climbed into the Jeep on the passenger's side, flopping down in the seat, then slamming the door shut. Actually, she hadn't made contact with the door. It just sort of slammed on its own.

That was the way her other abilities had come about—sort of by accident. The day she realized she could kick speed in the butt, she'd tumbled head first into the river that ran close to the colony when she hadn't been able to stop in time. She'd eventually learned to control most of what she could do.

Roan would probably tell Joe, and then they'd keep her hidden so they could study her more, and see what else she could do. She was starting to feel like a lab rat.

She laid her head back against the seat and sighed. All her life, she'd lived at the colony. Long after she'd finished any home schooling, she'd stayed because she couldn't bear to hurt her mother. But now that she was free, she wasn't.

What would happen if she just took off? Moved someplace where no one knew her. She could keep her skills under wraps. Of course, there was the problem of new ones popping up unexpectedly. Like the hangers this morning, and the Jeep door just now. She could always claim ignorance.

She jumped when the door opened on the driver's side and Roan climbed in. He started the Jeep, put it into reverse and backed out. His jaw still twitched. It wasn't like she didn't know she'd pissed him off. Joe had been very specific when he'd said he wanted to keep her under wraps.

Now might not be the best time to start a conversation so she looked out the window. He still hadn't said a word by the time they pulled up in front of the building.

Nope, this wasn't good at all.

Damn it, he really needed to see her side of things. She followed him inside. He went straight to the training room. At least he was aware why they were there and wasn't giving up on instructing her. Except he went straight to the classroom, then to the bookcase. He ran his fingers over the books in the case, drew out the thickest one, thumbed through the pages, then thrust it toward her.

"Read this. There'll be a test." He turned and strode purposefully out the door.

She glanced at the book. *Policies and Procedures*. Man, she must've really pissed him off. She had a feeling taking the book to the woods and reading beneath one of the trees wouldn't be a good idea.

On the other hand, he was already pissed at her. What did the degree of being pissed off really matter? She headed for the door.

She could almost feel his gaze on her as she headed into the woods. She didn't go far, not wanting to push her luck that much. She parked herself beneath one of the tall pines. Serenity washed over her. She closed her eyes, breathed in the heady fragrance of pine, and soon felt her troubles drifting away.

Really, what did it matter if Roan was irritated? Or Joe for that matter? Joe had recruited *her*, not the other way around. They were all excited about what she could do so she really doubted they would stamp FAILED across her paperwork. At least, she didn't think they would.

She flipped to the back of the book and looked at the last page—412 of them. Good grief. Okay, whatever.

Two hours later, she closed the book. Her eyes were permanently crossed. Most of it had been so boring she'd barely gotten through it. The chapters on investigative techniques had been really cool, and there'd been some other chapters that hadn't been too horrible to read through.

She couldn't put it off any longer, though, and came to her feet. She would have to face Roan sooner or later. Besides, she was getting hungry. As she walked across the gravel parking area, she glanced up and caught a movement at one of the windows. Roan? Probably.

Lunch was an excruciating experience. Roan didn't speak and as soon as it was over, he stood, dropping his linen napkin on the table. "I have to leave for a while. Keep reading." He didn't say another word, just left.

Oh, yeah, he got to leave while she was still stuck here. This was not how her life was supposed to be. And did he care? No. He was probably going out with the guys or maybe he had a hot date.

She marched back to the training room and crammed the book between two others, then skimmed her fingers across the rest and drew one out that looked as though it might be interesting. It was about killing people. She might need that sooner than she thought. She took it to the living room and made herself comfortable on the sofa.

The day passed slowly. She could hear every tick of the clock. She read the same paragraphs more than once, then had to go back and read the passage again.

If he was with another woman, what did she look like? Was she pretty? More than likely. They were probably having a nice dinner—candlelight and wine. He would laugh when he told her about the rookie he was trying to train, then they'd laugh together.

Evening fell. Dinner was a disaster. She couldn't even work up a good appetite. She stabbed her vegetables until they were mutilated, finally gave up, and went back to the living area.

After Frances and Cole left for the night, an eerie silence filled the building, and even though Cole had started another fire to ward off the evening chill, it didn't seem to help.

But then the silence was broken. She could hear the Jeep

getting closer and sighed with relief. Would he still be angry with her? Not that she cared. He'd gotten out for a while and played while she'd been stuck here reading a book that didn't even tell her a good way to kill him and get away with it.

She didn't turn around when the door opened, but continued to stand in front of the fire warming her hands.

He went into the living room and stopped. His building anger was palpable. It almost matched hers. He either snorted or growled, she wasn't exactly sure which, then he walked away from her. Apparently, he changed his mind because he came back inside the room.

"I thought it was understood that you wouldn't go to the woods alone?" he practically growled.

So, he wanted to start a fight. Fine with her. And if he needed to use her going to the woods as an excuse to drop her from the program, that was fine, too, but she wouldn't go out like a little lamb. Nope, he'd just opened the storm doors to all her anger and frustrations. Bring it on, baby!

She turned from the fire and faced him. "No, *you* said I couldn't go to the woods alone. I didn't agree. You also said we would work alone. You've told me exactly what I can and can't do, and it's getting pretty damn old." It was irrelevant at this point in time that Joe was the one who'd made the decision for her to train one-on-one. She was pissed at Joe, too, and if he was here, she'd tell him exactly how much!

Roan stepped in front of her. "I thought you wanted to be an agent. Is it too tough for you? Are you backing out?"

"Why can't I train with the others? They'll have to know what I can do sooner or later. Why not sooner?" Her anger rose to the surface. The log in the fire split and cracked, spewing embers up the chimney.

He crossed the room, not stopping until he stood right in front of her. "Because you can't take orders. You've proven that only too well today."

She planted her hands on her hips and glared at him, but she had to raise her head to do so since he was so close, and so tall. "You can't tell me you like the situation any more than I do. You said so yourself that you want to go back into the field. How do you think I feel? I wanted to be around other people who are training. I want to feel like I'm a part of something. I'm tired of being . . ." Her words trailed off when she realized how much of herself she was exposing.

His anger seemed to vanish in a heartbeat. At least, his jaw stopped twitching and the hard glare in his eyes was replaced with a softer, kinder look.

He brushed her hair behind her ear, then smoothed his knuckles across her cheek. Lyraka realized just how much she'd yearned for his touch. Or was it just the touch of another person. She loved her mother, but Aasera hadn't been one to hug. The Nerakians weren't a demonstrative race.

"Tired of what?" he asked softly. "Tired of being alone?"

He dropped his hand down to his side and cold enveloped her. Did he sense how much she longed for more?

She didn't want his pity. She squared her shoulders. "Yes, but you already know that."

"Yeah, I do."

"Of course, you've read my file."

"And you."

"What do you mean, and me?"

"I see it in your eyes. All your hopes and dreams. You have very expressive eyes."

Lyraka wasn't sure she liked the idea that he could read her thoughts so well. What if he . . .

"And yeah, I know you want me as much as I want you."

"No, I don't," she lied, trying to bluff.

He brushed his palm over the front of the thin shirt she wore, across her breast. Her nipple immediately hardened and a flash of heat spiraled downward and settled between her legs.

"Don't you? Even now your body tells me exactly what you want. Do you deny that you want me to unbutton your shirt and slip it from your shoulders? Or that you want me to unhook your bra and let it fall to the floor so I can look at your breasts, touch them, squeeze them . . . take one tight nipple into my mouth and suck on it while caressing your other breast? Do you deny that's what you want?"

"I . . . we . . . can't." But, oh damn, she wanted to do that and a whole lot more.

She needed air, and distance. She abruptly turned and walked to the window. Her body trembled with need.

He followed her, resting his hands on her shoulders. "What are you scared of? I promise I won't hurt you."

"But I can't promise I won't hurt you," she whispered.

He turned her around until she looked him in the eyes. "What's that supposed to mean."

She bit her bottom lip. "I've been with one other man. A poet. He said . . ." God, this was so embarrassing.

"He said what?" Roan prodded.

"That I burned him."

His eyes widened. Then the worst thing that could've happened, happened. He laughed. She'd known it wouldn't go well, but she'd hoped Roan wouldn't laugh.

"I'm sorry," he quickly told her before pulling her into his arms.

His warmth circled her, filled her with a sense of peace and the knowledge that this was exactly where she was supposed to be. But no matter how much she wanted to be there, she had to make Roan understand.

"I'm serious. Rick, the poet, left that very night." She frowned. "My mother might have had something to do with that, though. I think she might have paid him off. My mother doesn't like men very much."

"Tell me what happened." He lightly ran his hand up and down her back.

It felt good to just stand there in his arms. She wished she could stay forever.

"Do you really want the sordid details?"

"I don't think you can burn people."

"You didn't think I had speed, either, or that I could fade

into my surroundings, or move objects without touching them. Oh, and I finished that book you gave me and two others. I read very fast."

He leaned back and looked into her face. "You really finished the book? It was the most boring one in the bunch."

"It wasn't that bad." She frowned. "You wanted to torture me?"

"I was angry. You spoke to Gavin. Even after I gave you the book, you went against the rules, and headed to the woods alone. You disobeyed a direct order."

"I'm sorry." She snuggled back into his arms.

"So, tell me how you burned this guy."

"Rick."

"Okay, how did you burn Rick?"

"I'm not exactly sure."

"But it was while you were having sex."

When he put it like that, she pretty much wanted a hole to open up so she could crawl inside. Actually, why was she even talking about her sex life, or lack of, with Roan? But she already knew the answer. Because she wanted him to fix whatever was broken inside her so that she could have sex again. The little she'd experienced had been really, really good.

"Yes. While we were having sex. We didn't actually finish, I don't think. He said I was defective. Broken." She still remembered how she'd felt when he'd run away. Up to that point, it had been so much fun. She sighed.

He lightly caressed her back. "Then there's only one way to find out what's wrong," Roan said. "We'll just have to have sex."

"And if we incinerate?"

"They can scatter our ashes over the mountainside."

She wasn't so sure she liked that solution, but his hand was causing all sorts of things to stir inside her. Maybe they could just take things as far as a first degree burn.

Chapter 12

Lyraka shook her head, stepping out of the comfort of Roan's arms as fear filled her. "I'm not going to be responsible for watching you go up in a puff of smoke."

"Does that mean you care about me?" He ran his hand lightly through her short black hair sending tremors over her body.

"I care whether you die or not, especially if I'm the cause." If the truth were known, she was starting to care for him more than she wanted to admit. For that reason, she couldn't put his life in danger, no matter how badly she wanted to have sex.

That, and he was a really good instructor. Joe would probably be pissed if something happened to Roan, too. It seemed to her that she was in a lose-lose situation. Well, except for the hot sex. Hot sex would be nice.

"Why don't you let me decide if I want to take the risk? You don't know for sure that I'll burn to a crisp, do you?"

She should lie and tell him she'd corroded a case of batteries and as many vibrators, but before she could, he gave her a warning look.

"The truth."

She'd never been very good at lying. Why couldn't she have that skill?

"I don't know anything for sure," she admitted.

"Then if it gets too hot, I'll stop."

"And if we both incinerate?"

"Then we'll die happy."

She wasn't sure if she was ready to die for sex. Before she could decide one way or the other, he slipped the top button on her shirt through the buttonhole. Her body trembled as she watched his hands move to the second button, then the third and down to the last one.

This would be a good time for her to demand he stop. Just open her mouth and tell Roan, no. He would stop. She already knew that much about him. He would never force her to do anything against her will. She should tell him. Then again, maybe they could stop before the heat got too unbearable.

With a feather-soft touch, he fanned back the edges of her shirt and pushed it over her shoulders, tracing his hands down her arms. Trembles followed in his wake. Their gazes met just before he let her shirt drop to the floor.

Maybe they *would* just die happy, consumed by the heat of their passion.

"You're so beautiful," he said.

She was glad she'd worn her white lacy bra. It was cut low and pushed her breasts up, barely covering her.

He ran the tips of his fingers over the curve of her breasts. "Not even scorched." He raised his hand and wiggled his fingers.

"That's not funny." But he was right and she was glad, although she could feel the familiar heat as it began to build inside her.

He reached behind her to unfasten her bra, but she moved away slightly.

"I won't hurt you," he said.

Heat of a different kind flooded her face. "It's not that."

"Then what is it?"

"I don't want to be the only one without a shirt on." How did she tell him she wanted to see him naked without dying from embarrassment? What she wouldn't give to be more experienced.

"An easy remedy." He reached for the hem of his olive green T-shirt and pulled it over his head.

Ohmygod. She tried to swallow, but her throat had suddenly gone dry. His naked torso was better than she could've imagined. He was all hard muscles and sinewy ridges. She couldn't force her gaze away from his six-pack abs.

"It's okay if you want to touch me, too," he said with barely restrained laughter.

"It's not funny—again." But her words were barely a whisper.

"Hey." He grabbed her chin and raised her head. "Haven't you ever touched a man before?"

"Only Rick, but he didn't look at all like you. I mean . . ."

He drew in a sharp breath. "I feel as though I'm taking advantage of an innocent young woman. Maybe this isn't such a good idea." He reached for his shirt.

"No!" If he stopped, she had a feeling she'd never have a real orgasm with a man. "I'm not innocent. I'm twenty-eight years old, Roan, but I feel like I'm dying a slow death."

"It's okay." He pulled her against his chest, kissing the top of her head. "I won't stop unless you change your mind. Just do me a favor and don't wait too long to decide you've changed your mind."

"Deal."

Good, she was glad he hadn't changed his mind because now that she was against his naked chest, she didn't want to move. He began to lightly caress her back. She felt the heat again, but not so bad that she couldn't stand it. She began to relax against his chest. He smelled wonderful, manly.

When he unfastened her bra, she closed her eyes. He slid the straps down her arms until the only thing holding it in place was his chest. If he stepped away, she'd be naked from the waist up. What if he found her lacking?

"I want to see your breasts," he said close to her ear. "I want to look my fill, then I want to caress them and tug on the nipples. You have sensitive nipples, don't you?"

She nodded, unable to speak. Her whole body was as tight as a well-strung bow.

He took a step back and her bra fell to the floor. "Stunning. Just like I'd known they'd be." He brushed his palm over one hard nipple.

She gasped.

He stopped. "Do you want me to stop?"

"No."

"Good."

Roan knew Lyraka hadn't been exaggerating about the heat. He could feel it coming off her in waves. Not so bad that it burned, but it did make him wonder just how hot it was going to get. He had a feeling she'd be worth getting burned over.

He pinched her nipples between his forefingers and thumbs. He watched her expression, enjoying what he was seeing. She bit her bottom lip, her eyes drifting closed.

"Do you like when I pinch your nipples?"

She nodded.

"Look at me."

She shook her head.

He grinned, knowing she was embarrassed, but at the same time not wanting him to stop. He was afraid he was going to make her a whole lot more embarrassed before this night was over, but by morning, he doubted she'd have any regrets.

She was innocent. She had been with this Rick, but apparently he hadn't known what he was doing. Lyraka might as well be a virgin. Roan would take it slow, but he wanted her to find pleasure in every aspect of making love. That included being a part of foreplay.

"Open your eyes," he told her again.

And again, she shook her head. He stopped. Her eyes flew open.

"That's better. How can I teach you if you have your eyes closed?"

"Is this part of the training?" She cocked an eyebrow.

He leaned forward, running his tongue across her upper lip, then her lower. He felt her sigh, her surrender. He straightened.

"No, not part of your training as an agent. This is a training exercise in the proper way to make love." He rolled a nipple between his finger and thumb again.

She gasped. "I think you're using emotional warfare."

"But you enjoy it."

"Oh, yeah. A lot." She nodded.

"Touch me."

For all her bluster and external toughness, she was really nervous. He saw it in the way her hand trembled just slightly. In the way she didn't quite meet his eyes. But once again, just like in everything she'd done so far, she wasn't backing down.

He took her hand and guided it to his chest. "Touch me," he said in a softer voice.

She ran her hand over his chest. "You're really firm." She licked her lips and he wondered just how long he'd be able to last. Hell, he'd wanted her from the moment he'd seen her, even though he hadn't been ready to admit it to himself.

She brushed across his nipple. He closed his eyes, relishing her touch on his naked skin.

"Are you sensitive there?" she asked.

He opened his eyes and laughed down at her. "You catch on fast." He had a feeling this was going to be a test of his own endurance.

"I've been told I'm a fast learner."

And she was beginning to come into another kind of power. One that women had held over men through the ages. Roan didn't mind.

"So if I rub your nipple like this . . ." She lightly massaged the pad of her finger across the nub. It immediately hardened. "Oh, look, it got hard, just like mine."

Time for lesson two. "I can make it feel even better."

She stopped, and looked at him. He almost regretted drawing her attention away, but he had to stay in control or he wouldn't last very long. This night should be about her, and he wanted to make it one she wouldn't soon forget.

He cupped both her breasts in the palms of his hands, then lowered his head to one, scraping his teeth across the hard nipple before sucking it inside his mouth. He immediately felt the heat of her body enveloping him.

"Oh, God, that feels good," she moaned.

He swirled his tongue around the nipple. She clutched his head, bringing him closer. He still needed better access. He released her nipple and she made a noise of disappointment.

"I only want to get more comfortable." He'd seen some throws in the cabinet where the games were stored. He went to it, opened the bottom drawer, pulled out the blankets, then laid them in front of the crackling fire.

He glanced at her as she semi-shielded her breasts. Shyness would not do. He wanted her to feel comfortable because he planned on stripping her out of everything else that she was wearing, so he switched off the overhead light. There was enough light from the fireplace that he wouldn't miss seeing a thing. When he looked at her, he saw that her shoulders weren't quite as stiff.

"Move your arms from in front of your breasts. I told you I wanted to see them."

She arched an eyebrow.

"Or we can stop. I don't want you to feel uncomfortable."

She paused, then moved her hands away.

Damn, her rose-tipped breasts were perfect.

"Take off your shoes." She wore tennis shoes so it was easy for her to toe off first one, then the other. "Now unfasten your pants."

Her hands trembled, but he had a feeling it was more from anticipation than the fact he was ordering her to undo them.

She pushed the metal button through the opening, then slowly slid the zipper down. Did she know how much she was torturing him? Probably not.

He swallowed hard. "Now take them off."

Again, she hesitated, but he wanted her complete surrender. He wanted her to let go of all her inhibitions and just feel the pleasure he was going to give her.

She peeled her pants down her legs, then kicked out of them. The only thing that shielded everything from his view was a very thin strip of white silk. His dick throbbed. Sweat beaded his brow. He didn't know if it was from the heat of the fire or the heat from her.

"Lie down."

She went to the makeshift bed and laid on top of the throws. He stood at her feet. He wanted to tell her to remove her panties and spread her legs. He wanted to look at her, see all of her, but he didn't want to push her too fast.

Instead, he slipped the metal button out of the buttonhole of his jeans, then just as slowly as she had done, he brought the zipper down. She watched his striptease, her breathing becoming more ragged. He wanted her to be as turned on as he was.

He removed his shoes, then tugged his jeans over his hips, and down his legs before kicking out of them.

"Hurry," she breathed.

"You don't have to wait."

Her eyes widened.

"Touch yourself."

"I . . . I can't."

"You've never touched yourself?"

Her cheeks turned a rosy hue, and he had his answer.

"Touch your breasts." He didn't need to add, or we can stop, but his words hung in the air. Damn it, he didn't want her to be afraid of anything around him. He wanted her to experience it all.

She ran her hand across her nipples, then bit her bottom lip. God, watching her touch herself was such a fucking turn-on.

He grabbed the waistband of his briefs. Her hands stilled. He stopped. She tweaked both nipples. He pushed his briefs over his hips and down his thighs.

Heat pulsated from her. He could feel it even from where he stood. Colors began to swirl around her. It felt as though he was on drugs.

Her legs opened. Roan didn't think she even realized she was spreading them. He kicked his briefs out of the way and moved to his knees between her legs.

He touched the insides of her thighs, then jerked back. Damn, her skin was hot to the touch. Not so much that it blistered him, but hot enough. When he looked at her, he saw the disappointment on her face.

"I burned you, didn't I?" She turned her head away. "I'll just have to accept I'm doomed to a life of celibacy."

"You'd give up so easily?"

She met his gaze. "You like the idea of becoming burnt toast?"

"Remember, I'm a member of an elite force. The best of the best. Our motto is never give up, never surrender." He grinned. "I'll be right back." He jumped to his feet. "Don't move."

She smiled and shook her head. "I'll stay right here."

He hurried to the kitchen and filled a bowl with ice. In less than three minutes he was on his way back to the living room. She rose up on her elbows, frowning, then peered into the bowl.

"Ice?"

"Ice," he said. "Trust me."

"That's what you keep telling me, but I'm not so sure I want to."

"Lie back."

She did, but hesitantly. He took one of the cubes, touching it to her leg.

She sucked in her breath. "It's cold."

"That's the idea." He ran it slowly up her leg from her knee to mid thigh before it melted. The lady was still hot.

Good.

He picked up another ice cube and ran it up and down the crotch of her panties. She sucked in a breath and raised her hips.

"Do you like that?"

"Um, yes."

That one melted. He took another one and ran it over first one nipple, then the other. When it melted, he moved his tongue over one tight nub before sucking it inside his mouth. Her skin wasn't too hot, but then, he always did like the heat.

He moved to her other breast, heard her moan when he sucked the tight little nub inside his mouth.

"Roan, I can't stand it anymore. I need you."

He sat back on his heels. "Need what? To do this?" He tugged on her panties until he could see her pussy. Sweet. Just as he'd imagined it would be.

"I love looking at you," he said as he bent her knee. He slid one side of her panties over her knee and down her leg, caressing her smooth skin as he did. She started to lower her leg, but he stopped her. "No, keep it right like this." He wanted her to open all the way for him.

Heat pulsated from her body in waves. He took an ice cube and started at her mound, running it along the perimeter.

"Roan, please. I can't stand anymore. I feel as if my body is on fire."

He didn't want to stop. There was so much more he wanted to do. He wanted to lower his head and suck her inside his mouth, taste her. But he understood her need, because he felt the same way.

He took another ice cube. "Tell me if I hurt you." He slid

the ice cube inside her, taking his time so he didn't cause her pain.

"Crap, it's cold."

"Not too cold, is it? I can stop."

"It's kind of sexy."

Kind of sexy? God, she was killing him. He was already about to explode. He grabbed his jeans, reaching inside the pocket for a condom and quickly ripped open the packet and slid it down his length.

He eased inside her, breaking past the thin barrier. He hesitated.

"Don't stop, please," she said.

He felt as though he were diving inside an active volcano. Sweat beaded his forehead and upper lip as the colors swirling around him deepened to fiery reds and wild purples, hot pinks and vibrant greens.

But then the heat changed, as though it accepted him and began to creep up his body. It started at his toes, and like flowing lava it poured over his body. It was fucking fantastic.

She wrapped her legs around him, pulling him closer and he sank deeper. He pulled nearly all the way out, then plunged inside her again.

"Do you feel it?" she breathed.

Did he feel it? "Oh, yeah." He felt every nerve as though it had a life of its own, but he felt her too. He felt the beat of her heart, and her lungs as they filled with air, then exhaled. Their bodies seemed to fuse and become one. Never in his life had he ever felt this alive, this aware of his surroundings, of the woman he was making love to.

He slid inside her slick body, then drew out. The blood pounded through his veins, drumming inside his head. Their ragged breathing filled the room.

"Ah, God, Roan, now . . . now!" she cried out.

He moved faster, she rose up and met each thrust.

"Yes, yes!" She stiffened beneath him.

He clenched his muscles as the lights exploded into thousands of shimmering stars that rained down on them. He couldn't breathe. He gasped for air. Lyraka took a deep breath, but *his* lungs filled. He collapsed on top of her and with his last bit of energy, rolled to his side.

"Something strange happened," she said with awe. "It was as though I felt everything you were feeling."

"Me, too."

"But more than making love."

"As if we'd become one person."

"We blended together."

"Weird."

"But exciting."

He nodded. "Oh, yeah, it was that."

"And we're still alive."

He hoped they were. He wasn't quite so positive, but if he had died, it'd been a hell of a ride!

Damn, what had they done? What had he done!

"I thought you said you'd been with a man?"

"I have. Rick. Remember, I told you."

"You're a virgin. At least, you were." Guilt flooded him.

She rolled to her side, facing him, her breasts rubbing against his arm. Damn, she was killing him.

"And now I'm not." She frowned. "I guess I should thank you. It was fantastic."

He laughed. Oh, Lord. He'd never been thanked by a woman before. Not that he thought he wasn't pretty good in that department. But then, all Lyraka had to compare him to was Rick. From what she'd told him that probably didn't say a lot.

He moved closer. Bad move. Now her breasts were against his chest. She sighed and snuggled against him. Her thigh bumped his penis and he reacted like any normal, red-blooded American male would react.

"You're getting hard again," she said with awe. "Do we have more ice?" She looked up at him.

Do we have more ice? He certainly hoped so.

Chapter 13

Sometime during the night, they'd staggered up to his room and crawled into bed. She languidly stretched as she woke up the next morning. God, so this was what it was all about. Relaxed didn't even come close to how she felt right now. Contented? Yeah, closer to that. Like a cat. *Meow.*

That was what it was like to have an orgasm. No wonder Nerakian women were addicted to sex. She briefly wondered if chocolate would be as good. Maybe one addiction per lifetime would be enough to handle.

She turned on her side and opened her eyes, glancing at the clock. Six o'clock. She'd overslept.

And she was in her bed. Her forehead wrinkled. Had she dreamed sex with Roan? She moved the cover back. Her body still looked the same. Then she smiled. She didn't have a stitch of clothes on. So, it hadn't been a dream.

She shoved the covers to the side and got out of bed feeling as though a new kind of vigor filled every part of her body. Having sex was better than any energy drink she'd ever had.

There was a tap on her door right before it opened. Roan poked his head inside her room.

"Are you . . ." His words trailed off and something close to a gurgle came out of his mouth. He opened the door the rest of the way and strode inside her room, not stopping until he stood in front of her. "God, you're the most beautiful woman I've ever seen." He lowered his mouth to hers.

She raised her lips to meet his, pressing her naked body against him. His tongue stroked hers.

Heat infused her, she jumped and moved back, touching her lips. "Your lips are hot."

"You can say that again."

She shook her head. "No, I mean, you're hot-hot."

He touched his finger to his lips. "You're right, I am hot. I think I might have absorbed some of your heat last night."

Her shoulders slumped. "Oh, no, I've cursed you."

He laughed, drawing her back against him. "If that was a curse, can you curse me again tonight?"

She drew in a sharp breath as a visual filled her head and a rush of heat coursed through her. "I could curse you right now if you want."

He sighed. "Frances and Cole will be here soon, and I don't want to hurry through making love with you. But it is tempting."

He cupped her breast, squeezing her nipple before the heat began to spread. "I'll meet you downstairs."

"Ass."

He laughed.

She grabbed clean clothes and hurried to the bathroom. She didn't want to spend another moment away from Roan. Maybe this one-on-one wasn't going to be so bad after all.

She rushed her shower, then dressed, and ran a brush through her hair. It didn't take her long before she was ready, but she stopped long enough to study her reflection in the mirror with a critical eye. Until now, she'd never thought much about her looks. She turned her head to one side, then the other. Not bad, she guessed.

Make-up hadn't been a top priority for her. Who was going to notice if she wore any or not? Aasera had never worn make-up so there hadn't been much of a chance to experiment.

Lipstick might have been nice. If she had any. Roan might think she was trying to fix herself up for him. He'd be right, but she didn't want him to think it. Last night might not have meant as much to him as it had to her.

Ah, last night. Her body trembled just thinking about it. The incredible heat and the swirling lights. She'd wondered if she would ever get to see the lights at their strongest. She hugged herself. Roan had given her so much.

Roan. Darn! He was waiting downstairs for her.

She rushed out of the bathroom and down the stairs. He was in the kitchen drinking his coffee. She slowed her steps as she walked the rest of the way inside. *Keep it casual.* Their gazes locked, then his gaze swept over her, really slow. Her blood began to heat.

She heard the sound of a car coming up the hill. "Cole and Frances," she said.

"I don't hear anything."

She shrugged. "I have better than average hearing."

A couple of minutes passed. Roan went to the window while she poured herself a glass of juice.

"You're right. It was them," he said as their car pulled into the parking area.

"Of course I was right."

"That must be some hearing."

"It can get bothersome. It's noisy in the city with all the cars and people. In the country there's crickets and other noises that used to drive me crazy." She took a drink, then lowered the glass. "What are we going to do today?"

A smile lifted the corners of his mouth.

Oh, yeah, she'd like to do what he was thinking.

Just as abruptly, his smile dropped. "Classroom."

She grimaced. "I read all the books."

"Sorry. This is part of it."

"That doesn't mean I have to like it." She finished the rest of her juice and placed her glass in the sink. She wasn't looking forward to the classroom. She cast a longing glance out the window. It was going to be a nice day today. The sun was already coming up. The perfect day for being outside.

She followed Roan to the classroom, then sat at one of the smaller desks. There were eight total besides the instructor's larger desk.

"I want to go over the interview process this morning," Roan said, flipping open a book and turning to the page he wanted. When he looked at her, it was as though he was a different person. Gone was the man who'd made passionate love to her last night, and in his place, was the instructor. She would've liked to spend more time with the man from last night.

The morning moved slowly, they broke for a quick breakfast, then an even quicker lunch. By early afternoon, she was ready to run out of the building screaming.

"You're tapping the pencil again," Roan told her.

She looked at the pencil between her fingers. So she was. She laid it to the side and ran a hand through her hair, then stretched her arms above her head. "I'm tired of sitting at this desk. Has no one ever heard about cushions in seats? I want to be outside."

When he didn't say anything, she studied his face. Could he possibly be thinking it over?

"Okay."

Elation filled her.

"We'll go to the obstacle course."

That wasn't exactly what she meant, but if it would get her out of the building, she'd agree to just about anything.

"I just need to grab a few things. I'll meet you at the Jeep."

When she went outside, she stood by the Jeep and raised her arms high above her head. Aasera once told her the Nerakians worshipped the sun. Maybe that's why part of her longed to be outside.

There was something about the heat that made her want to feel it on her skin. Let the rays wash over her naked body. There had been times in her life that she'd sneaked away to the woods and removed her clothes. Patches of sun had found its way through the trees and bathed her in warmth.

Roan came out of the building with a backpack. He tossed it in the back of the Jeep. "Ready?"

She nodded and climbed in on the passenger side. What she wouldn't give to walk through the woods with Roan, both of them naked. She drew in a deep breath at the picture that formed in her mind.

How good would she be at seducing him? Would the instructor drop his guard and let the man come out?

Crazy thinking. She wanted to be an agent. She closed her eyes and remembered last night. The sex had been so good. Powerful, explosive.

"You okay?" Roan asked as he pulled into the parking area.

"Yes, of course. Why wouldn't I be?" She sat a little straighter in her seat.

"I don't know. You seem quiet." He turned the key and the engine stopped. "You're not rethinking your decision to become an agent, are you?"

She shook her head. "No, this is what I want."

"You said you wanted freedom. I'm not sure being on call most of the time is the freedom you're looking for."

Her gaze moved to the window. "Sometimes I used to wonder where I belonged. I'm not Nerakian, but yet, I'm not one hundred percent earthling, either." She looked at him. "Being an agent will give some definition to who I am. Does that make sense?"

He nodded. "I think I know where you're coming from." He hesitated.

"What?" There was something he wasn't telling her. She was curious to know more about the man he was, and what had shaped his life.

"Nothing." He reached for the door handle.

"Why did you want to become an agent?" she pressed, not willing to accept his silence.

"I guess I was a lot like you are now," he finally said. "I don't have any family. Not left anyway. An aunt raised me. My mother was killed in a car accident when I was twelve. I never really knew my dad. I don't think he wanted a kid. Mom never married. The one time I asked about him, she had such a look of devastation on her face that I figured whatever it was, it wasn't worth causing her that much pain. I never asked again. My aunt took over my care after my mother was killed."

"You never asked your aunt about your father?"

He shook his head. "I doubted she would tell me, or that she had even known him. But she tried to make up for my lack of not having a mother or father around. My aunt never married, and never quite seemed to know what to do with me so I wasn't sure exactly where I belonged. Not the situation you're in, but similar."

"I didn't know my father, either. I guess we're alike in more ways than one."

"I have a theory about mine; I was better off not knowing him."

"Yeah, I came up with the same theory."

"Ready for the obstacle course?" he asked, changing the subject.

She'd rather walk in the woods, but she had to admit that gliding through them was pretty fun, too. "I'm ready." She wasn't looking forward to running the course, though. It had kicked her butt the last time. Would he still want her if she was sweaty and smelly? Doubtful.

Twenty minutes later, she forgot about everything as she flew through the trees, then landed on the big air bag. She scooted off the end and unhooked. God, it was so beautiful here. She breathed in the fresh scent of pine. It was a heady fragrance.

She turned when Roan came sliding in. If she squinted her eyes, she could almost pretend he was Tarzan about to scoop her into his arms and take her high into the treetops where he would make wild, passionate love to her.

He landed on the air bag and unhooked. "I thought we'd check out the backside of the course today." He came to his feet.

"There's more?"

"A lot more. We haven't covered half of it yet."

Great.

For the next hour they trudged through the dense woods. They hadn't been this way before. She noticed the trees were getting thicker and she had to wonder if Roan knew where he was going.

"Roan?"

He stopped and looked over his shoulder.

"You do know where you're going, right?"

His grin was slow to form. Butterflies fluttered inside her stomach.

"Don't you trust me?" he asked.

They were back to the trust issue. "Yes . . . of course I trust you." That had to be the lamest response she'd ever given.

He shook his head. "You have to learn to trust me." He faced her, reaching into his back pocket. "Trust is what it's all about."

"What are you doing?"

He brought a length of silk from his back pocket. Okay, they were going to do the blindfold again. She could pass this time. She knew how the game was played.

"I do trust you." She turned around.

"We'll see." He placed the length of black silk over her eyes and knotted it in the back.

She heard him remove his backpack and drop it to the ground. Weren't they going to the platform where she would fall backwards onto the big air bag?

He put his hands on her shoulders and turned her around to face him.

"Do you trust me?"

"I said I did," she told him, but she was starting to get a little worried.

"You don't look as though you trust me. In fact, you look a little concerned."

"I trust you," she said between gritted teeth.

"Good." He unbuttoned the top button of her shirt.

She took a step back. What exactly did this have to do with trust?

"Change your mind?" he asked.

Ass. This was another test and she didn't plan to fail. She had no problem stripping outside. She stepped forward again. "Of course I haven't changed my mind." Besides, she knew what it would lead to—making love. She only hoped he could stand the heat. There wasn't any ice out here.

He unbuttoned her shirt the rest of the way and slipped it down her arms. "Black lace. Sexy." He ran his hand across the top of her breasts. "It barely covers your nipples."

Heat began to swirl deep inside her. She thrust her chest forward wanting him to touch and caress. His laughter was light.

"Is that an invitation?" he whispered in her ear, his hot breath fanning her cheek.

"What do you think?"

"I think you don't mind getting naked in the woods."

"I told you that I love the woods. They're like a second home to me."

"Good, because I plan on stripping every last article of clothing from your body." He ran his fingers across the top of her bra, scraping over her nipples and down her stomach. He stopped at the waistband of her pants.

She could barely breathe as she waited impatiently for him to take off her pants.

"Eager, aren't you."

She nodded.

First, he unlaced her hiking boots, then pulled them off. Next, he undid her pants and slid the zipper down. He didn't hurry. She could have counted the teeth on the zipper as he slowly took it downward. Then he was tugging the material over her hips, down her thighs and helping her to step out of them.

"Black lacy panties. Did you wear them just for me, hoping we'd have sex?"

Had she? She knew the answer. She had. She just wished he wouldn't point the truth of his words out to her.

"Did you?"

"Yes," she admitted.

"I like them."

Pleasure rippled through her.

"I'm going to take them off. Not right now, but soon. First, I want to see your breasts. I want to feel the weight of them in the palms of my hands." He slid his hands around behind her and unsnapped the clasp, then removed her bra.

If he didn't touch her soon, she'd die. Her body ached for him. Last night had awakened her sexual cravings. She wanted to experience everything.

"I love looking at your breasts, your rosy nipples." He pinched the nipples, her body quivered. "Sweet."

She moaned.

"Do you like that?"

She nodded, biting her bottom lip.

He slid his hands over her hips, tugging on the waistband of her panties. "I want to see all of you." He pulled them down, then placed her hand on his shoulder. He'd knelt in front of her so she knew he was looking at the most intimate part of her body, but she was so on fire for him right now that she didn't care.

She raised her foot when he nudged her, then he was removing her panties. She stood before him completely naked, and she loved it.

"I'm going to kiss you right here." He brushed his fingers through her curls.

She drew in a breath. "I don't know . . . I've . . ."

"Trust me." His mouth covered her, sucking and licking.

She gasped. No one had ever done this to her. Ohmygod,

the sensations were almost too much, but it was so fantastic. She reached out, connected with his shoulders and held on before she collapsed.

"I can feel your heat. It sears me, but it doesn't burn."

"Your skin feels hot . . . too," she finally managed to say. If they both burned to a crisp at least she would die happy.

He pulled her down to her knees. She didn't want to move. What he was doing with his mouth felt too damn good, but she was too weak to resist.

"I put a blanket in my backpack. Don't move."

She nodded, not knowing if he saw the movement or not. She couldn't speak. He'd drained all the energy out of her. She heard a rustle in the leaves, then he was reaching for her, helping her to lie down. He lay beside her, cupping one of her breasts, tweaking the nipple.

She reached toward him, the palm of her hand connecting with his shirt. She slipped her hand beneath it, sighing when she felt his rigid muscles. There was a lot more that she wanted to touch this time.

There was a rustle, then voices. She froze. His hand stilled.

"Someone's coming," she whispered. Why hadn't she heard them before now? Some agent she would make. She hadn't paid enough attention to her surroundings to hear whoever was stomping through the woods. She reached for the blindfold. He stopped her hand in midair.

"Trust me," he said.

"Someone is coming. I need to get my clothes."

"I'll protect you. Just lie quietly."

"No!" She kept her voice low. There were at least two of them and she could hear them getting closer. Being naked in the woods, making love in the woods was all well and good, but she'd just as soon not be caught outside like this by strangers.

"Trust me," he repeated.

Trust him? She didn't think so. Roan was still dressed. Okay, she could do this if she concentrated. She let out her breath, felt the blanket beneath her. All she had to do was concentrate, stay calm, and blend in.

Roan stroked between her legs, breaking her concentration. Damn! Did he even realize what he'd done? Probably not.

"I have to get my clothes. Now!"

"I told you, I'll protect you, if you'll only trust me. I swear I won't let you come to any harm or embarrassment."

The voices were getting nearer. She sat up, tugging at the silk fabric that covered her eyes. As soon as it was off, she flung it away from her. It took a few moments for her eyes to adjust. As soon as she could see, she scrambled into her clothes. Damn, why wouldn't her fingers work?

She buttoned her shirt crooked, but she didn't care as long as she was covered. She grabbed her pants and jerked them on. Forget her panties. She'd put them in her pocket.

Out of the corner of her eye, she saw that Roan hadn't made a move to get up. Why should he? He was dressed. He probably thought it was cool to be caught out in the woods with a naked woman. Well, she wasn't about to be a trophy he could parade around.

Finally, she'd had enough. "Aren't you going to at least get up?"

"Why?"

She whirled around and faced him. He was holding a small box. What the hell was going on? He pushed a button. It sounded as though someone was walking up on them. A tape recorder?

Anger boiled inside her. She'd never felt this much fury swirling inside her. She stomped her foot. "I hate you!"

He pushed the button and there was silence. No one was going to walk up on them.

"You still haven't learned to trust me."

"This . . ." She waved her arm. "It was all a test?"

He nodded.

"You used me."

He stood. "I'm trying to save your life."

She raised her chin. "Do you use this test on all your students?" She sneered. "Bring them out here and shame them?"

He rested his hands on her shoulders. "I didn't mean to embarrass you."

"Didn't you?"

He shook his head. "You might not like what I did, but I only did it to protect you."

"Go to hell, Roan." She turned and was gone in a flash. She would never let him touch her again.

Chapter 14

Roan wanted to kick himself. He shouldn't have done it. He doubted she would ever learn to trust him now. Damn it, he shouldn't have gone that far.

He raked his fingers through his hair. Damn it, he had because she did mean so much to him. That was the kicker.

Lyraka had to learn to place complete trust in him, in the team she would eventually be assigned to. What choice did he have? When it came right down to it? None. He sank to the ground, leaning his back against a tree.

He'd seen it in her eyes the first day—innocence. It would get her killed. If she hated him for the rest of her life, at least she might stay alive. He was teaching her some hard lessons.

His cell rang. He reached inside his pocket and brought it out, glancing at the caller ID displayed on the screen. Joe. Great, that was all he needed.

"Yeah."

"You sound like you're in a good mood."

"I couldn't be better."

"I have some news that might cheer you up."

"I'm going back in the field?" Not that he felt as though he could leave Lyraka right now. She still needed too much training.

And he still wanted her.

"I want Lyraka integrated into the training here—with the team she will be working with."

"There's a lot she still needs to learn." He shook his head. "No, she's not ready."

Silence.

"I need her back here," Joe finally said. "There's been some activity."

"What kind of activity?"

"The Roverts. King Ethgar has died. Prince Banyon is the new ruler."

A cold chill ran down Roan's spine. He'd never met the Prince, and didn't care to. The Roverts were nasty creatures, like vampires, who sucked the essence out of other species, draining them dry. It only lasted a week, but for that week, the victims were in a vegetative state.

If the Roverts wanted, they could keep their victims that way indefinitely, letting them come out of their coma long enough to realizc what was happening before putting them down again. It was an extreme form of torture and Roan pitied the victims.

"When do I leave?"

"You don't."

"But . . ." Then it dawned on him what Joe was saying. "Surely you don't plan to send Lyraka in. She's not even close to being ready. If you do this, her death will be on your conscience." And he would do everything in his power to stop her from going.

"She won't be alone. You'll be with her."

"This isn't a good idea, Joe." Damn it. There was no way she'd be ready.

"We need her skills."

"Speed won't save her."

"But her ability to blend in to her surroundings will."

Roan closed his eyes, raking a hand through his hair. "You know about that?"

"Yeah, I saw her do it once. It was right before she came here. I knew then she was something special."

"It doesn't matter what she can do. It's what she can't do that bothers me. There's more to being an agent then one or two special abilities."

"Then you'll need to make sure she learns. I want her here in the morning. Our spies tell me the Roverts are planning something. Right now, we're still on yellow alert, but that could change."

"They'd be stupid to go to war."

"Would they? The Nerakians are all bluff. They haven't fought a war in years. It wouldn't take much to get control, especially if they join forces with another species who wouldn't mind a fight." There was a pause. "Roan, we might not have a choice."

"Okay, okay. When do you want her back down the mountain?"

"Tomorrow morning. We'll see how she does working with a team, but I still want you to oversee her training."

They spoke for a few minutes, then Roan snapped his phone closed. Damn! He'd hoped for more time with her. Right now, Lyraka hated him with a passion.

He stood, grabbed his backpack, and headed up the hill. But when he got to the top, she wasn't waiting for him at the Jeep. Had she walked back? It was at least five miles. He glanced around before he climbed inside. A niggling of worry crept over him.

There was no sign of her as he drove down the mountain. He didn't like that she hadn't waited for him. Not that he blamed her. He'd acted like a jerk using that kind of tactic. He wouldn't have used it on anyone else.

He had hoped she would trust him—that they'd been through enough together she would know he wouldn't let anything or anyone hurt her.

He pulled into the parking area and got out after turning off the ignition, looking around as he did. The sun was slipping lower in the sky. He didn't sense her watching him. His gut said she was probably inside nursing her wounded pride. That made him feel lower than a grain of sand on the bottom of the ocean.

He found her in the living room sitting on the sofa, staring at the fireplace even though there wasn't a fire. Damn, she looked lost and sad. He didn't feel any better knowing he'd been the one to make her feel like this.

"I'm sorry."

She didn't look at him.

He walked around the sofa and stood in front of her. "I wanted you to trust me. After all we've been through, I thought you would."

"It was mean. I thought someone was walking up on us." She raised her head and looked him in the eyes. "You're the only person who's ever seen me naked. I did trust you. I trusted you enough to make love with you. Maybe it's you who needs to learn to trust me. I'm part of the team, too." She stood, looked at him with tears in her eyes, then walked from the room.

He thought he couldn't feel lower than he had a few minutes ago. Man, had he been wrong. He drew in a ragged breath.

That night they ate in silence. He noticed Lyraka didn't eat much at all. She spent most of the time moving the food around on her plate. She finally stood, dropping her white linen napkin on the table. When she brushed past his chair, he spoke.

"You'll be joining the others tomorrow."

She stopped immediately, and faced him. "What do you mean? Am I being kicked out?"

"No. It's not like that all. Joe wants you to train with the others."

Silence.

"And you?"

"I'll still train you, except now it'll be with the group. There'll probably be other instructors as well. Joe wants to . . . step up your training."

"Why?"

He stood, tossing his napkin on the table. "Because there's been some activity. Because he may need your skills to quell an uprising." He closed the distance that separated them. "Go home, Lyraka. Go back where it was boring and safe. You're not ready for this."

"I've been ready all my life. This is what I was meant to do. I've studied all the books. I faced the obstacle course, and I bet I'm as good at it as any other agent."

"There's more to it than that."

She raised an eyebrow. "You mean the trust thing?"

"That's part of it."

"Or were you trying to run me off and using trust as an issue?" When he didn't say anything, her eyes widened. "That's it, isn't it? You haven't wanted me here from the start."

"Of course that's not it." But he knew that was part of it. He sighed. "People get killed."

"Death is a part of living. Sometimes you have to take chances just to feel alive."

He placed his hands on her shoulders. "But I don't want you to take that chance."

"It's not your choice to make." Her words were soft, but carried a lot of weight.

He got lost in her eyes. "I'm sorry about today."

"I know."

There was a wealth of sadness in her eyes and he knew that he was the one who'd put it there. She had every right to hate him.

"I guess there's nothing left to be said." He dropped his hands from her shoulders and walked past her. "Be ready to leave at the usual time in the morning."

She reached her hand toward him, but he'd already left the room. Her steps were heavy as she walked from the dining room. She started past the front door, but stopped at the last minute and walked toward it. She eased it open and slipped outside.

The air was chilly. A shiver swept over her, but she didn't stop, continuing toward the trees. She didn't breathe easier until she was deep inside the cover of branches and bark.

But she didn't feel the kind of peace that usually came. What was happening to her? She felt as though Roan had ripped her heart out, then squeezed the very life from it. If only her mother was here so that she could ask her what was happening.

Maybe her life would return to normal once she was with others who pursued this career. Maybe then she would feel more in sync with herself. Maybe then she would stop feeling this incredible pain.

Maybe.

Chapter 15

Lyraka had never been this nervous in her life. Not even the first time she'd had to go to the dentist and heard the drill in the background, not when Rick had first kissed her nor when Roan . . .

Okay, she was pretty nervous from the time she'd first laid eyes on Roan.

But she held her head high as she walked into the room. She counted eight people. Everyone was standing except one man who had his nose buried inside a book in a back corner of the room. She recognized Roan, and Gavin, the guy from the firing range. He smiled and she relaxed a little.

Roan cleared his throat. "Lyraka will be joining the team," he told everyone.

Besides Gavin and Roan, there were four men and two women. One of the women was a Nerakian, probably a warrior, she looked a lot like Kia—who was technically Lyraka's niece, except Kia was older.

The warrior glanced her way, then seemed to dismiss Lyraka. She faced front, but then slowly brought her gaze back to Lyraka. The woman's eyes widened slightly. Their gazes locked. Lyraka raised her head and squared her shoulders. The woman nodded.

Okay, so the warrior suspected there was something different about Lyraka. No biggie. The Nerakian didn't know

Lyraka's blood was mixed. Let the warrior wonder what made Lyraka different.

Lyraka turned her attention to the other female. Definitely earthling. She was petite and blond. Everything about her looked soft. Blond hair, baby blue eyes. But when she met Lyraka's gaze, Lyraka noted the intelligence lurking in that one look. Lyraka had a feeling there wasn't anything soft about her.

The men stared openly at Lyraka, as if they'd never seen a woman. She met the gaze of one of them. He blushed before shoving his thick glasses higher up the bridge of his nose, but she noticed he didn't look away. The only man who didn't stare was the one who had his nose stuck inside the book.

She tried not to let her nervousness show. Roan had already said they would introduce her skills when the time was right, but for now, she would just be one of the group. She didn't feel like one of the group. She felt like a bug under a microscope.

The team she was joining had been training for months, though not together. Roan said it might not be a good idea to mention she'd only been there for a short time. She could understand his reasoning, sort of. After all, they were there to keep Earth safe. They shouldn't mind doing whatever it took to make that happen. But she would keep silent.

"Everyone take a seat," Roan said.

There were no desks here. Only one long table. She moved to the seat closest to the door and pulled the chair out. Nothing like a quick getaway. Gavin and Roan stood as everyone else took a seat.

Gavin looked at each of them. "You've each been handpicked to work as a team. Some of you have already been working together and some of you have been training longer than others."

"But now you're going to be taking it a step further," Roan said. "Everything you do, you'll do as a unit. There's no room for mistakes."

"Introductions first," Gavin said. He nodded toward the blonde. "Alesha Talbot. Graduated top in her class from Stanford. She's your numbers person. If you need to know how long you'll have to get in and get out before you're blown to hell, she's the person to go to."

Lyraka would not have expected that Alesha could add one plus one. She looked like a piece of fluff. Lyraka had a feeling this was one lady who better not be crossed. There was certainly more to her than she'd first thought.

"Reeka, as some of you already know, is Nerakian. She's an expert on alien species . . .

"Johnny, you have a problem with being on a team with a Nerakian?" Gavin asked. "If you have something against working with any person on the team, then I'm sure we can fix that."

His implication was clear. They worked together or that person would be dropped.

Johnny shook his head. "No, sir, of course not."

"That's what I thought." He looked at everyone else again. "Like I said, you're a team. Each of you will hold the others' fate in your hands. If you can't work together, then we don't need you."

Gavin looked at Roan, he nodded.

"Reeka is also a warrior and an expert in tactical maneuvers. Next is Warren."

The man with his nose still stuck in a book looked up.

"Warren is one of the best demolition experts I've ever run across."

Warren shrugged. "I like to blow things up, what can I say?"

Everyone laughed and the mood was lightened.

"Link is fondly known as the interrogator."

Link blushed. "I have a way with people."

"Johnny and Ray are the muscle of the group. If all else fails, they'll bulldoze their way through a brick wall with brute strength."

All brawn and no brains?

No, they wouldn't be here if that's all they were. Lyraka had a feeling that even though they were built like muscle men, they were smart, too.

"And Lyraka," Roan said.

She met his gaze.

"Lyraka is an expert in counter maneuvers."

Link pushed his thick glasses higher on the bridge of his nose. "What does that mean?"

"Exactly what I said." Roan quickly changed the subject, but she knew by the way Link continued to watch her, that he was even more curious.

Since when had she become an expert in counter maneuvers? She wasn't even sure she knew what that meant. But at least he hadn't said she had no experience whatsoever.

She glanced at the others. Each one of them brought something to the team. What right did she have to be here? Because she could run fast? Because she could blend in, literally? Suddenly she felt as though she were a complete fake. Roan and Joe had been right to begin training her one-on-one. If not for that, she wouldn't have a clue what was going on.

Was that why Roan's tactics had been over the top? So that she would learn faster? She had caught on pretty quickly. Except she hadn't given him her complete trust. She'd failed that test.

"We're going to be doing some mock escape and rescue procedures," Roan said. "Most of you have already been through this on paper, but nothing in the real world works exactly like it does in a textbook and you have to be able to think and act fast without any hesitation. And you have to be able to trust each man on your team. If that trust is broken, it could cost the whole team their lives."

She refused to look at Roan. She knew exactly who he was talking about.

"Relax and get to know each other today. Tomorrow, you'll have your first mock mission."

Roan and Gavin left the room. Reeka came to her feet. "I'm a warrior as the instructors said, and Nerakian."

"Yeah," Johnny said as he came to his feet and sauntered over to stand near her. "The perfect planet, except there aren't any men. All I want to know," he sneered, "is why the Nerakians killed off all the men, but everyone likes sex so much it's almost like a frenzy when you come to Earth."

Link stood. "I . . . uh . . . don't think this is what the instructors meant when they said they wanted us to get to know each other." He looked around the room at each person. "I've probably been around longer than anyone here because they've used me mainly on Earth, but I know whole teams haven't gotten any further than right where we are now because they couldn't work together." He looked pointedly at Johnny.

Johnny looked as though he might say something, then changed his mind and shrugged. "I wasn't being serious."

"I'm hungry," Ray said. He hadn't said much up until now, but he effectively diffused a tense moment.

Warren came to his feet, finally closing the book he'd been reading. "Ray, you're always hungry. In fact, I don't think I've ever seen a time when you weren't."

Ray grinned and socked Warren on the arm which almost sent the smaller man halfway across the room. "If you'd eat more, then you might be able to put some muscle on that skinny frame."

Actually, from what Lyraka could see, Warren wasn't skinny and had his share of muscle. It was just that Ray looked as if he probably spent a lot of time in the gym working out.

Ray and Warren seemed nice enough. She was pretty sure Johnny would never be a favorite with her. She wasn't as sure about the women and Link. She'd reserve her judgment until after she'd been around them a little longer.

"There's a snack bar down the hall," Ray said. "Since we were ordered to get to know each other, we might as well do it over a soda and a candy bar."

"Sure, why not."

"Chocolate?" Reeka said.

Johnny cast a disparaging look at Reeka. "Why do I get

the feeling that you would sell your soul to the devil for a bar of chocolate?" He sauntered past her and out the door.

Reeka glared at him.

"Hey, don't worry about him," Ray said. "Hell, I might sell *my* soul to the devil if it was Godiva." Everyone laughed and another tense moment passed.

Roan had talked about trust, and how a team couldn't survive without it, but she had no idea how she was ever going to be able to put her trust in Johnny. She didn't like him. He might be good at what he did, but he was in need of an attitude adjustment.

As she followed everyone out the door, she couldn't help wondering if being with other people was going to be all she'd imagined.

The lounge was filled with overstuffed furniture and a table with snack cakes, fruit, and candy bars. Lyraka could already see Ray was in heaven. She opted for a granola bar and bottled water. That looked like the safest choice. She'd love to try the chocolate, but was still leery about its addiction. Her mother had already warned her about it.

The brown loveseat was the kind you could sink into. She made herself comfortable, then wished she'd chosen a chair when Johnny sat next to her. She scooted farther over, but their legs still touched. Wearing sweats had been a good idea.

"So, why does a pretty lady like you want to be an agent?"

She set her water on the side table and bit into her granola bar, making him wait until she swallowed and giving her time to think about her answer.

"My reasons are probably the same as anyone here. Adventure, fighting the bad guys." She shrugged.

"Or species." He looked pointedly at Reeka.

"You have something against Nerakians?"

"You don't?"

"No."

"Yeah, that's what a lot of people say, but that's not how they feel when it gets right down to it."

"That's your opinion, but don't presume to know how I feel." He was an obnoxious ass. She started to stand, but he grabbed her arm.

"That doesn't mean we can't be friends," he said. He ran his finger up her arm. "We're team members. You can't tell me you don't feel something for me."

She started laughing. She couldn't help it. Maybe it was the stress of the last few days finally breaking through, but she couldn't stop.

"If someone tells a joke, then you have to share," Ray said as he sat in the chair across from them.

Johnny's disgruntled look only made it harder for her to stop laughing. Some of the others began to gravitate over to where they were.

"Lady, you're certifiable!" Johnny said as he jumped to his feet and stormed from the room.

Lyraka wiped the tears from her eyes. She really hadn't meant to laugh so much. Oh, Lord, now she was the center of attention and now everyone was looking at her.

Alesha sat on the arm of the loveseat. "Since we're going to be a team—"she began in a soft southern drawl—"you can't keep secrets. What did Johnny say that threw you into a fit of giggles?"

No one said anything as they waited for her to speak. Great, she'd already created a disturbance. Well, there was no getting around it.

"It wasn't that important."

They continued to stare, waiting patiently.

She hoped she was never interrogated because she'd cave in the blink of an eye. "He suggested that I felt something for him."

They just sat there.

"I told you it wasn't anything. I just couldn't stop laughing." Where was a hole when she needed one? She'd love to just drop down into it and pull the dirt back over her head.

Alesha chuckled.

Ray grinned. "His ego needed busting."

"I know we're supposed to be a team, but I just don't like him. He needed someone to bring him down a notch," Alesha said.

Warren and Link nodded their agreement.

Lyraka relaxed. This was what being a part of a team was going to be like, and it felt good.

They all started talking at once. She learned that Warren was from Ohio and came from a big family. He was somewhere in the middle of a brood of kids. Since he couldn't get a word in edgewise, he'd started reading everywhere he went. He still did.

Link was from Red River, New Mexico. He was tall and his hair was sandy blond. He said they had the best fly-fishing for miles around. She liked his smile. It seemed to envelop her like a gentle hug. He was a person she felt she could trust. Maybe that was why he made a good interrogator.

"Well, I'm from Atlanta," Alesha drawled. "I'm truly a southern belle."

Ray chuckled.

Her eyebrows shot up. "You don't think I'm a southern belle?"

"I saw you training last week. You were kicking some guy's ass and he was twice your size."

Alesha studied her perfectly manicured pink fingernails. "Just because I know how to defend myself doesn't mean I don't remember how my momma brought me up. I just happen to hold a black belt in karate." She smiled sweetly at Ray. He seemed to melt in the chair when she batted her long lashes at him.

"I'm glad you're on our side," Warren said. "I might demolish buildings, but I bet you could bring a guy to his knees with one look."

"Thank you, darlin'." She grinned, then winked at Lyraka.

Why couldn't she be that easy around people? Maybe if

she'd been raised differently she wouldn't feel quite so awkward. A rush of guilt ran through her. Her mother had done what was best to protect her daughter.

"Where are you from, Lyraka?" Ray asked.

Startled, she jumped. "Me?"

He smiled. "Yeah. Where are you from?"

She cleared her throat. "Texas."

"Yum, land of the cowboys." Alesha leaned forward. "Tell us more."

"There's not a lot to tell. I was home schooled. I grew up at my mother's artist colony."

"You have the most unusual shade of eyes," Warren said, staring at her.

She picked off an imaginary piece of lint on the leg of her sweatpants. "They're just blue."

"Reeka, how long have you been on Earth?" Link asked.

Lyraka cast a look of gratitude in his direction. He smiled and she knew he'd taken the spotlight off her on purpose. They would have to know sooner or later. Would they be just as friendly then? She really doubted Johnny would.

"I've been here three years," Reeka told him. She took a bite of chocolate, closing her eyes. There was just a hint of color swirling above her.

"Ever want to return?" Ray asked. "I mean, and live there again."

Sadness crossed her face, but was gone in a second. "Sometimes, yes, but there is much to offer here on Earth that Nerak doesn't have. Nerak will never open up to civilization like Earth has."

"But it is changing," Lyraka spoke up before she thought. She had all their attention again. This wasn't good. "Nerak is changing. They're allowing changes to be made."

"Finally," Alesha said. "Someone who knows more about what's happening on other planets. That's what Roan meant by counter maneuvers." She chuckled. "I knew I'd figure you out before the day was over."

"It wasn't a big secret." Lyraka smiled and hoped it came off friendly. She thought it did. Well, until she glanced Reeka's way. Lyraka could tell the other woman knew there was more to her than she was willing to share.

She was trapped by omission of the truth. Would they hate her because she hadn't admitted everything? She didn't like deceiving them. They were her team members, and maybe she needed to trust them.

Ray began telling them a story about growing up on a farm. Roan had said to wait to tell them anything about her skills. On the other hand, she didn't want to start off on the wrong foot.

It was now or never.

She took a deep breath. "I can run really fast," she blurted out. They all looked at her as though she was slightly off balance. That wasn't the reaction she'd expected.

"I can run the mile in under ten," Warren said.

"Under ten?" Ray wore an expression of disbelief. "I can't even run it in under ten and I'm pretty fast."

Alesha snorted. "I can run it in under ten," she said.

"No, you don't understand. I'm really fast," Lyraka butted in.

"I can run it in under nine," Link bragged.

She was trying to be honest with them and they weren't even listening to her. She stomped her foot. Her bottled water tipped over. She grabbed it and sat it back upright, then she frowned at them.

"No, I mean I'm really fast."

Warren and Alesha smiled. They still didn't get it. She came to her feet. One second she was beside the sofa, and in the next, she was standing beside Reeka.

Their mouths dropped open.

Ray closed his, then visibly swallowed. "I think that beats the hell out of your under nine, Link."

"I think you're right," Link finally said.

"My father was from Earth," Lyraka said as she sat back down. "But my mother is Nerakian."

Warren sat forward. "Man, this is wild. I didn't know there were any mixed bloods that were your age." He blushed. "Not that I think you're old or anything."

"I think we're going to make a good team," Reeka said.

"Kick ass," Alesha grinned.

"One for all and all for one," Ray said.

She relaxed. "I like that."

"I stole it from *The Three Musketeers*."

"It's the thought that counts," she said.

Johnny walked back in the room. "Are you guys ready to act like mature adults?"

He sure knew how to kill a good mood.

"No." They all spoke in unison. Johnny didn't look any happier than he had when he'd first walked out.

Later that day, she spotted Roan across the wide yard of the compound. He was talking with Gavin and Joe. She sat on the bench and watched them. They were just out of her range of hearing. Their conversation sounded more like bees buzzing. But she didn't care about their conversation. She just wanted to sit and watch Roan.

Yeah, he'd been an ass. She understood about trusting your team members. She also knew that trust took time, no matter how intimate the relationship.

And theirs had been very intimate. A deep longing filled her. She missed their training sessions, their conversations, and even playing checkers. Her body began to tingle with awareness. She missed the way he touched her, the way his mouth would cover hers, the way he made love to her.

He looked up as if he sensed she watched him. He said something to the other two, then began walking toward her. Heat began to rise inside her. She stood.

"Is everything going okay?" he asked.

She nodded, not trusting herself to speak. She only wanted to look at him. Even though it hadn't been that long since she'd seen him, it seemed like forever.

"You sure you're okay?" His forehead creased.

She drew in a deep breath. "Everything is great." She looked at the building, then back at him. "I told them I could run fast and I'm half Nerakian."

He relaxed. "Good."

"But you told me not to say anything."

"Not until you felt as if you could trust them. Remember, it's all about trusting your team."

"I'm sorry I didn't trust you."

"I know."

"You do?"

"Yeah."

"I miss you. Is that crazy? I mean, you're standing right here, but I miss how you held me in your arms."

He drew in a deep breath. "Keep looking at me like that and I'm going to pick you up and carry you to my room."

"Promise?"

"Lyraka, how do you like everything so far?" Joe asked, as he joined them.

She jumped. So much for Roan carrying her off. She was pretty sure that was out of the question now. "I like it very well. Thank you so much for giving me this opportunity."

"No, thank you. We need people with skills like yours." His smile was warm.

But he wasn't a fool and the way he studied the two of them, it was almost as if he knew there was something going on. She tried to keep her expression impassive. He finally turned to Roan.

"I have something I need you to do," he told Roan. "You don't mind my stealing him away from you, Lyraka?"

Yes, she wanted to scream. "I need to be going anyway. Roan, it was nice talking to you."

"Same here."

Was that regret she saw in his eyes? She liked to think so. She smiled as she went back inside the building. It was nice to know he cared.

* * *

Roan barely paid attention to what Joe was telling him as he watched Lyraka walk back into the building.

"She's beautiful, isn't she?"

"Oh, yeah," Roan agreed before he thought. "I mean . . ."

"You're making a mistake. It's not good to get mixed up with someone on your team. It could cause problems."

"You know me, Joe. When it comes down to it, I don't let anything interfere with my work."

"Just make sure you know what your mission is." Joe patted Roan on the back before walking away.

Crap, was Joe that intuitive? Or were they that easy to read? Probably a little of both, but Joe should know that Roan would never jeopardize a mission.

He looked toward the row of windows where the trainees stayed. Did one of the curtains flutter or was it just a trick of the imagination? Wishful thinking?

He hadn't realized how much he was going to miss being with her or how jealous he'd get because she was with other people. Why the hell had Joe pulled Johnny for this team? The guy was notorious for hitting on the women. A known ladies man.

He'd talk to him. Tell him exactly what the score was, and if that didn't work—he'd clobber him.

Roan frowned. When had he started getting this territorial? But then, he knew the answer—since Lyraka had walked into his life.

Chapter 16

Banyon stood on his balcony, surveying all that he reigned over. It was his, all his. His father had . . . conveniently died, thanks to Kragen, but it had cost Banyon dearly. Kragen had wanted more power, more land. If Banyon wasn't careful, his chief advisor might decide he wanted to rule Rovertia.

He stepped back into his chambers just as there was a knock on the door. His weapon was on a table across the room. He walked to it, slipping it into the scarf at his waist. He trusted no one.

His gaze landed on one of the full length mirrors. He arched an eyebrow. Yes, he was quite stunning dressed all in black, except for the pale blue sash. He brushed a hair back into place. Better.

"Enter," he said.

The door silently opened. Kragen, of course. The man was becoming quite the nuisance.

"What is it this time? Are you here to tell me that Aasera is still on Nerak, safe and sound, and quite unreachable?"

"Your Majesty, I'm sorry, but yes, Aasera is surrounded all the time by other Nerakians, and untouchable."

Banyon fingered the weapon at his waist.

Kragen paled. "But we have located her daughter."

Excitement flittered through Banyon. Finally, revenge was close at hand. "I will leave tonight." He wasn't going to give her time to slip through his fingers, not like her mother. All these years and the bitch had been alive.

Kragen cleared his throat. "The ceremony to officially pass the crown to you is tomorrow. It wouldn't be wise to leave so soon after your father's death, not without throwing suspicion your way."

The palms of Banyon's hands began to itch. What he wouldn't give to end Kragen's pitifully pathetic existence right now. The day could not come soon enough when he had no need for his chief advisor.

His eyes narrowed. "How many days do I wait?"

"Three. No more than that."

Three days. Banyon could wait that long. He'd wait a lifetime if he thought the end result would cause Aasera so much grief that she would want to end her life.

"Leave me." He waved his hand. The door opened. "No, wait. Send me a female. I feel the need to inflict pain."

"Yes, Your Majesty." Kragen bowed as he left the room.

Banyon smiled. He was already planning what he would do when he brought Aasera's child to his planet. Her torture would last for a very long time. Maybe even years, if he were lucky. He knew all the ways to keep someone alive.

If this female had as much fight in her as her mother, she would prove quite entertaining. He might even let Aasera know he had her daughter, and that he was torturing her. Oh, yes, that would be perfect.

There was another knock on his door.

"Enter."

Two guards brought a girl into his chambers. She was already crying and pleading. He looked at her in disgust. Were there no females left with a little fight in them?

Chapter 17

They were all dressed in green fatigues out in the middle of nowhere surrounded by trees. Lots of trees. Lyraka could handle that part. It was the rest she wasn't so sure of.

They'd been taken to this remote area in the back of a truck with benches so hard that Lyraka knew she was going to be bruised for the next few days. She took a deep breath and glanced at her teammates. They looked about as uncomfortable as she felt. Except Johnny, but since she didn't like him, he didn't count.

Roan had told them yesterday they would be going on a mock mission. What exactly was a mock mission? Her heart pounded inside her chest as she silently prayed that she wouldn't totally screw everything up. She wasn't sure she was ready.

The sound of an approaching vehicle invaded her thoughts. Ready or not . . .

"Someone else is coming."

"Where?" Alesha looked around.

"You can't see them yet, but I hear them." She shrugged. "I have better than average hearing, too."

"What are you, Superwoman?" Johnny sneered.

She glanced his way. He hadn't been in the room when she'd made her confession yesterday. "No, I'm half Nerakian and half earthling. I have skills that someone like you wouldn't understand."

His mouth dropped open, then snapped shut, but not before he mumbled something about that being the reason she wasn't attracted to him.

Whatever.

Roan drove up in his Jeep, with Gavin in the passenger seat. Roan turned off the ignition after coming to a stop and they both got out.

"This will be a search and rescue." Roan looked at each of them, his gaze lingering a half second longer on Lyraka. It was enough to make her feel warm on the inside.

Gavin reached inside the Jeep and brought out a black satchel. "You have five hours before your victims are ruthlessly murdered." He motioned for everyone to come over to the Jeep as he brought out a map. "This is where you are." He circled the area on the map with a marker. Then he circled another spot. "This is where the terrorists are thought to be holding the captives."

Lyraka looked around at the group. She could get there faster than anyone. She could go in and . . . and what? No doubt it would be a lot more complicated than just going in and untying someone.

Roan and Gavin reached into the back of the Jeep and brought out guns and knives.

"You're on an unknown planet, in an area we don't know much about." Roan handed Lyraka a gun and a knife. "The guns are loaded with paint balls so don't worry about killing any of your team—this time. The knives are rubber." They handed out the rest of the weapons.

"We hope your mission is a success." Gavin climbed into the Jeep.

"That's it?" Warren looked at the gun as though it were a snake about to strike him. "Shouldn't we have a little more information?"

"Sometimes this is all you have to go on. Good luck." Roan got in on the driver's side and they took off. The transport truck left right behind them.

"I guess this *is* it," Warren said.

Alesha studied the map. "From what I can tell, the victims are about four miles north of here."

Lyraka's eyes narrowed. "This seems too easy."

Johnny snorted. "Wake up, sweetheart. This is what it's all about. I've been through these before. They'll have men waiting for us with guns of their own. If we get past them, then we have to make it past the booby traps."

She felt like an idiot, which is exactly what Johnny had wanted her to feel like. Of course the instructors wouldn't make it easy. All the intense training that Roan had put her through was about to pay off. At least, she hoped it would.

Alesha tucked the map in her shirt and slung her gun over her shoulder. "Anyone else feel the rush of adrenaline?"

"I have a feeling we're going to need it before the day is over." Ray reached in his pocket, but came back empty handed. "I bet they won't have a buffet waiting for us halfway between here and there, either."

Some of her apprehension eased. She wouldn't be alone. She was with her team.

"We can't all go clomping through the woods. Someone should be in the lead."

"That would be me since I'm the only experienced one in the group," Johnny volunteered.

"No. It should be Lyraka." Reeka kept her gaze leveled on him.

"It figures that you people would stick together."

"No, she's right," Link said. "We already know Lyraka can run faster than anyone. Her hearing is better, too. She's the obvious choice."

"What do you mean she can run fast? I can run a mile in under eleven minutes."

Lyraka moved behind Johnny in the blink of an eye. "But you're not as fast as me."

He whirled around, hatred in his eyes. "I don't like being made a fool."

"Then don't act like one," Ray said. "Lyraka will lead the team. And we will work together. Understood?"

Johnny looked as though he wanted to argue, but apparently changed his mind at the last second. "Try not to get us all killed."

Jerk.

"Stay focused, darlin'." Alesha smiled.

"And don't get too far ahead of us," Ray warned.

"Watch up in the trees, too. I read where the enemy will drop nets sometimes." Warren looked up as though someone might jump down on them at any second.

Everyone was talking at once. She finally held up her hands for silence. "I get it. It's not as though I haven't had any training. I'll do a quick scan of the immediate vicinity and report back."

"We'll start making our way forward." Reeka tucked her knife in her boot and adjusted the gun on her back. "Be careful."

"May the force be with you." Link grinned.

Lyraka slipped out of the clearing and into the denser woods. For a moment, she stood silent and listened. There were only the sounds of the woods. Her stomach fluttered as a rush of excitement swelled inside her. It wasn't real, but it was exhilarating.

She zipped from one tree to another, stopping to study the terrain. She was about a quarter mile deep in the woods and had criss-crossed back and forth. Johnny was right about one thing—it couldn't be this easy.

She started to move, but heard something snap behind her. She whirled around and ducked at the same time a red paintball splattered on the tree just above her head. Her heart pounded inside her chest as she ducked behind some cover and scanned the area. She rolled to the left, hiding behind the next tree over. The red paint had almost got her.

Someone was stealthily making their way nearer. She took a deep breath and moved quickly to the next tree. She still couldn't see anyone. No, wait, was that a flash of movement? She took a deep breath and forced herself to relax.

Breathe in, breathe out. Relax.

She could feel herself becoming one with the tree. She waited patiently for the shooter to come to her. She didn't have to wait long.

Lyraka watched from narrowed eyes. Dressed all in brown and olive green, a woman eased forward. Lyraka had to admire her for barely making a sound as she moved.

The woman looked to her right, raised two fingers to her eyes, then pointed forward. Lyraka glanced in that direction and saw a man creeping closer.

Were there more than two of them? Not that it mattered. She couldn't take out two people at once. She didn't have that kind of training. God, she was dead.

Get hold of yourself!

Lyraka needed to relax or she wouldn't be able to stay blended in with her surrounding. If the woman continued in the same direction, she would pass right by Lyraka. She would take the woman out with the knife, then go after the man. Very carefully, she reached down and brought the knife out of its scabbard. She barely breathed as the woman stepped even with her, then one footstep past.

Lyraka quickly slipped her hand around the woman's neck, knife to her throat. "You are so dead. I just slit your throat."

"Shit!"

"Shh, remember, you're dead."

The woman pulled a tag from her pocket and slipped it around her neck. Lyraka looked at it, then had to stifle her laughter as she read the words, I'M DEAD.

The girl slid down the side of the tree and sat on her butt. Her frown turned to a grin as she shrugged. "Roan said you were good."

A flash of jealousy rushed through Lyraka. The woman's lips were full and pouty, and she was pretty. Lyraka didn't even want to think of Roan talking to the other woman, maybe even kissing her.

Lyraka immediately stopped thinking about it when she heard a slight rustle behind her. The girl's partner was coming toward her. She was quickly coming to the realization that focusing wasn't going to be a strong suit for her.

She looked around the tree. The guy kept glancing to each side as he slowly moved forward. Looking for the woman probably. She slipped her weapon off her back and aimed.

Suddenly, it all seemed too real. What if the gun wasn't fake? Could she really end someone's life? Cold bloodedly kill them? Her hands trembled and her palms became sweaty.

There were people that she had to reach or they'd be slaughtered. Could she let someone innocent die because she had to take a life to save one? Yes, she could. She lined the man up in her sights again. She had the shot. All she had to do was squeeze the trigger.

The man jumped, and whirled around. Blue paint decorated his back. Another blue paintball splattered in the center of his chest. She whipped around. Johnny shot again. Another paintball sped through the air and splattered all over the man.

"I'm dead already," he growled. "Good thing I have a vest on or I'd be shoving that gun down your throat. Paintballs sting like a son of a bitch."

Johnny grinned. "I wanted to make sure you were good and dead." He turned his attention to her. "What happened? Get cold feet?"

Reeka stepped behind him. "Looks like she downed one of them." She nodded toward the woman who was still sitting on the ground. The girl gave a slight wave, then held up her I'M DEAD tag.

"Good job," Link said.

"She still couldn't take the shot."

"Give it a rest, Johnny. You always play the same old song over and over." Warren winked at her.

Alesha had the map unfolded and was looking at it. "I

think we need to head more to the north." She pushed a button on her watch, then turned a little to her left. They were all staring at her when she looked up. She blushed. "Compass. Never leave home without one."

Alesha might look like a bubbly cheerleader without a care in the world, but the more Lyraka was around her, the more she thought the other woman might be a nerd.

Warren dropped an arm across Alesha's shoulders. "You carry a compass, you like numbers. I think we were made for each other."

"I'm a lesbian."

He moved his arm as though she'd burned him. "Really?"

"No. But I thought it might shock you into remembering we're on a mission and this isn't the time or place to flirt."

"It worked," he grumbled.

She folded the map and put it away. "After the mission is completed will be another story," she said without missing a beat.

"Speaking of which, do you think we can get back to it." Johnny slung his weapon over his shoulder.

He was right. "Okay, I'll scout and make another sweep of the area," Lyraka said.

And hope like hell she didn't have to kill someone.

"You were right. She's good," Gavin whispered.

"Told you so." Roan couldn't stop the feeling of pride that came with Gavin's words. Lyraka was a natural at this even though she didn't have the confidence yet.

He watched through the binoculars from the camouflaged perch high in the trees. It wasn't a big space but from this vantage point and with the glasses, they could see almost everything that went on.

"What do you think about Johnny?" Gavin lowered his glasses and rubbed his eyes.

"I think if you look up dickhead in the dictionary, you'd see his face."

Gavin laughed. "I think you're right." He lowered his binoculars. "You don't think he's laying it on too thick, do you?"

"Nah, Johnny?" He laughed. "Of course I do, but they're buying it all hook, line and sinker."

He raised the binoculars again and watched as Lyraka methodically scoured the area, being careful to watch out for booby traps. They would come later, when she was tired.

"Damn, she's fast. All I see is a blur."

Lyraka stopped, cocking her head to the side.

"Shh," Roan whispered.

Had she heard them? Maybe. They were still a good distance away. Then again, she might have only heard a wild animal scurrying away. Apparently she thought so, because she went back to scouting the area.

Yeah, she was good, but would she get past the traps and the final test in this exercise?

Chapter 18

The air might have been cool this morning when they first started the mock mission, but it was hot and muggy now. A fine sheen of sweat covered Lyraka's entire body. It wasn't pleasant.

She took a cautious step forward, then jerked her foot back just in time as a heavy net flew into the air, bounced twice, then swayed back and forth before coming to a stop. Her breath caught in her throat, her hand flying to her chest as her heart pounded.

That had been way too close. Whoever had set up the booby traps knew what they were doing. She frowned. Probably Roan. He would make this exercise as difficult as possible. Not that she blamed him. She would do the same if their roles were reversed. Better to get caught now than later.

She scanned the area before cautiously moving to the next tree. There was a whirring noise. She ducked and rolled. A water balloon splattered against the tree, barely missing her. She must've tripped a wire. Did it reset?

She darted back in the direction the water balloon had come from, going toward it from an angle. Sure enough, there was a machine camouflaged by bushes and limbs. She waved her hand in front of it and another water balloon shot forward and splattered against the tree. Motion sensor. Clever. She looked around the base until she found a switch and disabled it.

Pride swept through her. Pride that it had missed her, pride that she'd been able to disable it. Pride that she was leading her team safely.

Hadn't she read something about pride going before a fall? She pushed that thought away. Besides, she'd also read somewhere that you should take pride in your work.

She quickly gauged her location. The team shouldn't be that far behind her. She made her way back to them, wanting to warn them there were booby traps.

In only a few minutes, she spotted Johnny, front man in the group. Figured. The guy really hated relinquishing control.

"I think it's all clear ahead." She stopped in front of Johnny. He raised his gun. She dodged when he fired.

"Shit! Don't sneak up on me like that. The next time I might have real bullets."

"Don't be so trigger happy." Ray nodded toward her. "How's it look up ahead?"

"There are booby traps. I took out what I ran across, but we should stay on guard in case there are more. I think if we continue the direction we're going, we should be okay."

"We're getting close." Alesha opened the map, folding it just so the area they were in was displayed. "Maybe a quarter mile farther."

"Good. I'm starved." To prove his point, Ray's stomach growled.

"For once, I agree with you about being hungry," Warren said.

Lyraka noticed everyone looked a little frazzled. The physical exertion wasn't as bad as the mental stress. Everyone wanted to perform well. It was no wonder they were a little edgy.

Everyone except maybe Reeka. She was practically bouncing on her toes, ready to move on. Lyraka's mother had told her that Nerak was perfect. The planet had no wars. They were at peace, but they had trained warriors just in case. She figured it would be like training for something you would never get to use. No wonder Reeka had left. She was finally getting to put her skills to the test.

"The sooner we rescue the captives, the sooner we get out of here." Lyraka turned, stepping off the path and a little to her right since Johnny seemed intent to push his way past. As soon as she set her foot down, she heard a barely perceptible click. "I stepped on something." She bit her lip, looking at everyone.

"Well, move off it," Johnny said.

"No! Don't move." Warren hurried forward. "What happened?"

"When I set my foot down, I heard a click."

"It could be a cluster bomb. If you let off the pressure, it'll blow up you, and everyone around you. Not that I think it's a real bomb or anything. They probably filled it with paint, but if we get splattered, we're all considered dead."

"Great going, Lyraka." Johnny grimaced. "We're all screwed because of you."

"Shut up, Johnny. If I can diffuse it, we'll be okay," Warren said.

"You said cluster bomb, right? Sorry, but I doubt anyone is that good. I'm not failing this exercise because of her." His gaze narrowed as Johnny looked at each one of them. "You want to be an agent, right? Who's coming with me?"

No one spoke up.

"It's okay." Lyraka didn't want anyone to fail because of her. "Go ahead and finish the exercise. You have to save the hostages. They're what's important."

"We're a team. We stay together," Link said.

"Then all of you stay. I'm outta here," Johnny ground out. He moved forward and was lost in the trees in only a few moments.

"Good riddance," Warren muttered.

"Can you diffuse it?" Lyraka didn't want them to die on her account, and if this was real, it would mean their death.

"We're about to find out. Okay, first thing is to see what

I'm working with. Don't ease the pressure. I'd just as soon not get an eyeful of paint."

Warren lay down on the ground, carefully brushing the debris out of the way.

"Is it a bomb?" Alesha whispered as if even the sound of her voice might set it off.

"Can't tell. I don't suppose anyone has a ruler?"

Alesha pulled one out of her back pocket. Warren's eyebrows rose.

"What?" She frowned. "I use a ruler for a lot of things."

Link laughed.

Warren took the ruler. "Okay, I'm going to slide this under your foot and take the pressure, but don't ease up." He slid the ruler beneath her foot, and without looking away said, "You guys might want to take cover behind a tree or something. There's no reason for anyone else to be splattered."

They hesitated.

"Go," Lyraka said.

Everyone stepped behind a tree for safety.

"Okay, it's do or die." He slid the ruler a little farther beneath her boot.

A drop of sweat slid between her breasts. She had an incredible urge to wiggle her shoulders, but instead, she held her breath and tried to think of something else.

What if this was real? She would never see Roan or her mother again. Was this really what she wanted to do for the rest of her life?

"Raise your foot nice and slow."

She took a deep breath and raised her foot.

Warren began to laugh.

She frowned, looking down at him. "Did you diffuse it?"

He moved the ruler. She jumped behind the tree nearest her.

"You stepped on a branch. The clicking noise was when it snapped."

"Oh, God, I thought we were going to die."

He shook his head. "Oh ye of little faith."

"Is it safe to come out?"

"It wasn't a bomb." She felt like such an idiot. The others stepped from the shelter of the trees. "Only a branch."

"Cool, then we don't need to have a mock funeral for you two."

"You would've had a funeral for us?" Warren brushed an imaginary tear from his eye. "I'm too touched for words."

Alesha batted him on the arm. "Let's get going before Johnny steals all the glory."

Lyraka was all for that.

They were silent as they moved through the woods. Lyraka went ahead as before. She didn't come across any more booby traps, but she did spot a small structure, one or two rooms at the most. The roof was thatch so it blended in well with the rest of the wooded terrain. The outer walls were a weathered brown stone, the windows boarded over.

Her heart began to pound again. She took a deep breath and slowly exhaled. She slowly backed away until she thought it was safe, then turned and hurried back to the team. This time, they weren't far behind.

She quickly told them what she'd found. "I didn't see anyone around the cabin."

"It's a trick," Reeka said. "They want us to rush in. Did you see Johnny?"

She shook her head. "No sign of him."

"He could be scouting the area." Ray didn't sound very confident. "I've seen his type in action before. He wants the glory, the medals, and all the hoopla that goes with being an agent, but when it gets down to the nut-cutting . . ." He cleared his throat. "Sorry. What I meant to say was that when it comes down to why we all chose this profession, then he falls short of the mark. I wouldn't doubt that he's been captured."

A scream filled the air. Lyraka jumped.

"What the hell was that?" Link warily looked around.

"Johnny." Alesha clicked the safety on her gun to the off position.

Lyraka looked at them. "They wouldn't torture him, would they? I mean, this is just a practice maneuver."

"Nah, we couldn't be that lucky," Warren said with a grin. "They'll want everything to be as real as possible. They won't hurt him too much, but they'll give him a taste of what it would be like if he ever gets captured."

"Do we really have to save him?" Reeka looked at them. "I'm just being practical. Nerakians are like that."

Lyraka saw the twinkle in Reeka's eyes and knew she teased, which was rare for a Nerakian, especially a warrior. She guessed anyone could adapt and change no matter who they were.

She turned her attention back to their problem. Saving Johnny wasn't very appealing to her, either. "Ray, you're better at rescue. Do you have a plan?"

"No, but I bet if we all put our heads together, we can come up with one." He picked up a rock, kicked away the debris to clear a spot on the ground, then set the rock down in the middle. "This is the building." He looked at Lyraka. "What's around it?"

"I didn't get too close when I saw it. I came back here instead, but it sits in a small clearing surrounded by trees." She made a circle on the ground using a stick, then set a smaller rock halfway between the trees and the cabin. "There's an old well right here. If a couple of us move up and use that for cover, then go the rest of the way to the cabin from that point, we'll only be vulnerable for probably less than thirty seconds."

"This is what we'll do then." He quickly mapped out a plan. They would go in twos and circle the cabin. Lyraka would be with Ray, Alesha with Link, and Reeka with Warren. The others nodded they were ready and they moved out.

When the building was within sight, Ray and Lyraka crept to the back side. The door was open.

"The door was closed when I was here before."

She glanced at Ray and saw his apprehension. She knew the feeling. It didn't look as if they had a choice other than to check out the cabin.

Ray pointed toward the well, she nodded, and the two of them moved forward. Her hands trembled when they crouched down beside it. She wasn't sure if it was from adrenaline overload, fear, or maybe a little of both.

Her gut instinct told her whoever was in the cabin had already gone, but she couldn't take that chance even though it cost them precious minutes.

Ray motioned for her to take the right side, he would take the left. Alesha and Warren had the front. Reeka and Link would have their back. Before he could take a step forward, she grabbed his arm.

"I move faster," she whispered.

After only a second's hesitation, he whispered back. "Be careful."

She made her move and was on the back porch in a flash. She gripped her gun as she hugged the exterior wall, and listened. She'd swear there wasn't anyone inside. There was absolutely no noise. She looked toward Ray, then touched her ear and shook her head.

He slunk down as he made his way across the yard and joined her. Once there, he eased around the side of the door and did a quick look, then shook his head.

What was this? Roan had said the hostages were here. She poked her head inside the structure. Nothing. Empty. She frowned. The interior was dim. As her eyes adjusted she noticed the wires running along the windows and the floor. When Ray started to step inside, she grabbed his arm, then pointed toward the wires.

"Crap, let's get the hell out of here." He didn't wait to see if she followed, knowing she would.

"It was wired with explosives. At least, it would've been explosives if this was a real exercise." Roan had thought of everything. So where had the hostages been moved?

The other four joined them.

"We found tracks," Warren said. "Johnny might have told them we were coming."

"Then we have to find them and fast. That is, if they haven't already simulated their deaths." Reeka spoke in a matter of fact voice. The Nerakian warrior was firmly back in place.

Reeka and Warren led the others to where the tracks were.

"Looks like they left in a hurry since they didn't cover where they were going," Ray said, then looked in the direction the footsteps were headed.

"Then we can catch up to them. At least, I can."

"It's too dangerous," Ray said with a shake of his head.

"It's the only choice we have. I'll be back before you can finish arguing." Lyraka grinned before she took off.

"Yeah, I'd say she can run the mile in under nine," she heard Link say before she was far enough away that she couldn't hear them.

Lyraka was careful to stay off the path even though there might be booby traps. It took her less than five minutes to catch up to Johnny and his captors. She kept her cover.

There were three men with guns. Really big men with ugly snarling faces. Where the hell did the government recruit these guys—from prison? This all looked a little too real.

Johnny's hands were tied behind his back as he was pushed and pulled along. There were three more men with their hands tied behind their backs, but she noticed they weren't pushed quite as hard as Johnny. She'd seen all she needed to see and headed back to the others.

Once she'd rejoined them, she quickly explained they were moving fast and yes, they had Johnny.

"I have a plan," she said. "I'll get in front of them and see if I can pick off the one in front. Two of you bring up the rear and one on each side and we'll have them boxed in."

"Be careful," Ray told her.

She nodded and took off again. She moved in place so that she was in front of the men and their hostages. She chose a spot that was just a little elevated, but would shield her in case she was caught in any kind of crossfire.

Then she waited.

As soon as she had the front man in her sights, she squeezed the trigger, hitting him dead center of his chest. He stumbled, looked at the blob of blue paint, cursed and sat down on the ground.

She smiled.

He was dead, and he knew it. The other two quickly took cover behind a hostage, guns to their heads. Their implication was clear—if they went down, so did the innocent men they had captured.

"We'll kill them!" one of them yelled.

"Let them go, and you will live. You have my word." All she had to do was keep them talking until the others caught up and got into position. But after three minutes had passed, she'd run out of things to say and was starting to worry.

"I think you're by yourself," one of the bad guys called out. "What are you going to do when you capture us?" he taunted.

"Like she said, put down your guns and we'll let you live." Link spoke from the side somewhere, but she couldn't see him. Relief washed over her.

"Back off or they're dead!" The bad guy spun around in the direction Link's voice had come from.

"You're surrounded," Warren said from the opposite side.

"You don't have a chance," Ray called from somewhere in the rear.

"It looks as though we don't have anything to lose 'cause no way are you going to let us go if we free them."

There was a pop and the bad guy's chest was covered in a big blue splotch of paint. He immediately went down.

"Do you want to be next?" Link asked the remaining guard. "Yeah, you might kill a hostage, but you'll definitely be going down. You drop your weapon, let the hostage go, and you at least have a chance."

Since the only one left had Johnny, Lyraka almost hoped the bad guy splattered him with paint. She really didn't like the guy. But he didn't, he carefully laid his gun down and stepped away, hands behind his head as he went down on his knees.

She came to her feet, smiling. Mission accomplished.

"It's a good thing I'm not a bad guy or you'd be dead right now," Roan spoke from behind her.

Chapter 19

Lyraka jumped and whirled around.

Roan knew he probably shouldn't have scared her like that, but he wanted her to be aware of all possibilities. Anyone could be just around the corner.

"I didn't even hear you!" She frowned at him, but she didn't look that pissed. After her initial scare, she even looked a little glad to see him.

For a moment he got lost in her eyes and the way she looked at him. Just as quickly, he cleared his throat and turned serious. This was important.

"When you're on a mission, you have to be aware of everything. If there had been someone on watch, you'd be dead right now."

She tilted her chin. "We did save the hostages, you know. Did anyone ever tell you that you really know how to kill a moment?"

"Yeah, they have."

"I thought as much."

There was a burst of laughter. Roan's gaze moved to the trail where the others were. Gavin had just joined the group of agents who'd acted as hostages. Roan noticed that he was taking his time cutting the rope from Johnny's wrists. Johnny was going to make him regret that later.

"You did very well," he said as he turned back to her.

Her smile widened. "You think so?"

Rookies. "Yeah, I know so."

"What's next?"

She looked like she was ready to shoot more bad guys. He'd created a monster, but one he was proud of. Lyraka just might make a good agent after all.

A very sexy one, too. She definitely filled out fatigues in all the right places. Whoa, what the hell was he doing? The training session had barely ended and he wanted to jump her bones. He'd never in his life been this infatuated with a woman. It made him nervous as hell. Time to leave while he still could.

"We'll head back so everyone can clean up and grab a bite to eat," he told her. "I've called a meeting at the training room afterwards so we can go over the exercise. Gavin will lead everyone back to the transport truck. It's not far from here." If he didn't get away soon, he would pull her into his arms and kiss her.

He turned and went deeper into the woods. Just over the ridge there was a clearing where he'd parked the Jeep.

She followed. "Did I really do okay?"

He grinned when he looked over his shoulder, then leaned back against a tree. "Yeah, better than I expected."

She frowned. God, he liked the way she frowned, the way her lips pursed. If he pulled her into his arms and kissed her, her body would press against his, her soft curves molding to his harder body.

"Hey, Lyraka, where are you?" one of the guys called out.

"They can't see us. Better join your team before they think you were eaten by a wild animal."

She hesitated, then threw her arms around his neck and planted a quick kiss on his lips, then pulled back before he could do more than catch his breath.

"I've missed you." She turned and scrambled down the small hill.

He took an involuntary step after her, realized what he was doing, and turned in the opposite direction toward his Jeep.

She missed him? He smiled, liking that she did. Not that either of them would have a chance to do a lot about it. The next few weeks were going to be the most intensive exercises any of the trainees had ever been through.

He remembered what it had been like when he went through training, but this would be different. Each one of them had been handpicked for what they could bring to the team. This was the best of the best—they just didn't know it yet. That is, if they made it through the course.

He opened the door of the Jeep and climbed inside. This had been a relatively easy day. The next ones would be a lot more difficult.

And more realistic.

He stopped with his hand on the ignition key. The next exercises would also be dangerous. What they would face in the weeks to come would push them to the brink of their endurance and then some. Joe had said he wanted them ready to roll in four weeks in case they were needed. His spies were telling him something was up with the Roverts and maybe the Adnams. He didn't like either one of the species.

A few years ago, he'd had a chance encounter with a Rovert. Everything about the Rovert said he was human. Women would probably drool over him because of his dark looks. He'd been charming and pleasant, until Roan looked into his eyes. There was no soul inside him. Just a coldness that reeked of pure evil.

He wasn't as worried about the Adnams. Not as long as he kept his distance. They had a tendency to explode smelly slime. Gross, but not deadly. They acted a lot tougher than they were. Nasty creatures.

He started the Jeep and headed back to the main buildings. If the Roverts and Adnams were stirring up trouble and combined forces, it could get really messy. He didn't like to think of Lyraka being in the middle of it.

He rested his arm on the door and leaned back in the seat. Relationships could be so damned complicated sometimes. More so if it was two agents involved.

But they weren't involved. They'd only had sex. His gut clenched. He hadn't had sex like that his whole life. Lyraka was special.

She was so eager to learn everything, and didn't mind getting dirty. He laughed. They were the same in that respect. She damn sure didn't back away from anything he'd asked her to do except when it came to blind trust. She had a problem with that, but he was certain she would learn to trust as the team worked together over the next few weeks.

He pulled into one of the parking spots, turned off the ignition, and climbed out. He had to write his report. More paperwork. He was getting sick of it. If Joe didn't get him out of here he was going to put in for vacation time. Joe couldn't continue to hold him hostage in the hopes that he would train everyone who'd ever thought about becoming an agent.

Joe was in his office. Roan tapped on the door, then went inside.

Joe looked up. "Roan, come in."

"Sally wasn't at her desk."

"I let her off early. How'd the exercise go?"

"Good."

"Lyraka?"

"Better than I'd expected."

"Did they work together as a team? That's the most important thing."

"Yeah."

"And Johnny?"

"Exactly as I expected."

Joe nodded. "Did they use Lyraka as lead?"

"Right from the start, even though Johnny had wanted to take it. The rest of the team didn't budge."

"Smart move. I knew they would make a good team. They each bring something to the group that makes them special." He picked up a pencil and tapped the eraser end on the top of his desk. "Will they be ready?"

Roan shrugged. "I think so. Maybe. If they don't break.

What you're planning hasn't been done before. It's a tough call."

Joe set the pencil down and leaned back in his chair, a grim expression on his face.

"What?"

Joe shook his head. "My head tells me that we have plenty of time. My gut is yelling at me to hurry and get this team together."

"We have other teams."

"Not like this one. Besides, we're spread too thin. The government doesn't think we need to train agents for intergalactic patrols. The president is listening to his advisors, and the advisors are looking at what this is costing. They'd rather use the money to fund research on how long it takes catsup to run out of the bottle." He tossed the pencil down in disgust.

"Then we'll just have to hope your gut is wrong."

If they were spread that thin, it would be hard to protect the borders, and they would be ripe for an invasion. That wasn't good.

"It's surprising how a hot shower and a good meal can turn a man's disposition around." Ray patted his stomach.

"What I'm wondering is how you could hold so much." Link shook his head as everyone headed toward the training building.

Reeka snorted. "Between the two of you, I was wondering if you were going to leave anything. Next time, both of you start at the end of the buffet line."

Lyraka smiled. They were already forming a nice easy friendship. It felt good to be part of something.

"Did y'all notice someone was missing?" Alesha looked around pointedly.

"Johnny, and good riddance. I'd had all of him I could take."

Lyraka had to agree with Warren, but it made her wonder

if Johnny'd gotten kicked out of the program. Her heart wasn't breaking because of it.

They walked inside the building and down the hall to the training room, then filed in, and sat at the long table. A few minutes later, Roan walked in. Her heart began to thump loudly inside her chest as she drank in the sight of him. He wore jeans and a dark green T-shirt. Her breath caught in her throat as a familiar heat began to sweep over her.

"Is it getting warm in here?" Ray asked.

"Maybe you're having hot flashes." Alesha snickered.

"Not funny."

Time to think of something else and not about having sex. If she was the one generating the heat, it could get embarrassing.

"The other instructors will be along in a few minutes," Roan told them.

"There are more instructors than you and Gavin?" Reeka asked.

"You'll have one other instructor. You're about to start intensive training. You'll be asked to push yourself further than you've ever thought you could. Today was a walk in the park compared to what you're about to go through." He looked at each one of them. "But when you finish you won't *think* you're the best of the best, you'll *know* it."

Pride filled her. This was what she was meant to do.

"Here they are," Roan said as he turned toward the door.

"You've got to be shittin' me," Ray said

Everyone turned and looked toward the door. Lyraka's mouth dropped open. There was no way this was happening. No way!

"Meet your third instructor, Johnny Hayden."

She had a feeling she would never make it through the coming weeks of intensive training. Well, damn!

Chapter 20

Roan could tell by the team's reaction that they weren't happy. It couldn't be helped.

"He was a ringer." Ray's look said it all for the rest of them—he was disgusted.

"We had to see if everyone could work and play well with others. And we wanted to see if you would stand by each other if the chips were down," Johnny said. "You proved it when you refused to leave Lyraka. It might be different in other branches of the government, but when you work for the elite force, you work as a team, and you watch each others' backs. Together, you're a well oiled machine. Separate, and you become weak."

"So, are you really an asshole?" Alesha drawled. "Or were you pretending?"

He grinned and it completely changed him. "By the end of the training, you'll probably think we're all assholes." He suddenly turned serious. "Everything you thought I was, I'm not. I don't care who you are as long as you believe in what you're doing. We're the good guys, and everyone should have the right to live in peace."

Gavin went on to tell them exactly what they'd be doing over the next few weeks. Roan had to give the team credit for not walking out right then and there. They would be expected to do a lot.

Time passed quickly as they went over the mock mission. The afternoon turned into evening. Gavin and Johnny left Roan with the last part of what needed to be done so they could start setting up for the next day. He figured from the slumped shoulders and the yawns, they'd been at it long enough.

"That's it for today. Get some rest and I'll see you back here tomorrow morning." He began to gather up the papers on the desk as everyone filed out of the room, but when he looked up, Lyraka was still there.

She sat on the long table, feet swinging, patiently waiting for him to notice her. Man, why the hell had he taken their relationship as far as he had? But the longer he looked at her, the more he knew exactly what had possessed him.

He went back to stacking papers. "You're going to have a long day tomorrow. Better get some rest."

"You think so?"

"I know so."

She crossed her legs. He caught the movement from the corner of his eye. It seemed innocent enough, as though she hadn't planned on it being provocative, but it was, and he was finding it hard to concentrate.

She'd changed into red shorts and a thin white shirt with short sleeves. Trouble was, the shirt was really thin and he could see the lacy cups of her white bra. Had she worn it on purpose, knowing what it would do to him?

"It's not that late. I won't even go to bed for at least another couple of hours."

The thought of her crawling into bed, pulling the sheet slowly up her body, the cotton caressing her, was a vision he didn't want, or need, right now. He set the papers down and leaned his hip against the desk. "We shouldn't have made love."

"Is there a rule against it?"

He frowned. "No, but you're going to need all your concentration to get through the next few weeks and . . ."

"I want to make love with you. My body burns for your touch. I want your mouth on me. I want to taste you."

He turned and strode to the door.

Disappointment filled her. She felt such an incredible need to be closer to him, to have him take her into his arms, to feel his warmth wrapping around her. She didn't think it was her passionate Nerakian side, either. If it had been anyone else in the room, she would've walked out the door without a problem. It wasn't just the man, it was the person that she wanted, and now he was walking away. Incredible disappointment filled her.

Roan shut the door, then turned the lock.

"You've quickly become an addiction for me," he said, then turned. "From the first moment I saw you, I knew I was attracted to you, even though I refused to acknowledge it."

His words sent a thrill through her. She hadn't thought she could live another minute and not feel his body pressed against hers.

"This could get complicated."

"It already is." He sighed. "I've seen other relationships get screwed up when two agents were involved. It'll be tough when we're on a mission. Will you be able to think of me as your team leader?"

She raised her chin. "Yes, but will you be able to think of me as an agent?" She had to know if she would be putting him in danger.

He walked toward her. "Probably not completely. I'll worry about you more than the other agents, but I'll train you just as hard as the others. I'll probably push you more because I want to know that you can handle yourself in any situation. You might even start to hate me."

She shook her head. "That will never happen."

He lowered his head, brushing his lips across hers. The familiar heat began to build, there was an intensity that flowed between them. She leaned into him, licked her tongue along his neck. She felt the tremble that went through him, just barely perceptible, but it had been there. There was something empowering knowing that she could make him tremble.

"Will anyone bother us in here?" The conference room was at the end of the hall so she wasn't that concerned. She would hate for Gavin or Johnny to come back for papers or something. They could always prop a chair against the door.

"I'm the only one with a key." He began to unbutton her blouse. "But there will be one problem that can't be helped."

"What's that?" She undid the first few buttons on his shirt, exposing a light sprinkling of dark hair. She remembered how the hairs had tickled her nipples.

"There's not a snowball's chance in hell that I'll ever look at the table in the same way because I plan on stripping off your clothes and making love to you on top of it."

She sucked in a breath.

"Do you know what I'm going to think about every time I look at the table?" he continued. "I'm going to be thinking about you lying naked on top of it, your legs spread wide as I slowly enter your hot body."

What had started out as a fluttering from deep inside her belly suddenly moved downward and tickled between her legs. She liked the thought of Roan picturing her naked on the table, but she had a different vision, and she liked hers a lot better.

"And what if you're the one on the table?" She unbuttoned the last button and pushed his shirt off his shoulders. It fell to the floor with just a whisper. She shrugged her shoulders and her shirt was the next to go.

He cupped her breasts. They were barely covered by a bit of white lace. She watched as he lightly stroked across the lace. It was sensual, sexy.

"What did you have in mind when you had me naked on the table?" he asked. "Having your way with me? Taking control?"

"That feels good." She was so lost in her own pleasure that

it took a moment for his words to sink in. Damn it, he was making her forget that she was seducing him. She pushed his hands away. "Would it bother you to let me take charge?"

He shook his head, a slow smile curing his lips. "Not one bit. I think I even like the idea."

"Good, because I want to do the exploring this time."

His smile changed to a frown. "Is it getting warm in here?"

She'd noticed it, too. "Yeah, but it feels different from the last time."

"As though it's coming from both of us, and not just you."

She placed a hand on his chest. "You're right." Heat radiated off him in waves. "It's almost as though I've transferred some of my heat to you. That's odd."

"You don't feel as hot to me."

She cocked an eyebrow. "Are you saying I'm not as hot?"

He reached behind her and snapped the clasp on her bra and had it off before she could even make one little sound of protest. Not that she would have.

"Oh, you're real hot." He stared at her breasts.

It was all she could do to swallow.

"But the heat doesn't burn like it did the first time."

"It's almost as though you've accepted my heat, taking some of it as your own."

"Is that possible?"

She shrugged. "I don't have a clue. Does it bother you there might be a chance you could burn an earthling if you made love to her?" She hadn't thought this would happen. Nor the fact that Roan might have sex with another female. She didn't like that thought at all.

On the other hand, if his body temperature rose when he was horny, she might be the only one he would ever be able to have sex with. She certainly didn't want to think of him with another woman, but she sort of felt guilty that she might have ruined him for them.

He looked as though he was still thinking of the possibility that he might not be able to have sex with anyone besides her. She slipped her hands inside his pants and unfastened the top button.

"I doubt you would get so hot that you could actually burn a woman." She didn't want to get into a discussion of whether he could sleep with anyone besides her. That was kind of a mood killer for her.

"But you're not sure."

"No, not exactly."

She quickly pushed his pants and briefs down. She didn't think she would ever get tired of looking at him, especially naked. The one night she'd been with Roan, she hadn't had a chance to examine him because he'd kept her in a frenzy of passion all night. But now, in the well-lit training room, she could look her fill, and she planned to do just that.

He caught her shoulders. "I'm not sure about this."

"I'm absolutely, one hundred percent sure we should have sex." She stroked her fingers down the front of his penis. He was nice and hard. She liked the way he quivered when she touched him.

He drew in a sharp breath, his eyes closing.

"You really don't want me to touch you like this?" She grasped him full in her hand before sliding his foreskin down, then back up. She bent down and ran her tongue over the soft tip. He tasted salty. She liked the way he felt against her tongue. She wanted to do more but she straightened, letting her breasts brush across his chest hairs. "Are you sure you don't want me to do any of that?"

Something close to a growl erupted from him. He quickly kicked out of the rest of his clothes, but when he reached for her, she pushed against his shoulders. He moved back. When his butt was against the table, she pushed a little harder and he sat down.

"I want you naked," he said.

"I want you inside my mouth." She leaned down, bracing

her hands on either side of him and sucked his penis inside her mouth.

He groaned and grasped her head.

She knew she was pleasing him just as he'd pleased her. His mouth on her sex had been an incredible experience, but knowing she was giving him pleasure was nice, too. She liked the way he felt inside her mouth, the way it felt to run her tongue over the ridges.

And there was the heat. She could feel it even more now. Almost like stepping into a furnace, but the heat didn't burn. And there were the waves of color that swirled around them, caressing them like tiny fibers of sensual tingles. It took her a moment to realize he was pulling her up.

"My whole body is on fire for you."

Worry filled her. "Does it hurt?"

He laughed, shaking his head. "No, it just makes me want you more." He unfastened her shorts and pushed them down.

She quickly kicked out of them, standing before him wearing only a white lacy thong. The way he looked at her with such burning intensity made her feel like the sexiest woman on Earth.

"Have I mentioned how I love the white lace?"

"Want me to leave it on?" She stepped back, sliding a finger beneath the top band.

For an answer, he moved off the table and scooped her in his arms. She yelped, then quickly stifled the sound. They might be at the end of the hall, but she didn't want to take any chances.

He set her on the table. She lay back against the hard surface. Her body heat warmed it up nicely. "I want you so badly."

"I know the feeling." He climbed up and lay beside her, cupping her breast.

It was all she could do to think when he touched her like this. She rolled to her side so that she faced him, sliding her hand over him, caressing his arm, his waist, the curve of his butt.

He nuzzled her neck, nipping lightly with his teeth. Incredible sensations swirled low in her belly. But she wanted more. She nudged his shoulder until he was on his back, then she straddled him, her body pressed against his.

"Ah, yes, that's good," he moaned, clutching her hips. "Your pussy feels good against my dick."

Her body trembled. She never would have imagined his words would turn her on rather than embarrass her, but they did.

"You like that? I mean when I talk dirty."

She stopped moving. Her face grew warm. It was one thing to know he turned her on with his naughty talk, but another to admit it.

He reached up, stroking his fingers across one nipple. "Never be embarrassed to tell me what you like. It turns me on, too."

He was right, and she wanted to give as much as she received. "I want to feel you inside me." She moved against him. He grasped her legs. "I want to feel you buried deep inside me, moving in and out."

"You're a quick learner," he said, his words strained.

"I think I like sex talk."

He rose up a fraction creating more pressure against her. She gasped, not expecting the rush of sensations caused by the friction of his dick against her. Nor was she expecting him to slide his fingers from her thighs up to her sex.

"I love looking at your pussy," he said before he opened the folds.

She gasped, reaching her hand down to shield herself.

"No, let me look at you. I want to know everything there is to know, to see everything there is to see, to touch and kiss all of you." He rubbed his thumb up and down her labia. "Do you like that? Does it feel good?"

She nodded, tried to swallow and couldn't.

He wet his thumb, then ran it up and down her again, a feather touch only. She whimpered.

"What?" he asked.

She nudged toward his thumb. "More." She closed her eyes, her hands resting on her thighs. "I need more, Roan. Please."

He pressed harder. She couldn't take a deep breath. She could only lose herself in what he was doing to her body.

"I can feel your body tense. You like me touching your pussy, massaging it faster and faster."

She bit her bottom lip. "Yes, right there. Don't stop. Yes. Almost. Almost." Pleasure rippled over her in hard waves. Her body stiffened. She cried out, gasped for air. She sank down to Roan's chest, her breathing ragged. She barely knew when he moved her to her back, then grabbed his pants. She heard the foil packet tear, then he was nudging her legs open, sliding inside her body.

He went deep, then slowly came out. That felt good. She wiggled her butt into a better position. He slid deeper the next time. Even better.

"I love fucking you. The heat, the swirling lights. It's like plugging into a 220 outlet except the shock isn't there, only the charge and it feels fantastic."

Heat began to build inside her.

"Next time I don't just want to caress your pussy with my fingers. I want to taste you on my lips, with my tongue. I want to slide my tongue up and down you."

Her body clenched. She raised her legs, wrapping them around his waist.

"Now you're ready."

She was more than ready.

He moved harder and faster inside her. She tightened her inner muscles. He gasped.

"Oh, God, yeah, just like that."

He pushed harder, deeper. She met every thrust as the lights spun above her, as the heat began to build once again. She clutched his shoulders, her body trembled. Roan growled from low in his throat, his body jerked. She gasped for a breath. He jerked again, moaned, then eased to the table.

"Don't pull . . . uh . . . out yet." She still needed the connection, but now that they had both reached a climax, she was a little embarrassed by what she'd experienced. Would it always feel like this? Every time she was with him, would it be like the very first time? She hoped so.

"I'm not leaving anytime soon," he said into her hair, then rolled to his side, taking her with him. "It's a good thing this is a long, wide table."

She smiled. Yeah, it was, and a sturdy one, too.

"Have I mentioned how beautiful you are?"

She shook her head, enjoying the sound of his voice.

"You're the most beautiful woman I've ever met."

She heard a door slam down the hall. It reminded her how near other people might be.

"Want to get dressed and grab a soda out of the snack room?" he said.

"That sounds good. I suddenly feel starved." They got off the table. She knew she was smiling like a fool, but she didn't care. She glanced away as he disposed of the condom.

And saw the table.

It was as though an impression of her back and butt had been burned into the wood. "Oh no," she breathed.

Roan walked back to the table and looked down at it, then laughed. "This wasn't exactly what I meant when I said I'd be imagining you naked on the table."

She glared at him as she reached for her clothes and began to jerk them on. "It isn't funny. An impression of my ass is burned into the table."

He lightly stroked the outline. "But it's a very sexy ass."

Butterflies fluttered inside her as she watched him lightly caress the burned area. An all too familiar ache began to grow inside her. She wet her suddenly dry lips.

No, damn it! She cleared her mind of anything remotely sexual. "It can't stay like this. There is no way I'm going to walk in here tomorrow morning and see my ass on the table."

He grinned. One of those slow seductive smiles that curled

her toes and made her pulse beat faster. It was all she could do to concentrate.

"We have to get rid of the table," she said.

His eyebrows rose. "Tonight? Now?"

"Yes, tonight." She went to one end and tried to pick it up, but it didn't budge. It was really solid, in fact. She gritted her teeth and tried again. There was no way she would be able to help him move the table.

"Heavy?"

"Yes." She frowned. He wasn't being a bit of help.

"Look. I think it's starting to fade."

She examined the area. He was right. It was kind of like resting sweaty palms on a glass surface, then watching them slowly disappear. She wiped her hand across the impression. Nothing changed. If it faded, then it would have to do it on its own time.

He walked around to her side and took her into his arms. "Let's go get something to drink. We'll talk a little, maybe walk to the small park, then we'll return to see if the rest has faded."

She laid her head against his chest. "And if it hasn't?"

"Then I'll blow up the building and all the evidence will be destroyed."

She smiled. "You can't do that. There are people in the building."

"That might be a problem. Maybe I'll just get a sander and go over the surface."

"That might work better."

"Then it's settled."

He let go of her and started for the door, but stopped. "Oh, one other thing. You might want to grab your bra off the back of the chair."

She whirled around. He was right. She automatically reached up to her chest, but knew she hadn't put it back on.

"Want me to check for you?"

Her nipples hardened. "Hush." She scooped up her bra,

and keeping her back to him, removed her shirt and put on her bra, then followed with her shirt.

"You could've told me I'd forgotten to put it on."

He shook his head. "I loved watching the way they bounce just a little when you walk. It's a hell of a turn on."

She wondered if she would survive his naughty talk. Even now, she could feel warmth spreading over her.

"Later," he promised as if he could read her thoughts.

His words sent a riot of hot sexy emotions through her. She would so hold him to his promise. But how much later? Sheesh! She was certainly making up for years without sex.

He grabbed her hand and squeezed after they left the training room, and he didn't let go. She loved feeling this connection with him.

He'd said she might grow to hate him over the following weeks. There was no way she would ever hate him. He'd opened up a whole new world for her. Hate him? No, that would never happen.

Chapter 21

Lyraka hated Roan. She hated the ground he walked on, the air he breathed, his family—if he had any hidden under a rock somewhere. He'd only talked about his aunt. She hated everything about him.

"Lyraka, you're not trying hard enough," Roan said.

Speak of the devil.

"I am trying. Have you ever thought that I might not be any good at throwing knives? It's not as though I wanted to grow up and join the circus."

Warren snickered, but stopped when Roan frowned at him.

Everyone had mastered throwing knives. Alesha and Reeka had it down pat. Lyraka was the only one who couldn't get the hang of it.

"Keep trying." She stuck her tongue out at him when he turned his back to her. Warren grinned. She felt the heat rise up her face. That had been childish—even though it had felt damn good!

She was tired all the way to her bones. They'd been working everyday for the last three weeks. Every . . . single . . . day. Twelve long, grueling hours. If they weren't running the obstacle course, they were in the training room. At least her butt impression had faded by the time they'd returned to check it.

But Roan had been right that she would probably hate him

before all the training was over. Hate might be too strong a word. It was more like intense dislike.

He picked on her. Even some of the others on the team had commented on it. Roan pushed her harder. He always rode her more.

Her forehead wrinkled. Not literally rode her. Not since that night in the training room. She closed her eyes and sighed as she remembered just how well he had ridden her. Maybe that was her problem. She hadn't had sex since then.

Major horniness. That's the word she'd picked up from Reeka. Reeka had seen the swirls of light above the building that night and casually mentioned it the next day, but Lyraka had kept her face expressionless. At least, she hoped her look had been one of innocence. She'd just as soon not shout out the fact every time she had sex. The swirling lights were bad enough.

Hey, look, another Nerakian has had an orgasm.

Why couldn't a bell lightly jingle when a Nerakian had sex? That would be much easier to live with, except in her case it would probably be some big-ass bell. For whom the bell tolls. Yeah, right.

"Lyraka, pay attention," Roan said.

She opened her eyes and threw the knife toward the target with all the strength and accuracy she could muster. It whistled through the air, the sound clean and sharp. She held her breath. The knife landed on the flat side against the solid target with a loud klunk.

"Bad throw."

"Ya think?" She drew her gun from the holster at her hip, aimed, and fired. She hit the target dead center. "I didn't miss that time." She holstered her gun and turned on her heel.

"Where do you think you're going?"

"To pee." That had been crude, but he'd really ticked her off. He'd been pushing her all day and telling her what she was doing wrong, but not one little word about what she was doing right. Yeah, she was pissed.

She headed back toward the dorms. They were a mile away. She could've run it in nothing flat, but she wanted to walk off her anger. She heard his Jeep start, then he was driving beside her.

"Get in," he yelled above the rattle of the engine.

"No!"

"If I have to stop the Jeep, pick you up, and put your cute little ass in the passenger seat, I will."

She stopped. "You couldn't catch me, even in your Jeep. I can outrun you both."

"Please." His gaze held hers.

She faltered.

"We need to talk."

What kind of agent was she going to make if she caved this quickly when the enemy gave her one disarming look and said the please word? Please got to her every time. He was technically not the enemy so maybe this time didn't really count.

"Okay, I'll get in," she said and jerked open the door. "Stay on your side of the Jeep, though."

"Anything you say." He took off once she was inside, but rather than stay on the road to the main buildings, he turned down a road that didn't look, nor feel, as though it was used very often.

"Where are we going? Damn it, I thought you were going to take me back to my dorm."

"Did I imply that? I apologize. I didn't mean to."

Ass.

She crossed her arms in front of her and looked straight ahead. Well, until he hit a pothole the size of Rhode Island. She reached out to keep from impaling herself on the stickshift, lost her balance, and landed face-first in his lap, her face only inches from his zipper.

"Careful," he said.

She should bite him. It would serve him right. She could say it was an accident. Yeah, right. Instead, she pushed up, shoving her hair out of her eyes.

"You might want to hold on to the door. I know it'll be difficult breaking your stiff demeanor, arms crossed tightly in front of you and all, but it might save you the embarrassment of falling face first into my lap again."

Maybe she did hate him. But she grabbed the door just in case.

He turned off the road, pulling between a group of trees and cut off the engine. "Let's walk." He opened his door.

Fine. She climbed out. "Where are we going?"

"I'll show you. Trust me."

Trust him? Yeah, right. But she followed.

Water flowed somewhere. She could hear it bubbling over the rocks. She began to relax. They walked deeper into the woods. The fragrance of pine hung heavy in the air. A deer looked up, startled by the intrusion, then with graceful speed, was gone.

This was what she'd needed. The woods were her solace, her comfort. The training had been so intense that she'd collapsed on her bunk each evening. The silence, the peace, had been missing from her life and made her out of kilter—as though two people had separated, the outer from the inner. Now they were joining back together and she was becoming whole again.

Her mother once said that you could go through life reaching for everything you want and maybe getting it, but true happiness came when the mind and body were in perfect harmony. Only then could you find true pleasure. That's why her mother meditated. The woods were Lyraka's meditation.

The sound of water rushing over rocks became louder. She suspected there was a waterfall near. They stepped into a small clearing. White frothy water from higher up the mountain cascaded over shelves of small rocks. It was a dramatic effect.

There'd been a river that ran through the woods where she'd lived in East Texas, but nothing that compared to this.

The water was so clear she could see the grains of sand at the bottom.

Roan reached down and picked up a rock, tossing it in the river. The rock rolled and tumbled as it was swept farther downstream. "When I first came here to train, they gave us an occasional day off. Most everyone on the team would sleep or go into town for a beer. I came here." He met her gaze. "Not exactly to this spot. But I would come to the woods and just walk. One day I heard the water and decided to find the source. That's when I found this place."

He sat down on the grass, then patted a place next to him. Her hesitation was brief. After she settled herself on the ground, he began to talk again.

"Sometimes I push you too hard. I know that."

"Yes, you do." She wasn't going to lie.

"It's because I care."

"Stop caring so much, you're killing me. I know why you're doing it, but look over the last three weeks; where I was, and where I am now. I'm damn good." Her forehead wrinkled. "Except at knife throwing."

"You need to be better than good. There's no room for mistakes."

"Then I won't make any."

"I'm being serious."

"So am I."

"It's dangerous."

"I knew that coming in. I'm not afraid to face it."

"You should be." He picked up a small rock and rubbed his thumb over it. "You could get killed."

"I could get run over by a car while I'm walking across the street. When it's my time, there's nothing that will stop it."

He dropped the rock and met her gaze. She saw the worry in his eyes.

"You think I won't worry about you, too?" she asked.

"That's different."

She laughed lightly. "Why? Because you're a man?"

"Of course not. It's because I have more experience."

"But I have special abilities that will give me an edge." She drew in a deep breath. She understood why he worried about her safety. She worried about his, too. "This is what I want to do. I know it's the same way for you. I see it in your eyes when you talk about the missions you've been on. They sparkle with excitement. That's the way I feel on the inside. I think I've been ready for this all my life."

He came to his feet and stood looking at the water. "I know all that. I think you're the best I've ever trained even without your special skills."

She stood, brushing off the seat of her pants. "Then you have to let me spread my wings and fly. You have to trust me."

"It's not fair to throw my words back in my face."

"Sometimes I don't play fair." She moved closer, snuggling against his back, wrapping her arms around his waist. "Like right now. I want to make love with you."

"I didn't bring you out here just so I could make love to you."

She pressed her lips against his shirt. "But you wouldn't be opposed to the idea, would you?" She let her hands slide down until they were against his zipper, then she lightly squeezed and was happy to hear him groan.

She unfastened his belt, then slipped the metal button through the buttonhole. He didn't move, in fact, he barely breathed as she tugged his zipper down.

"I'm going to have my way with you." She smiled, enjoying the role she was playing.

"I think I'm going to let you."

She slid her hands under the waistband of his briefs, grazing her fingernails on either side of his erection, but careful not to touch it. He sucked in his stomach.

"You're killing me." He moaned.

"No, only torturing you a little."

"Turnabout is fair play."

"I'll hold you to that."

She encircled his penis, rubbing her thumb over the tip. He thrust his hips forward. Slowly, she brought the skin down, then back up. "I love the feel of you in my hands. You're thick and hard. When I'm ready, I'm going to strip out of my clothes and spread my legs wide. When you plunge deep inside my body, I'm going to wrap my legs around your waist so you can go even deeper."

"Have you been practicing talking dirty?" His words were raspy with need.

"Practicing? No, but I've been dreaming of making love again. My body grows warm just being near you." It was easier when she didn't have to look right at him. Standing behind him, she was bathed in a cloak of invisibility. It made her braver.

She slid her hands lower, pushing his briefs down before cupping his balls. She liked the way they fit in her hands. She continued pushing his clothes downward, scraping fingernails over the top of his thighs, then running them back up and lightly caressing, teasing.

"Enough."

He turned in one movement and took her in his arms before she could complain that she wasn't through touching him. But when his lips brushed hers, all thought of what she'd been doing was gone. She only wanted to taste him. The cinnamon of his toothpaste, the heat of his mouth.

She lost herself in the fierce power of his kiss, then he gentled, becoming tender as his tongue stroked hers. She caressed his as her arms went around his neck, her fingers tangling in his hair.

He pulled back, burying his face in the crook of her neck. "You're going to be the death of me. I worry that you'll get hurt if I don't push you hard enough during training. I worry that you'll hate me if I do. You were meant to be an agent.

You have the skills, and you have the instincts of a seasoned agent. And every time I look at you, all I can think about is making love to you."

"Then make love to me now, and don't worry about anything, because nothing else matters."

He moved away and unlaced his combat boots. She didn't waste any time stripping out of her boots and clothes. Then they were standing naked in front of each other.

"You don't think we'll catch the woods on fire, do you?"

"Maybe, but if we start smoking we can always jump in the river."

He scooped her up in his arms. Laughter bubbled out of her. She tightened her arms around his neck, afraid he was going to toss her in the river, but he only laid her gently on the ground. He stood above her, staring at her. "You're so damn beautiful."

She could feel the heat rise up her face.

He laughed. "You're lying naked on the ground, yet you blush when I tell you that you're beautiful." He laid beside her.

"I can't help it. I'm not used to compliments."

"Then I'll have to tell you just how hot and sexy you are more often." He cupped her breast. "Like your breasts. They're just right. Nice and firm. I love watching the way they bounce just a little when you walk. I love how your nipples harden when I brush my fingers across them."

She drew in a sharp breath.

"You like that?"

"You know I do."

He lowered his mouth and sucked a nipple, swirling his tongue around it before moving to the other one. Her body arched as a deep ache began to grow inside her.

He moved back to her side. "And that? Did you like that."

She nodded.

"I want to hear you say it." His words were hoarse, his eyes glazed with passion.

"I love when you suck on my breasts, when you run your tongue over my nipples."

"And this? Do you like this?" He ran his fingers through the curls at the juncture between her legs.

"Yes." That one word was all she could manage.

"Spread your legs," he whispered close to her ear.

She did, and he moved between them. She cried out with pleasure when he ran his tongue over her labia, then sucked her inside his mouth. Her body began to tremble as heat spread through her. Before the trembles could overtake her, he quickly slipped on a condom and entered her.

She wrapped her legs around him as she'd promised, and he sank deeper. The sounds of the water rushing over the rocks filled her mind, the scent of their desire mingled with the heady scent of the woods.

"Oh, God, yes," he cried out as he thrust into her body.

He slid deep, then pulled almost all the way out. In and out, in and out. Faster and faster.

She clenched her inner muscles, heard him gasp with pleasure. Heat infused them both. Bright oranges, deep purples, fiery reds caressed their bodies.

She cried out, her body trembling with the impact of her orgasm. His body tightened. He moaned, then slowly collapsed beside her. The only sounds were the ones in the woods, and their breathing.

As she caught her breath, Lyraka realized something, she was falling in love. Damn it, she didn't have time for love. She wanted to be an agent.

Chapter 22

Banyon had wondered all this time what Earth was like. Now that he was here, he wasn't that impressed. Rovertia was far superior.

But he enjoyed playing games, especially the one he played now. He smiled at the woman and watched as she fluttered her hands in front of her. Did she actually think he would ever be interested in someone like her? Apparently.

She revolted him. He was used to perfection and she was far from perfect. She had wrinkles. Disgusting wrinkles.

Kragen had found where Aasera had been hiding—in some sort of colony that his old nemesis had begun for artists and poets and other wasteful pursuits. The Nerakians were like that. They meditated constantly. It was a ridiculous habit.

Long ago, Roverts had been sent to the planet Earth, discreetly blending in with the population as they learned earthling ways.

When he'd arrived, three men had met him. They had rented a transport unit called a limo. While two of them stayed on the outskirts of the artist compound, another acted as his driver. They'd provided him with luggage to avoid suspicion. He already knew a lot about this planet and its people's ways. Unlike the Nerakian, he liked knowing his enemies.

"I bet you're a painter," the woman said. She'd told him her name was Anna.

"You're very astute." He bowed slightly at the waist.

Her hands fluttered again. It was very annoying. She reminded him of a pesky Nagem, small creatures that were like an irritating bug fluttering fast and close to one's face. He hadn't been able to swat one yet.

"Let's see what I have." She set a book on the counter between them, then opened it. She studied it for a moment, then looked up with a smile that stretched across her face. "We have one cabin available."

"Good. Can you tell me if Aasera is here?"

Her eyes widened. "You know Aasera?"

"We are old friends from long ago."

Her shoulders slumped. "Oh, that's too bad. She's on an extended vacation. I don't know when she'll return. I'm in charge until she does." She suddenly brightened. "Do you plan on staying for a while?"

He smiled warmly. "Who knows what the wind shall bring."

"Oh, that was very poetic."

"But her daughter is here, correct?"

"Lyraka? Oh, no, she's gone, too."

Anger swept through him. He gripped the counter to keep from lashing out at this hideous creature in front of him. As soon as he felt calm once more, he asked, "Where has she gone?"

"She's . . . uh . . . you say you're an old friend?"

The woman wasn't as stupid as she looked. "It doesn't matter. If I don't see them this time, I'll leave a note and an address where they can reach me."

She relaxed. "Yes, that will be fine."

He let his gaze linger on her. "Will you dine with me tonight? I don't know the area."

Her face took on an odd, rosy hue, and she began to flutter again. "I'm sure you could find a younger, beautiful woman. Why would you want to have dinner with me?"

"I think older women have a wisdom that goes far beyond that of youth. Please, don't break my heart." He bowed his head.

"In that case, I would love to."

She giggled when he took her hand and lightly placed his lips against it. She smelled of age, not at all like the young woman he'd been with last night. It had been a shame he'd had to leave her the way he had.

"I'll show you to your cabin."

Anna knew she was blushing. She hadn't blushed in years! Not since she was in her thirties, but here she was sixty years old and blushing like a school girl.

She cast a glance in his direction again and almost had an orgasm. She hadn't had one of those in years, either. The man was sexy as hell with his dark sensuous looks. She'd almost melted when he'd walked into the office.

When she'd asked his name, he'd told her it was Banyon. Just Banyon. Like Cher or Madonna. That was it! Maybe he was a star and this was going to be his retreat from the paparazzi. She'd never heard of a Banyon before today, though. He talked kind of strange. He could be from another country. Maybe Italy. He looked Italian. She'd heard Italian men couldn't get enough sex.

But then, they'd never met her. Oh, she was so bad!

She cleared her mind and removed the key from her pocket. "Here we go." She unlocked the door and pushed it open, letting him step inside first.

He looked around. She waited anxiously, hoping he wouldn't change his mind. The cabins were pretty bare. If he was used to a five star hotel then this might not work for him. There would go her chance for a romantic evening. And maybe sex.

"This will suit me." He faced her.

She relaxed. She'd been so afraid. But none of that mattered now. Especially when he looked at her like he wanted to devour her right on the spot.

It was all she could do to take a breath. "Then I'll see you tonight?"

"Yes."

Her hands fluttered. It was a nervous habit, but she couldn't stop doing it. Banyon didn't seem to mind.

Heat crept up her face again. God, she was standing there staring at him like a moron. She hurried out the door, shutting it behind her. She was going to take a long, hot, rosewater bath, then she was going to dust rose powder all over her body.

Banyon watched her run across the space back to the main building. He was disgusted. Women didn't interest him that much. They were toys to be used, then discarded. Simple creatures with very small brains.

If he'd known the daughter wasn't here, he would have sent someone else to gather the information. Normally, he wouldn't dirty his hands, but he wanted to see the daughter for himself.

Did she look like Aasera? He could feel himself growing hard just remembering the last time he'd seen Aasera.

There had only been one woman with whom he'd wanted to mate, but Aasera had cringed when he proposed they copulate. He'd been furious and grabbed her. She'd grabbed a glass dish and hit him.

He fingered the scar on his face, remembering it as though it were yesterday. Anger burned deep inside him, festering over the years like rotting flesh. Now that he was this close, he wouldn't let anyone stand in his way. He would have his revenge.

The communicator in his pocket buzzed. He brought it out, setting it on a nearby table, then pushed a button. A screen rose and clicked on. Kragen.

"Your Majesty." He bowed slightly.

A thrill went through Banyon. He'd waited a long time to be addressed as such. He should've had his father killed years ago. It wasn't as though they had cared for each other, but his father had been useful when Banyon was growing up. He'd taught his son what was important in life—if there was a weak link, you got rid of it. His father had been right. Now that the weak link was gone, nothing could stop Banyon.

He looked at the screen. Kragen was another weak link. "Do you have information that I can actually use this time? Neither Aasera nor her child are here."

"You should've let me send a soldier to discover the child's location."

"That's why Aasera wasn't killed last time. I sent someone else to kill her and Aasera has lived in peace all these years because I was told she was dead. I carry the scar she gave me, while she paid no price for inflicting it."

"Yes, Your Majesty." Kragen bowed again.

"Do you have new information?"

"Aasera is still on Nerak."

Anger fused through him. He was surrounded by incompetence. But then, he already knew that.

"You requested daily updates."

"Then you have done your duty." Banyon snapped off the communicator. "Imbecile."

His men would take the child when he located her. Once she was back on his planet, he would begin the torture. He would know that he caused Aasera pain.

The day passed slowly. He had no desire to explore this planet. He sat in the chair instead, and thought of everything he would do to get revenge.

There was a knock. He would have his answers. He stood and walked to the door. He'd learned quickly that everything was manual on Earth. Very primitive. Why anyone would want to defect was beyond him. Nerak might be disgustingly bright, but at least the Nerakians were far more advanced than earthlings.

He turned the knob and opened the door. This woman would give him all the information he needed, then he would destroy her.

He sniffed. "What is that smell?"

"Roses. I hope you like them."

He didn't. It was a disgusting odor. "Wonderful," he exclaimed. Her hands began to flutter. He wondered if she would take off in flight. Yes, she was much like an irritating little Nagem.

There was only one species worse than a Nagem that he'd come across. The Adnams. They were puffers. A shiver of disgust ran through him. The Adnams grew bigger and bigger in size when they were threatened, then exploded an odorous substance all over their victim. It usually wasn't enough to kill anyone, but the gray slime took forever to remove. Nasty, slimy creatures.

But they could be useful, and they owed him. They'd caused a disturbance so that he could enter Earth undetected. Not that he thought earthlings had detection equipment that was high tech enough to know he'd landed. However, he wasn't positive they hadn't advanced over the years. His father had restricted travel after the incident with Aasera had almost caused an interplanetary uproar. But his father was no longer ruler of Rovertia and things were going to change. One day soon the Roverts would be a force to be reckoned with.

"I thought we could go to a restaurant not far from here. I hope you like fish," Anna said, breaking into his thoughts.

For a moment, he'd forgotten where he was. "It's my favorite."

He wondered how Aasera had adapted to Earth life. That must have gone against everything she had been taught. Nerakians didn't eat. Nor were there any men on Nerak except for companion units, which were only machines. They had gotten rid of all their temptations.

Since arriving on Earth, he'd encountered some of these spoils and hadn't been impressed. His planet had just as much, if not more, to offer.

He smiled at the thought, then frowned. Aasera had been a purest and shunned all he could offer. It must have been difficult being banned to a planet that had many indulgences.

He curled his hands into fists. Obviously there had been one indulgence she'd succumbed to since she had borne a child. She'd refused to copulate with him, but had lain with a man from Earth. For that alone, he would eventually kill her child, and he would make sure Aasera knew there would be nothing she could do to stop him.

"I've never even seen the inside of a limo," Anna said as she got in and slid across the seat.

"I am glad I can give you pleasure."

That was the last thing he was able to say. The female Anna chattered incessantly on the way to the restaurant. She talked about everything except Aasera and her child.

Once inside the restaurant, they were shown to a table and seated. When she took a drink, he was finally able to talk. "Tell me about my friend and her child. It has been many years and I long to hear about them."

She set her glass down, still looking unsure. He reached across the table and took her hand in his. Hers felt cold and clammy. A shiver of revulsion swept over him, but something else, too. Anticipation. He enjoyed the thought of leading her on. Making her think she was important to him, then later, being able to tell her she meant absolutely nothing. He wanted to see the dark despair enter her eyes. The tears fall from them. He wanted to laugh at her ridiculous idea that he could be remotely interested in someone like her. The hunt was exciting because the kill was close on its heels.

"I have worried you," he spoke softly. "That wasn't my intention. I realize I'm a stranger to you. Maybe we should go. It wasn't my wish to make you feel uncomfortable." He started to stand.

"No, no!"

Her face lost some of its color. He'd won, but then, he'd already known he would. Women were silly creatures. Aasera had been the only one whom he'd felt challenged by.

He took his seat again. "I would do nothing to cause you distress. It's just that it's been so many years since I have seen my friend. Aasera and I lost touch and it pained me very deeply. I would like to look upon her face and see if she is still the same."

"I guess it wouldn't hurt. I mean, you are friends and all." Her eyes widened. "I have a picture of Aasera."

His gut clenched. "I'd like very much to see it."

She reached inside her purse and pulled out a small book, then opened it. "Here she is."

He took the book and looked at the picture. Aasera. She had aged without the compounds Nerak had to offer. It pleased him to see the wrinkles on her face.

He flipped to the next page. His heart pounded inside his chest as heat unfurled inside him. The woman in the picture gazed at the sun as though she worshipped it. There must have been a slight breeze when the picture was taken because her clothes hugged her body like a lover.

The next page was a close-up of the same woman. Her pale blue eyes drew him in and captured his attention. There was something familiar and mesmerizing about her. He would have this woman before he left Earth. Maybe he would even take her back with him, enjoy her until she bored him.

He looked at Anna. "And who is this?" He turned the picture toward her.

"Oh, that's Lyraka, Aasera's daughter. Isn't she a beauty?"

Excitement rushed through him. Not so much the child then. No, this was a grown woman. "Yes, she is very beautiful." He smiled inwardly. The contemplation of revenge had never been sweeter. "She is on vacation?"

"Yes. Such a sweet child. I hope you get to meet her."

"I'm sure I will." He only had to locate her. That might prove difficult.

"I'm her godmother," she said. "I knew Aasera when Lyraka was born. She opened the book to the last page and showed it to him. "I even have a lock of her hair."

He almost laughed. This foolish woman had just given him Lyraka's location. Not as simple as a drop of her blood, but in just a few hours, he would know where to find the daughter. First, he had to end this farce.

He looked at Anna. She met his gaze, then blushed. He

knew the effect he had on women. It made him feel powerful that they couldn't resist him. He doubted it would be different this time.

"Have you ever met someone and knew that was the person you wanted to spend the rest of your life with?"

She began to shred the paper napkin she was holding. "You're teasing me."

"This is too sudden for you. I'm sorry, but I couldn't stop myself." He looked away.

"You're serious?"

He took her hand, rubbing his thumb across the palm. "I have never wanted a woman as much as I want you right now."

"But you're so handsome and I'm . . . I'm . . ."

"The most beautiful woman I've ever met. You stir my blood with a fire I haven't felt in a very long time. I want to take you back to the cabin and make love to you all night long." He sighed. "Now you probably hate me."

She squeezed his hand. "No, I don't hate you at all." She looked away. "Not when I feel the same way."

Of course he would win. He had no doubt about his ability to seduce. "Then we will leave now while my passion burns inside me."

"Oh, yes, I wouldn't want it to die out. Let's hurry." She jumped up, grabbed her purse and stuffed the photo book inside. The waiter hurried over, but Anna waved him away. "We've changed our mind."

She practically ran to the limo, pulling him alongside her. The driver hurried to get inside. They climbed in the back. As soon as the door shut, he pulled her into his arms. Roses filled the space between them and he thought he would be sick. The odor was nauseating.

"I want you," he said.

She trembled in his arms. "Yes, yes. Take me now!"

His mouth covered hers. He cringed when she stuck her tongue in his mouth. He closed his eyes, completed the seal, and began to inhale. She struggled at first, but it was useless of course.

When she was completely limp, and in a state of limbo, he let go of her and belched loudly. The air around him was filled with the disgusting smell of roses. He coughed, which only made it worse.

He leaned forward, pushing the button that lowered the glass between him and the driver.

"Return to the compound."

The driver waved his arm. "Ugh, the smell."

"It was her! Not me! She bathed in something she called roses. Just drive."

He refused to have someone so far beneath him say he smelled. Kings did not smell. What had she done? Drank a gallon of that awful stuff?

The smell had only worsened by the time they returned. The driver stopped the limo, opened the door, then quickly stepped back.

"Take her to her cabin and place her on the bed." Anna would be in a state of limbo for at least a week. By then, they would have found the daughter and returned home.

That was the only big problem with the Roverts. They couldn't actually kill someone by sucking out their essence. They could only leave them in a state of inertia, but it served his purpose because Anna wouldn't be able to warn Lyraka about him.

Yes, he could taste his revenge. He belched and filled the back of the limo with the putrid odor of roses again. Ugh, it would take at least six moon cycles to be rid of this odor, but it had been worth it.

Chapter 23

Roan opened the door to Joe's office and walked in. Joe looked up.

"Have a seat. Something has happened."

He sat across from Joe's desk. "What's up?"

"The Adnams are causing a problem. I'm pulling Johnny and Gavin to take a team to meet with their leaders."

Better them than him. An Adnam had sprayed his leg once and it had taken a month for him to get off all the slime. The smell had been as bad as the boiled cabbage his aunt used to cook. After he'd been slimed, everyone had stayed clear of him the entire month.

"You'll have the new team by yourself," Joe told him.

"They learn fast so that won't be a problem."

"We may need them to go out sooner than we'd expected if this turns into a full fledged uprising."

"It'll be too soon. They haven't trained enough, maybe in another month."

"We might not have a choice. I doubt it will be anything but a show of manpower. I only wanted to keep you up to date on what's going on. They've cut our funding, and we're having to manage on a shoestring budget." Joe massaged his temples. "Sometimes I wonder if this is all worth it."

"The public might feel differently if they knew what we do."

"Either that, or there would be all-out panic. Look what happens when aliens monitor us like we monitor them. New Mexico, Arizona, and not too long ago, Stephenville, Texas, of all places. It was in all the blasted papers. Intelligence did a quick cover-up and made a joke out of it. So now it's even more important that we fly below the surface."

"Still . . ."

"Yeah, I know." Joe leaned back in his chair. "Do the best that you can do. That's all I can ask. What are they doing today?"

"Taking the day off." When Joe frowned, he continued. "They've been at it solid for the last few weeks. I had to give them a break."

"I guess you're right."

"I am."

As he left Joe's office, Roan had to wonder if deceiving the public was the best thing. People had a right to know other species existed. Most aliens were good, some not so good.

He looked up, then stopped in his tracks. Lyraka was walking across the yard, talking with Alesha and Warren. As usual, Warren carried a stack of books. He wondered how long before there would be no books left for Warren to read.

Lyraka laughed at something someone said and looked up. Her gaze met his. She waved the other two on, then changed her direction and started walking toward him.

Damn, she was so beautiful she made him ache with longing to hold her in his arms. She had a natural easy grace with just the slightest sway in her hips.

"Did I tell you thanks for the day off?" she asked when she was closer.

"I just spoke with Joe. It may be the last day off for a while."

Worry crossed her face. "Why?"

"The Adnams are stirring up a few things. Johnny and Gavin are taking a team up."

"So we're on call?"

"Not yet. It's probably nothing. This isn't the first time something has happened to stir up another planet. Usually, a mediator can set things back in order."

"What are we supposed to do now?"

"The team continues to train—tomorrow." He grabbed her hand. "Come on, let's get the hell out of here. I think we both need a day off. Besides, I have a pager."

"I thought we weren't supposed to leave the area?" She cocked an eyebrow. Damn, she was cute when she was a little sassy.

"It's allowed if you leave with the instructor."

"Really?"

"Do you want to go or not?"

"I don't know. Exactly where are you kidnapping me to?"

"Does it matter?"

"No." She laughed.

God, he loved the sound of her laughter. He grabbed her hand and headed toward his Jeep, and didn't release it until they were in front of his vehicle. Her hand was small and soft and he felt it growing warmer. It was nice to know he could do that to her.

He went to the driver's side and she to the passenger's side. After he started the Jeep, he backed out from the parking place and headed down the hill, rather than up.

"I thought you'd whisk me off to the obstacle course. Where exactly are we going?"

He shook his head. "The closest town is about an hour away. It's all downhill until you get to Springtown. I've been there once. I think you'll like it."

"Is it big?"

"About one hundred and ten thousand. The river that I showed you the other day runs through it, there's a park, a shopping mall, a few bars. It's a nice town."

"I didn't go into the city much. My mother was always afraid for our safety. It seemed she was always looking over her shoulder."

"Was she afraid of other Nerakians? Weren't the elders the ones who exiled her, rather than her leaving of her own free will?"

"I hadn't thought the elders would harm her, but I wondered if it might have been someone else. That she might have an enemy or something." She shrugged. "Maybe she was just afraid we'd be found out by the government here on Earth. Either way, she was very protective."

"Does your mother know what you're training for?"

"I think she knew she didn't have a choice but to let me go. Maybe I finally convinced her how much this meant to me. Who knows? But she cut the apron strings, and for that, I'll be eternally grateful."

"And yet you've been stuck on the mountain training."

"But I'm away from my mother's colony."

"Was it that bad?"

She combed her fingers through her hair and looked out the window at the scenery. There were fewer trees the farther they drove. The woods had been replaced by fenced pastures with cows grazing on the thick, almost knee high grass. Occasionally, she would see a farmhouse. It all looked so normal. Not that her life had been abnormal, just isolated.

"Bad? No, it wasn't that bad. It was lonely." She'd wanted to be with other girls but Aasera had continuously drilled it into her that they were different. Even her mother's best friend, Anna, hadn't known who they really were. Her mother had been caged as much as Lyraka.

A smile curved her lips. But now they both had their freedom. Her mother was training other interplanetary travelers, and soon she would take to the air again.

A few times, her mother had told stories of the places she had traveled, but not often. For the most part, she hadn't talked about her life on Nerak. Lyraka hadn't pressed the issue. When her mother had spoken of her home planet, there had been such deep sadness in her eyes that it had hurt Lyraka almost as much.

How long had she been lost in her thoughts? She sat up as they approached the town. "Is that a Ferris wheel?" She pointed toward a slowly turning circle of chairs that appeared to dangle in midair. She'd never been on one. There were a lot of things she'd never done. She glanced toward Roan and wondered if they might at least drive by it.

"Looks like there's a carnival in town." He gave it a cursory glance.

Sometimes men weren't that good at taking a hint. "I've never been to one."

"You know what a carnival is?"

She frowned when she looked at him. "I can read." She'd read a lot growing up. Her mother had let her get a library card and she'd always had a stack of books checked out. She probably hadn't read as much as Warren, but she'd bet it would be close to his count.

"Reading isn't the same as experiencing one."

It was all she could do to not wiggle in her seat. "I suppose." She didn't want to act as though she were ten years old.

He parked the Jeep near the entrance, then glanced her way. "You can barely contain your excitement."

She shrugged. "It looks like something that will pass the time."

"We could walk in the city park."

"No!"

He laughed.

Ass. She grinned. "Okay, I'm excited."

"Then let's go."

He got out, then locked up as she stood in front of the Jeep and stared at the flashing lights and the crowd milling about. He was right, she was more than a little excited. Her mother would have never allowed her to go to a carnival.

But she was here now. She grabbed Roan's hand when he joined her, then pulled him toward the entrance. Everything looked magical and she felt like a fairy princess.

"Have you been to many carnivals?"

"Two or three."

A man twirled something pink onto a paper cone.

"What's that?"

"Cotton candy. Want some?"

She nodded. He paid for one and handed it to her. She took a bite. The pink sugar confection stuck to the tip of her nose, but melted in her mouth. Roan leaned over and licked it off. Laughter bubbled out of her.

This was what it felt like to be a kid. To laugh with someone you enjoyed being with. To feel as though she could conquer anything.

"Come on and I'll take you to the top of the world." He tugged her along with him.

"You already have."

"I wonder if we could start a new mile-high club."

"What's that?"

"Never mind. I have a feeling it would never work."

He gave the operator some bills, and they sat on the bench. A bar was dropped in place and then they were climbing. She grabbed his arm and held on. The Ferris wheel stopped at the top and gave her a clear view of the river that ran through the town.

"It's beautiful."

"Not as beautiful as you."

When she turned to look at him, he lowered his mouth to hers. Warmth filled her. She wrapped her arms around him, drawing him closer as his tongue caressed hers. She never wanted this day to end. She wanted it to go on forever and forever.

She vaguely felt the jerk of the wheel as it began its descent. But she heard the clapping when they got to the bottom. They pulled apart. Great, an audience.

"You make me forget where I am."

He grinned. "Yeah, well you do the same thing to me."

They went up again, but not as high as he'd taken her. She snuggled into the crook of his arm when he pulled her closer.

It felt so right sitting next to him. She couldn't imagine ever not being with Roan. He made her feel complete, that she'd only been going through the motions of living until he'd come into her life. It was more than Roan being her instructor. It was as though he were the other half of who she was.

She'd fallen in love with him. Giddiness washed over her, until she realized he might not feel the same way. Roan had been with many women and she probably wasn't nearly as experienced. Just the thought of their not being together made her feel sick. The cotton candy she'd had earlier only added to the nausea.

They came to a stop at the bottom. She wished the ride could've gone on forever, but there always had to be an end. The operator unlatched the bar and they got off.

She realized that no one ever mentioned the downside to loving someone. She wasn't sure she liked the queasy feeling that went along with it.

"Having fun?"

She looked up at him. He still had his arm across her shoulders. Maybe people were just supposed to enjoy the moment and not worry about what would happen tomorrow.

She smiled. "It's the best day of my life." Maybe Roan would fall in love with her, too.

Banyon kept his distance, but followed the couple. Anger burned inside him as he watched the way the earthling held Lyraka close. He had no right to touch what belonged to Banyon. And Lyraka *would* belong to him.

Soon.

Maybe he would kill the man with her. He thought he might enjoy it even though he'd never killed anyone. He could always have it done and just watch. That might be exciting. Yes, that would be good. It looked as though she cared for this man. It would be exhilarating to see her suffer. To make her afraid.

He continued to follow them, watching the way the man

would brush his lips against Lyraka's hair. He didn't blame the man for being fascinated with her. Lyraka was even more beautiful than the picture Anna had shown him. Her skin fairly glowed with a golden tan. He would have preferred her hair longer, not cropped short like a warrior.

He might keep Lyraka for a while. Dress her in gossamer gowns and keep her in a golden cage so that he might look upon her. She would fight him at first, but before he killed her, she would be begging him to take her.

Revenge would be sweet.

Chapter 24

Roan couldn't get enough of watching the different expressions cross Lyraka's face. He would say she reminded him of a child, but she was snuggled against him and her curves told him that she was anything but a little girl. No, she was all woman.

"Want to try the shooting gallery?" He pointed toward a booth where stuffed dogs and bears hung from the ceiling.

"I want a stuffed dog. My aunt has four of the cutest puppies." She looked up at him. "Did you have a dog growing up?"

He shook his head. "A cat."

"A cat?"

"Yeah, I liked to hear her purr."

She frowned, then punched him on the arm. "That was bad. You didn't really have a cat, did you?"

He laughed. "It was my aunt's cat and the darn animal hated me. Every time I came close, she would hiss and spit. I never touched a hair on that cat. I think my aunt secretly thought I might be torturing the poor beast. I'd swear the animal was just damned unsociable, though."

"That's okay, you can make me purr later and I promise not to bite or scratch."

Everything around them stopped. It was all he could do to keep from flinging her over his shoulder and carrying her off to the nearest motel. Had she really said what he'd thought she'd said? He might have imagined it because he'd been thinking how later he wanted to make love with her. Wishful thinking, maybe?

He trailed behind her like a zombie. The only thoughts going through his mind were of him slowly stripping off her clothes, peeling off the lacy wisp of material that covered her luscious breasts.

The pop of an air gun drew him out of his fantasy. When he looked up, Roan noticed a man dressed all in black. Just as quickly, the man ducked around the side of another booth and was out of his line of vision. Intentional? Maybe. He could work for the carnival.

There had been something odd about him, though. He'd reminded Roan of a Rovert, but what would a Rovert be doing on Earth? He mentally shook his head. Joe had him seeing aliens around every corner.

There was another pop, drawing his attention back to Lyraka, then another.

"And the pretty little lady wins!" The operator of the booth sounded happy, but his expression was grim. "And which stuffed animal would she like? How about a parrot?"

"The dog. The big brown and white one." Lyraka pointed to the one she wanted.

He faked a sad face. "Oh, sorry sweetheart. You'll have to hit three more bulls-eyes to win the big animal."

"But that's not what your sign says." She glared at the man.

"She's right," Roan said. When the operator looked as if he would argue, Roan eased back the jacket he wore so the man would see his gun.

The man paled. "And right she is! The big brown and white dog it is!" He hurried and brought it down, then handed it to Lyraka.

She hugged the dog as they walked away. "I guess I told him. I was not leaving without my dog."

"The look you gave the guy probably scared the hell out of him."

"That and when you pulled back your coat just enough to show him your gun."

"You saw that, huh?"

"You taught me to see stuff like that." She smiled, but just as suddenly, her expression turned serious. "Kind of like the man in black who's been following us all evening. Who is he?"

He hadn't spotted him until a few minutes ago. Once again, Lyraka had surprised him. He didn't know why the fact she'd picked up on the man in black should surprise him. Lyraka was a fast learner, and he'd trained her well.

"Roan? Do you think he is following us? I only spotted him a couple of times." She looked up at him.

"I'm not sure who he is." He aimed her toward a table at a small outside café within the carnival. "What about that guy you said stayed at the colony? Rick?"

She shook her head. "Not him, besides Rick was scared of his own shadow."

He pulled out a chair and she sat, then he took the one across from her.

"What about you? Any enemies?" she asked.

"More than I want to count, but none that would stalk me. Let's just hang out here for a little while and see if we can spot him."

"Sounds good."

A gum-smacking waitress came to take their order, then quickly left to get the sodas.

"I'm sorry this man has ruined your first time at a carnival." When Roan caught him, he would make sure the man apologized properly.

By the time they'd finished their drinks and still hadn't spotted the guy, he had to wonder if the man actually was a part of the carnival. He'd run across his fair share of crooked carnies.

"Maybe we were wrong." She glanced around as they stood.

"Maybe."

She swung her gaze back to him. "But you don't think so."

"Let's just say, I'm not completely satisfied." He frowned. "Have I gotten that easy to read?"

"No, but I know you well enough that you don't trust many people."

She was right, he didn't. "There's a small group moving toward the parking lot. We'll go out with them. If there is someone following us, he won't make a move when there are witnesses around."

They followed close behind the group of laughing, talking people, but had to separate from the crowd when they got to the parking lot. He didn't relax until he was standing beside the Jeep, unlocking the door.

He heard the sound of footsteps pounding the pavement.

Lyraka screamed.

He jerked his head up. Her mouth was quickly clamped to quiet her. She struggled against the beefy arms that easily held her, dropping the stuffed dog.

Roan reached for his gun. Something slammed against his head. He tried to stay conscious, but darkness quickly enveloped him.

"Lyraka, I've waited a long time to meet you." The man's high-pitched laugh was the last thing Roan heard.

Fear swept over Lyraka. Was Roan dead? She bit down on the hand that covered her mouth. He moved it, muttering something she didn't understand.

Before she could scream, the hand she'd bitten was securely in place again, but tighter, practically cutting off her air supply. She could only glare helplessly at the man in black.

"I can see by your expression that you don't want me to hurt him." He sighed nodding toward Roan. "There's not a thing you could do if I killed him right now." His eyes narrowed. "My words cause a fire of hatred to flare in your eyes. I like that. You'll be very entertaining. I would expect nothing less from Aasera's daughter."

She stilled. Aasera? He knew her mother.

He fingered the scar above his eyebrow. "All these years I didn't know she was alive, but she's on Nerak, safe and sound and I can't get to her." His smile was evil. "You'll do, though."

She breathed a sigh of relief. Her mother was okay.

"Take them both. He might prove useful. And I don't want her trying to scream again. If she bites, choke her just until she passes out."

Lyraka kicked the man holding her. She had the satisfaction of hearing him grunt in pain, but then he squeezed his hand over her mouth. She couldn't breathe!

The last thing she thought about was that she wasn't a very good agent if she couldn't even escape from this brute's hold.

Chapter 25

Man, he must've really tied one on last night. Roan reached up and touched the back of his head, then winced. Memory came flooding back, followed by a cold chill of dread. Where was Lyraka?

He slowly sat up, blinking several times until his eyes adjusted to the dim light. As soon as the pounding inside his head eased, he glanced around. At first, he thought he was in the middle of some kind of void. It took him only a moment to realize he was in a room with glass walls. Beyond that, shadows. He stood and walked the perimeter. Eight by eight.

An eerie feeling crept over him. Now he knew how a bug felt when it was kept inside a jar. Only one difference. He wasn't a bug.

How to escape?

His captors left him dressed, but had taken his gun. He checked his pockets. Empty. But he still wore his ring. They must've thought it was worthless. Good thing for him. Did they not know a diamond could cut glass? He ran his hands over the wall. How thick was it?

"I see you're awake," someone spoke from beyond his cage.

Roan whirled around. The room beyond filled with light. He could see he was in a larger room with solid walls. A man walked toward him. Roan squinted. It looked like the same man from last night. He was still dressed all in black.

"Where is she? What have you done to her? If you hurt her, I'll make sure you die a slow and painful death."

The man laughed. "And how do you propose to do that?" He waved his hand as he stopped in front of Roan. "There is no escape."

Roan's glass prison was the only thing between them. He slammed his hand against the glass and drew a small measure of satisfaction seeing the man jump back, but then anger flared in the other man's eyes.

"That wasn't smart," he snarled.

Roan at least knew more about him. The man might swagger, but he was only overcompensating because he was a coward.

"Why wasn't it smart? Because I scared you?"

"Because I hold Lyraka in another cage." He gloated. "Because I can do anything I want to her. Does that scare you?"

Roan refused to let the man see how much it did scare him. Instead, he went another route. "Who are you?"

The man stood straighter. "I am Banyon, son of Ethgar, and King of the Rovert nation."

He'd suspected as much. They were all similar in their looks. What Roan couldn't understand was why he'd taken them hostage.

"Why would a king take two people who have no worth?"

"Because I can."

"You'll be hunted down, king or not."

"Will they travel to Rovertia? I think not." He laughed again. "Oh, I assume you must have thought we were still on your disgusting little planet. We left many hours ago, and I covered my tracks well. The Adnams have been very helpful. Nasty, but helpful."

"What are you going to do with us?"

Banyon looked as though he thought Roan would never ask. "When I tire of playing with the both of you, I will kill you. Maybe I'll let you watch her die, see the absolute terror in her eyes just before her life force burns out. Would you like that?"

Roan slammed his body against the glass. "I'll kill you. I'll make you wish you'd never been born!"

Banyon only laughed as he turned and left the room. Roan pounded on the glass, but the leader of the Roverts didn't turn around. A door slid open and he walked out leaving Roan to worry about what would happen to Lyraka. He didn't doubt Banyon would kill them. There had been a look of satisfaction when he'd told Roan what he planned to do.

As far as Roan knew, he hadn't pissed off any Roverts, and he was pretty sure Lyraka hadn't, either. But Aasera was another matter. Lyraka had said her mother was an interplanetary traveler. He probably had figured out the why, he just needed to know the how. As in, how the hell was he going to escape?

He went to the glass wall on his right and placed the palms of his hands against it. How thick was it? He knew it was solid, from when he'd slammed against it. He looked around. Other than a scratchy blanket and a few pillows, the cage was empty. He only had one choice, try to weaken the glass enough so that he could eventually shatter it.

This side would work the best. If anyone else came to check on him, or to taunt him, they might not notice that he was cutting into the glass.

He fisted his hand so the diamond in his ring could make contact, and drew it across the glass from one corner to the next, then felt along the line he'd just made. Barely a scratch. He kept repeating the action as his mind formed a vision of Lyraka being tortured by that maniac.

His gut clenched. Every possible way there was to kill a man flashed before him. Each line he drew in the glass was like cutting Banyon's throat from ear to ear.

After the twentieth pass there was still just the barest scratch on the surface. It would take him days to weaken the glass enough so that he could break through it.

God, Lyraka must be scared out of her mind by everything that had happened. His stomach churned. What if he couldn't save her? No, he wouldn't think like that. Not when he loved her so much.

His hand stilled. Love? He rested his head against the glass. When had that happened? He had a feeling he knew—the first time he'd seen her. She'd been a little unsure, but hadn't backed down. No, she'd met his gaze head-on, as if telling him she was there to stay.

He drew in a shaky breath. All the more reason to escape and free her. Roan had to tell her how much he loved her.

Lyraka was pissed off as she walked the perimeter of her glass cage again. It was eight by eight. The middle of the floor was covered with satin pillows in an array of jewel-toned colors. It was a gilded cage. On the other side of her glass walls, it appeared she was in someone's bedroom. There was a massive bed with a velvet draped canopy.

Where was she? Why had they kidnapped her? She refused to think about what they might have done with Roan. If they'd harmed one hair on his head, she'd make sure they suffered horribly.

At one point, they'd forced her to drink a bitter liquid that left her coughing and feeling woozy. Her clothes had been stripped from her body. A shiver of revulsion rippled over her as she remembered lying on a cold table, her hands tied down, and the man in black standing over her, staring at her nakedness.

He'd touched her, cupped her breasts in his hot, moist hands.

"Beautiful."

"Yes, Your Majesty," someone else spoke.

She'd cringed away from the man in black. "I'll kill you," she spat, but her words were thick. She'd pulled against the ties that bound her wrists.

He laughed. "I think not." He trailed his fingers over her stomach and through the curls at the juncture of her legs, then moved back to her breasts.

She caught the scent of dead roses when he breathed close to her face. She tried to turn away, but he caught her chin. "You are mine, my sweet captive. How does it feel to know I can do anything I want to you and there's not a thing you can do?" To prove his point, he moved his hand back to her breast and squeezed her nipple.

She gritted her teeth to keep from crying out. Just when she thought she would give in to the pain, he laughed. A dark, raspy sound that sent shivers of fear over her.

Abruptly, he moved away and ordered her dressed in the thin white gown that she still wore. It hid little.

She was forced to drink more of the bitter liquid, then she was bathed in darkness and oblivion.

A door opened and the man in black entered the bedroom. She stood tall with her head held high. She refused to shield her body. What did it matter? He'd already seen everything there was to see.

He noted her rebellion and smiled. "You're so much like your mother. Aasera fought, too. If the guards hadn't been surprised, I would have tamed her. But she escaped. A shame. She would have provided many days of entertainment. As will you."

"Go to hell."

"I don't believe in your religion, but I know of it. Hell is the place where evil goes. I think I would enjoy ruling there." He walked closer to the enclosure.

"What have you done with Roan?"

"Your friend is dead."

Suddenly, she couldn't breathe and sank to the pillows. Roan, dead? No, she would've known if that were true. Wouldn't she have felt his heart stop beating? He couldn't be dead. Not when she had just realized she loved him.

She looked at the man in black and saw the way he watched her reaction. There was something about him that told her he was lying. Hope sprang inside her.

"You're lying." She met his gaze, daring him to tell her differently.

"Yes, I am."

Her eyes narrowed. "Who are you and why are you doing this?"

He bowed slightly. "I am Banyon, Ruler of the Roverts. Welcome to my planet."

Her gaze swung from one side to the other. "No, you couldn't . . ."

"But I did. It was quite easy, in fact." He raised his eyebrows. "You call yourself an agent with an elite force? It took very little effort to take you."

"Easy for you to say when you had someone else doing your dirty work."

"True, but then I am the king so I can do whatever I want." His gaze moved slowly over her. "I'm going to have you. You do know this, don't you? I'm going to mate with you often."

"I'd rather you just kill me."

He brushed an imaginary fleck off his dark coat. "Yes, I will do that, too. Then I will send your head to Aasera. When she comes after me seeking revenge, I will also kill her."

"Is that how you got that scar? Did my mother give it to you?" She sneered. "You have the audacity to think you can beat her? That you will be able to kill her? I don't think so."

His face turned dark red, then he visibly forced himself to relax. "Yes, you are like her. It will be fun breaking you."

"You'll never touch me," she promised, raising her chin and glaring at him.

He smiled, then pushed a button on her cage and everything went dark. She couldn't see. Fear swept over her. She could take just about anything except being caged in the dark.

"Rest, my sweet. I will return."

Anger flared inside her, but it was short lived. In the dark, she had time to think about what was going to happen to Roan, to her. She knelt down, then curled up on the pillows, hugging one close to her. Damn Banyon! If she got the chance, she would give him more than a scar to remember her by.

* * *

Banyon could see Lyraka, but she couldn't see him. He enjoyed watching her. She was probably the most beautiful woman he'd ever seen. She was dark like a Nerakian warrior and had a lot of the fierce determination that he saw in their genetic make-up. Usually he had no desire to mate with a warrior. They were often cold and analytical.

Lyraka was different, though. Her eyes weren't dark like a warrior's. Her eyes were pale blue, and when she looked at him, it was as though she looked deep into his soul. They were mesmerizing.

He wanted her. He wanted to spread her thighs and plunge deep into her body again and again. He wanted her to cry out his name, to do his bidding. Then, and only then, would he kill her.

He watched her as she flung the pillow away and rolled to her back. She hugged her middle, her breasts pushing up. He licked his lips as he stared. The thin material hid nothing from him. He wanted her begging him to plunge inside her.

Maybe he would let the man watch them mate. He knew the earthling had deep feelings for Lyraka. It would give Banyon great pleasure to have him watch them mate. Yes, he would arrange for that as soon as she was submissive.

Life was good.

Chapter 26

"We've found the Jeep." Reeka and Link strode into the training room where the others were gathered.

Joe looked up. Dread filled him. He'd been worried since yesterday morning when Roan and Lyraka hadn't shown up. He'd known there was something between the two. A blind man would've seen the attraction, but Roan wouldn't have skipped training. Not when the Adnams were raising hell.

He looked at Reeka and Warren, and hoped they weren't going to tell him that it was at the bottom of one of the deep ravines that snaked through the mountainside.

"Where?"

"In town. The one just down the mountain. Springtown."

"And Roan and Lyraka?" he asked.

Reeka shook her head. "No sign."

"There's a carnival in town," Warren said. "We talked to some of the people who run the booths. We showed their pictures. One of the guys remembered them. Said the woman could shoot as good as a man."

Alesha snorted.

Warren looked apologetic. "His words. Not mine. The Ferris wheel operator said he noticed a man dressed all in black glaring at them when they . . . uh . . ."

Warren's face turned a bright shade of red. Knowing Roan,

it didn't take much imagination to figure out what they were doing.

Warren squared his shoulders. "He said that people started clapping when they kissed. He wouldn't have thought much about it, but the guy in black was evil looking. Someone you wouldn't want to meet on a dark deserted street."

"I knew there was something going on between them." Link leaned back in his chair, crossing his legs at the ankle.

Ray frowned. "Hell, I thought they hated each other the way he always rode her." He cleared his throat. "I mean, the way he wanted her to be the best and all. Do you think they might have gotten a motel room and time sort of slipped away? That happened to me once."

"There's something else." Warren reached into his pocket and pulled out a set of keys. "We found these just under the Jeep. Roan wouldn't have left them. That isn't all There was a spot on the pavement. It tested positive for blood."

"Damn." Joe stood, walking to the window. What had Roan and Lyraka gotten into? He scraped his fingers through his hair.

"What do we do, boss?" Alesha asked.

Joe turned from the window. He still didn't think she fit his idea of an agent, especially with the elite force. Her scores reflected otherwise. She'd made the highest ones ever on a written exam.

She'd played football in high school. She was right there in the middle of a bunch of smart-assed boys, but she'd held her own. She might look like a cheerleader, but she could kick some serious ass.

"What would you do?"

"I'd take a sketch artist and have the guy who saw the man in black describe him," Alesha said.

"Did either one of them have any enemies?" Reeka asked.

Joe shook his head. "I'm almost positive Lyraka didn't. Roan had his share."

"Do you think they're still alive?" Ray's expression was solemn. "You'd think if someone was after money, they would've asked for a ransom or something by now."

Joe shook his head. "I don't know." He'd never felt so useless in his whole life. All he knew was that whoever had them better make damn sure he didn't harm them because no place, no planet, was big enough for them to hide. He'd hunt them down if it was the last thing he ever did.

Roan thought he'd been in the glass cage for two days. It was hard to tell. Time seemed to have slowed to a crawl. Food would be waiting when he woke up. There was a pot to relieve himself that would be replaced with a clean one while he slept.

He had a feeling there was something in the food that made him sleep so he'd started hiding it beneath the pillows. Banyon had been in one other time to taunt him with what he was doing to Lyraka. Roan hadn't let the other man goad him. He only stared at Banyon, which had infuriated him.

But Banyon's tactics had worked better than the ruler could've hoped. He just didn't know it.

If Banyon was harming Lyraka, Roan would kill him. He just had to escape. He worked at scoring the glass every chance he got. The grooves were getting deeper. It wouldn't be long now.

There was a familiar whish of the door opening. He quickly moved away from the glass and positioned himself so that it shielded that side.

"I was beginning to wonder where you've been." Roan stood nonchalantly, one hand resting on the glass in front of him. He'd never before felt such a burning desire to kill someone. Until now. He wanted to choke the life out of the smug bastard.

"It's nice to know I'm missed."

"I'd miss a worm if I thought it would relieve the boredom of sitting in here day after day."

"That's why I have brought something to entertain you."

Roan knew by the smirk on Banyon's face that whatever he was about to do, Roan wouldn't like it.

Banyon clapped his hands and the door opened again. A video screen was brought into the room and placed in front of him. The men who carried it in left as quietly as they'd come. The screen was blank until Banyon touched a button.

Roan's breath caught in his throat. Lyraka was in a glass cage much like his, but she was obviously in a bed chamber. She wore a thin gown that showed more than it hid. She was being treated as less than nothing, an object on display for Banyon to enjoy at will.

"Let her go," Roan said quietly.

"She is beautiful, isn't she," Banyon said as though Roan hadn't spoken.

"Let her go now, and I might let you live." Roan turned his gaze on Banyon. The other man didn't look quite as sure of himself as he had a moment ago.

He quickly recovered, and said, "Enjoy what you will never have again." Banyon turned on his heel and left the room.

"Lyraka," Roan breathed. He rested his hands on the glass and drank in the sight of her. "Hang tight, baby. I'll get us out of here."

She glanced around as if she'd heard his words. He held his breath.

"Can you hear me?"

She moved to the cushions and sat in the middle of them looking dejected. For just a moment, he'd thought she'd heard him. Even with her sensitive hearing, there were too many walls that separated them.

But she was alive. He'd been afraid for her. He rested his forehead on the glass and drew in a deep breath.

As he lifted his head he looked at the video screen. Banyon was walking into the room where Lyraka was in her glass cage. God, he was a sick bastard. Roan got more irritated the nearer Banyon got to the cage.

Lyraka turned her head and saw Banyon. She slowly sat up, wobbling slightly. He'd given her something. Probably the same thing he'd been putting in Roan's food.

Banyon brought a golden key out of his pocket and inserted it into an area of the glass that had looked flush before. Roan felt as though he'd been plunked down in the middle of a dark fairy tale.

"Stay the hell away from her," he growled. He began to pace, his gaze never leaving Lyraka.

Banyon's face suddenly filled the screen and he smiled. The son of a bitch knew exactly what this was doing to Roan. Banyon liked to play games. Well, Roan didn't, and when he was free, he'd rip off Banyon's head.

Banyon entered the glass cage, then knelt on one knee and ran a hand through Lyraka's hair. She lay there in her drugged state. Roan's hands curled into fists as Banyon leaned closer to Lyraka's face. But rather than kissing her, as he'd probably planned, Lyraka came alive and hit him in the nose as hard as she could.

Banyon screamed and slapped Lyraka across the face, drawing blood when he busted her lip. Roan slammed his fist against the glass.

Lyraka jumped to her feet as Banyon ran from the cage, locking the door behind him. Two guards rushed into the room and escorted their leader away.

Roan turned his attention back to Lyraka who was laughing uncontrollably as she fell back on the cushions. God, she was nervy, and not as drugged as he'd first thought.

He grinned. Knocking the hell out of Banyon was something he would have done. No matter what the cost. It was the principle of the matter that counted. Lyraka had thumbed her nose at Banyon and said screw you.

Damn, he loved her.

And had more reason to free her. Banyon was going to exact revenge, and Roan didn't want the axe to fall on her head. Would he be able to break free in time?

How damn thick was the glass, anyway? He'd been working at making it weaker since he'd awakened. He wouldn't stop until he was free. He scored across the top, down the side, across the bottom, up the other side. The muscles in his shoulders ached, but he concentrated on what it would feel like to hold Lyraka in his arms again, to pull her against him.

"Hang in there, babe, I'm coming for you." Across the top, down the side, across the bottom, back up the other side. His arm burned. Pain was good. It made him remember just what was important in his life.

Lyraka carefully touched her lip. "Ouch," she hissed.

Damn, Banyon had hit her square on the lip. She should be thankful it had been an open handed slap rather than a balled fist.

He hit like a wuss. Had the man never been in a fight before? Probably not. He was a king and before that, a prince. He'd probably had other people doing his fighting for him.

But her fisted slam to his nose had been dead on. That had been priceless. She would do it again if she got the chance. She rubbed her sore knuckles. Even if it had hurt her almost as much as him.

She lay back on the pillows and tried to concentrate on blending in. If Banyon thought she was gone, he might open the door and she'd be able to escape.

Something in the food had made it impossible for her to blend, though. Some kind of drug had been added. She still felt a little woozy. And she was starving since she'd stopped eating and started hiding the food beneath the pillows.

She sighed and sat up when the blending still wasn't working. Hitting Banyon hadn't been a smart move. He might force the liquid down her again.

His touch had been hot and moist. A shiver of revulsion swept over her. His breath was like rotting roses and she couldn't stand the nauseating smell.

She glanced around her glass cage. Would she ever escape?

She could only go without food for so long. Where was Roan? Was he in his own glass cage? Was he alive?

Tears formed in her eyes, then slowly slid down her cheeks. Great agent she was. She quickly brushed the tears away. She wasn't going to give up hope that someone would rescue them. But how would the team know where they were? Banyon had a vendetta against Aasera. No one would suspect a Rovert had taken them.

The door swished open. She braced herself as Banyon strode into the bedroom, his guards behind him.

Her eyes narrowed. Was his nose crooked? It looked as though it was a little to the right. Had she broken it? Damn, she'd laid a good one on him.

"Leave me," he said to the guards and waved his hand.

Her mouth dropped open. His voice was nasally and high-pitched.

The guards left, and he turned back to her. "I'll make you pay for breaking my nose," he snarled.

She snorted with laughter. Oh, Lord, she had a feeling her situation was getting worse by the minute. She should be terrified, at the very least, scared, but she was finding it hard to be frightened of someone who smelled like dead flowers and talked like he had been snorting helium . . . a lot of helium.

Hadn't her mother told her once that Roverts didn't heal like everyone else? She looked at the scar on his face. That's why Banyon hated her mother so much. And now he probably hated her even more. Oh, hell, what did she have to lose?

"You sound funny," she taunted as she came to her feet and sauntered over to the glass. "Does your nose hurt?"

"Your death will be slow and painful."

She should probably stop pushing him, but she hated this glass box. Besides, he was the best entertainment she'd had in a long time. She leaned into the glass. "When I get out, I won't kill you."

His eyebrows rose at her words.

"How do you think it'll feel if I break your legs? Maybe your arms? Do bones heal on Roverts?"

He paled, and she had her answer.

"Or maybe I'll just cut another scar into the other side of your face. I bet the ladies wouldn't think you were so handsome after that. Not that they will now, once you speak."

"I don't think you'll do any of those things."

"Open the door and we'll put it to the test."

"The next time I open the door, you will lie on the pillows and willingly let me do whatever I want."

Even though he still sounded like a cat with its tail caught in the door, her humor fled. Her situation was real, and there wasn't anything funny about it. She wanted to cover herself, but she wouldn't give him the satisfaction of thinking he was getting to her.

"I'll do whatever I want," Banyon repeated.

She stepped back. He laughed.

"You'll spread your legs and beg me to mate with you. Your arms will draw me close, your lips will cover mine."

"Never! I'd rather die than let you touch me."

"But would you let Roan die? Would you watch me torture him just to keep from giving me the satisfaction of fucking you?"

Her body began to tremble.

"I'll give you until tonight to decide. I'll have a video screen brought in so you can watch as the flesh is slowly stripped from his body. It's very painful. Even the bravest of men start screaming like crazed madmen after the first hour has passed."

"I've changed my mind." She met his gaze. "I think I will kill you."

He laughed as he left the room. A few minutes later, food was slipped inside through a small door. No chance that she could escape by grabbing an arm.

But maybe if she ate all the food, she'd be drugged enough that she could let Banyon touch her, have sex with her. She swallowed past the bile that rose in her throat. How was she going to get through it?

Her spine stiffened. The how didn't matter. She just would. She'd grit her teeth and pretend she was some place else. Her mother had talked about cosmic meditation where a person could actually travel outside their body. She would pretend it was happening to someone else, not her. She would get through it.

And Roan wouldn't have to die.

Chapter 27

"I'm going to get a team together," Joe told the group. "Johnny and Gavin should be back by day after tomorrow. By then, we should know more about who took them."

"No." Ray stood. "Lyraka is a member of our team. We should be the ones who get her back."

Joe shook his head. "You're not trained enough."

"We're good." Reeka's words were a statement, not bragging, just fact.

Reeka was right, the team was good, but good didn't make up for a lack of experience. "No, I can't put your lives in danger. Besides, we have no idea who took them.

"Yes, we do," someone spoke up from the doorway.

"Aasera?" A rush of excitement went through Joe. She was even more beautiful than the last time he'd seen her. She was the one woman who could throw his whole world out of kilter, and she didn't even have a clue. Lyraka's father must have really done a number on her because she wouldn't have anything to do with Joe or any other man. Now here she was, and he hadn't protected her daughter. He'd sworn that he wouldn't let anything happen to Lyraka.

"Joe." She nodded her head, then walked the rest of the way into the room.

"I'm sorry. I broke my promise about keeping her safe."

"She was taken because of me. I'd forgotten about my enemies. It happened so long ago that I thought it was no longer important. Now we must save her."

"We can have a team together by tomorrow."

She shook her head. "He'll kill her."

"Who?"

"Banyon. His father is dead. He's the new leader of the Roverts. Many years ago, he wanted me and tried to take me by force. I scarred him." She looked at the others. "Roverts don't heal like others. I cut his face. He swore to kill me, but I escaped. Before he could even seek revenge, I was . . . exiled to Earth and everyone was told I had died while on a mission. He'll get his revenge on Lyraka."

"And Roan," Reeka said.

"Warrior." Aasera bowed her head.

"Traveler." Reeka returned the gesture. "Roan is a trainer and a skilled fighter."

"Then I have caused two lives to be in jeopardy because I didn't take precautions."

"No, Banyon has put them in jeopardy."

Aasera raised her chin. Joe had seen that look before and knew exactly what it meant. He had a feeling he wouldn't be able to dissuade her from going after Lyraka. Not that he could blame her. If it was his daughter, he'd do the same damn thing.

"Well you can't just go barreling in there with guns blazing," Joe said.

"Sounds good to me. Roverts aren't known for their fighting skills," Ray said. When everyone looked at him, he continued. "I've been reading about them. I do know how to read. Warren isn't the only one."

"We can make a lot of noise and divert their attention." Warren looked at everyone. "I've been working on a device that will fit in a shirt pocket, but when I trigger it to explode . . ." he pursed his lips and made a noise like something exploding.

"Bomb to go?" Link cocked an eyebrow.

Warren's cheeks brightened to a rosy color. "Yeah, something like that. It might be small, but it works."

"You've tried it?" Joe wasn't sure he liked the idea of one of the trainees making devices that would blow something up. At least, not out of the classroom.

"I sort of blew up the dog house back home."

Alesha cringed. "Please tell me the dog wasn't in it."

Warren straightened. "Of course not. He was already dead." When everyone stared at him, he quickly continued. "From natural causes a couple of years before. The dog house wasn't being used and I thought I'd see what the bomb would do. It worked, but it still needed a little tweaking. I've been working on it since college."

"We might need it later, but what if we go in as traders. I read the prince, king now, has a thing about buying women of other species. He likes to toy with them. The slave trade is illegal, but he still does it," Ray told them.

"That's horrible," Alesha said.

Aasera looked at her as only someone could who had more years, and more wisdom. "As is the drug trade, starvation, and much more. Corruption breeds corruption."

Alesha looked around. "If someone is going to pose as a trader, then they'll need someone in bondage. Hell, the last time I did anything with bondage, I was the one tying the ropes."

Ray grinned, then wiped the smile off his face, and cleared his throat. "They won't question me but once," Ray said.

Joe figured Ray was probably right, and it was a sound plan. But damn it, they were green. Aasera was a traveler, not a warrior. He looked at each of them and saw the looks of determination on their faces. This is exactly what a team would do.

He sighed. "Okay, but I'm going with you." Their expressions quickly changed to surprise. "I was a damned good agent before I moved to recruiter. I know what I'm doing."

"Then let's go." Link came to his feet.

"Not so fast. We need to ready one of the larger crafts, we need supplies, and we need to know what the others will be doing every second we're there. Aasera, you've been to Rovertia, we'll need a layout of the planet."

"We have to move fast," Aasera said.

"I know."

"Thank you for doing this, Joe."

"We'll get them back."

"Damn right," Ray said. "We're a team."

Chapter 28

Roan quickly stopped moving the diamond over the glass and went to the front of the cage when the door whished open. Banyon walked in, his nose slightly to the side of his face. Lyraka had really punched him a good one. Served the guy right. As soon as they escaped, he was going to dig out the book on keeping your cool. Lyraka definitely needed a refresher course.

"I will have Lyraka tonight," Banyon gloated in a nasally, high-pitched voice. "There is nothing you can do to protect her. How does that make you feel?"

Roan's mouth dropped open. Yeah, he'd say Lyraka had tagged Banyon good. Roan laughed which infuriated Banyon more. Hell, he couldn't help it. Banyon sounded like the guy from that sitcom. What the hell was his name? Oh, yeah, Urkel. Steve Urkel.

"Are you sure you can take her?" Roan shook his head. "If I were you, I'd keep my distance. Roverts don't heal very well, do they? Do you think you'll talk like that the rest of your life? That would be a shame."

Banyon stomped his foot. "Neither one of you will be laughing when she willingly gives herself to me."

"You know, I can't really see that happening."

"But you will see it all happening, every second, every minute." His smile was pure evil. He looked pointedly at the screen. "You'll watch Lyraka giving herself to me willingly over and over again until I tire of her."

Banyon was too self-assured. A tingle of apprehension ran down Roan's spine.

"It will be my name she cries out," Banyon continued. "If she doesn't do everything I want, I'll force her to watch my men strip every inch of skin from your body. She'll hear each scream, see the blood running down your body, and she'll watch it puddle on the floor."

"You bastard." Roan slammed his hand against the glass.

"Yes, I am, but I'm sure you already knew that." He nodded toward the screen. "You can watch her surrender on the screen." He turned to leave, but then turned back as if he'd suddenly remembered something else. "Oh . . . I'll still torture and kill you as soon as I finish with her tonight, and I will let her watch. I think that might put the anger and fire back in her. You have to admit that even you like a little fight in your women."

"I'll kill you. That's not a threat, it's a promise."

"But an empty one, none the less. And just so Aasera will know, when I finish, I'll cut off Lyraka's head and send it to her." He left the room.

Cold dread filled Roan. His gaze moved to the screen. Lyraka had picked up the bowl of mush she had been given. She dipped her hand inside and raised it close to her mouth.

He knew what she was contemplating. The drugged food would make it easier when Banyon came. Damn it, Roan wanted her to fight, to scratch the bastard's eyes out.

But Roan knew without a doubt, she wouldn't do that. She would do whatever it took to save him. He watched her as she dropped the food back into the bowl, then set it to the side, and shoved the pillows against the back glass.

Once she had them arranged, she moved closer to the side glass and closed her eyes. It took him a few seconds to realize that she was trying to blend in but it was impossible against a clear surface. After a few moments, she lay down. The floor was a dark solid surface.

Fascinated, he watched as she began to disappear. She didn't quite vanish completely, though. The drugs she'd been given must be affecting her ability to blend. But she didn't give up. She kept trying.

And so would he.

He went back to the glass and moved the rough diamond over the surface. Up one side, across the top, down the other side and across the bottom. Then he repeated the sequence over and over and over.

Lyraka knew if her plan didn't work, she would have to endure Banyon's touch, no matter how much she loathed him, but she had to at least try to escape or everything would be lost. She had no doubt Banyon would kill them both.

She lay on the floor and closed her eyes. Immediately a vision formed of Roan, his wrists bound in chains, arms stretched taut. His screams echoed inside her head as Banyon began to rip the skin from his back.

She sat up with a start. Damn it, how was she going to blend if all she saw was Roan's death?

Deep breath. She could do this.

She closed her eyes again and slowly exhaled, then inhaled, wishing she'd paid more attention to meditating when Aasera had tried to teach her. Aasera had told her that meditating was a part of who Lyraka was, that it was something inborn in all Nerakians.

Aasera had talked about cosmic meditation, too, where the spirit could actually leave the body. Lyraka had only experienced deep out of body meditation once when she was young, and she had to admit, it scared the hell out of her. She'd never tried again, much to the disappointment of her mother. But maybe if she could empty her mind, she could blend more easily.

She took another deep breath and exhaled. Calmness began to wrap her in its comforting cloud. She felt her body getting lighter. She lay on the floor, legs stretched out. The familiar rush swept through her. She could feel the floor, the solidity of the surface. It enclosed her in a protective cocoon.

She smiled, knowing she had reached the place she needed to be. Banyon would probably freak out when he returned and thought she'd escaped. That would give her the element of surprise, and might buy her a little time. If she could get a weapon, she would free Roan. She only hoped they could come up with a plan together from there.

It was weak at best, but it was all she had. If she was caught, she would suffer Banyon's touch hoping for a little more time because she really didn't want to die. Not when she'd finally felt as though she'd just started to live.

She began to materialize.

Concentrate!

Deep breath, exhale slowly. Relax.

The space around her became calm once more. She emptied her mind of all thoughts and went into a deep relaxation state. She could almost see her lungs filling with air, then emptying.

Something popped and she felt a whoosh of air.

She opened her eyes and suddenly was looking down on the glass cage. It looked empty. So this was what deep meditation was all about. She hadn't even gotten this far the first time.

She felt as if she were flying. She left the room, searching for Roan.

How would she find him when there were so many rooms and long winding corridors? There were Roverts and captives in chains everywhere. They looked frightened as they shuffled along. Would that be her one day?

No! She would never be anyone's slave. She would kill herself first.

But that wasn't going to happen. She closed her eyes and

concentrated, listening with her heart, rather than her head. Her spirit felt as though it were being pulled in a specific direction. She let it go, opened her eyes, and watched so she would remember the way.

She entered a room where there was another glass cage. And she saw him. Her heart began to melt. It seemed like forever since the night of the carnival, since he'd held her close, since his lips had touched hers.

She reached toward him. He looked around, as though he could feel her presence.

Roan, her mind whispered.

He flexed his shoulders, then tilted his head from one side to the other. What was he doing? She watched, and saw him use his ring to score the surface of the glass, stretching to reach from one corner to the next. Of course Roan would try to escape. Banyon wouldn't be able to keep him in a cage for long.

She was being pulled away. God, she wanted to stay longer even if he didn't know she was there. She would never get tired of looking at him. Deep down she knew this might be the last time she saw him alive. Her plan was flimsy at best.

She left Roan and left the building they were in and saw that it was actually like a castle and made of dark, dreary gray stone with turrets that stretched high into the sky. Everything about the land surrounding the castle was barren as if there had been a recent fire and only the stubble of plants was left.

Dark gray huts stretched out for a great distance in long rows in front of the castle. If this was where Banyon's people lived, then their existence was dismal at best.

Air rushed around and through her as she was pulled back inside her body, but before she was sucked into the glass cage, she saw Banyon coming toward the room. As her spirit rejoined her body, she sat up with a gasp.

Wow, that had been a different experience, but she didn't have time to think about what she'd just done. She quickly lay back on the hard floor and closed her eyes. Just seeing Roan had given her renewed determination not to go down without a fight.

Almost immediately, she could feel the density of the floor, and became one with it. Seconds later, she heard the swish of the door to the room as it opened.

"Guards!" Banyon screamed in his nasal voice.

If nothing else, she was proud of that punch. Her knuckles were still sore, but it was so worth it.

She heard heavy footsteps as the guards came running into the room.

"Where is she?" Banyon screeched. "You have let her escape."

"No, Majesty. No one has come inside the room. She couldn't have escaped."

"Then tell me where she is?"

Silence.

She didn't dare peek to see what they were doing, but she bet the expression on Banyon's face was priceless.

"Find her now or you'll pay with your lives!"

Again, she heard footsteps as the guards ran out of the room. She only hoped Banyon would unlock the door. She breathed a sigh of relief when she heard the key inserted in the lock, then the door opened.

"There's no way you could have escaped," Banyon said. "Are you hiding beneath the pillows?"

She peeked. The door had closed and he was bent over the pillows, tossing them to the side, one by one. She jumped to her feet. He whirled around and screamed. She used his moment of shock at seeing her become solid to smash her fist in his face.

His scream was garbled as he grabbed his face and quickly turned away from her.

She raised her foot and shoved it against his butt as hard as she could. He plunged headfirst into the glass and crumpled to the cushions.

She was getting so good at kicking ass.

The door opened. She spun around. Instead of guards, Roan slipped into the room. She started to run toward him, but knew that would have to come later. They still had work to do. She grabbed the key out of Banyon's pocket, then partially covered him with the pillows before leaving the cage and locking the door behind her.

"I didn't think I'd ever see you again," Roan said as he came up behind her.

"You broke the glass," she said as she turned and flung her arms around his neck, giving in to temptation.

"How'd you know about the glass?"

"It doesn't matter. We need to get to a spacecraft or something before the guards return."

"You can't go running through the halls dressed like that."

She looked down. He was right. There wasn't much of her that was hidden beneath the nearly transparent fabric. She hurried to Banyon's closet and flung the doors open. She could wear something of his. It was a good thing he had a small frame.

"Now this is what I call a closet." It was bigger than the cage she'd been stuck inside the last few days.

"Can we hurry?"

God, he was so sexy when he was anxious. She was a whole lot giddy that they were together again, but she knew they were far from being out of danger.

"What'd you do to Banyon, anyway?" he asked as he began to open drawers and dig through the contents.

"I punched him in the nose, then when he doubled over and turned, I shoved him into the glass, and knocked him out."

"That's going to leave a mark."

He held up a small knife that would probably only make someone mad if he were to use it, but she guessed it was better than nothing. She watched him slip it into his pants pocket.

She grinned. "Yeah, I know. I hope he has to look at scars

every day for the rest of his life." She pulled the diaphanous gown over her head and tossed it to the side. His indrawn breath drew her attention. She arched an eyebrow. "Have we got time for a quickie?"

He mumbled something unintelligible.

"I didn't think so." She pulled on a pair of black pants and a dark black tunic top. She had to roll up the legs and the sleeves, but they were better than what she had been wearing. His shoes would be too big so she didn't even bother with any.

She faced him. "How does this look?"

His swift glance swept over her. "Naked was better, but since we're trying not to draw attention, I guess this will do for now. Once we're safe, I'm going to steal you away, and I'm going to make love to you all week."

A ripple of pleasure burned through her. "I like your plan."

They eased out of the closet. Banyon hadn't stirred.

"You do have a plan, right?" she asked in a low voice.

"Yeah, don't get caught."

She pursed her lips. "I could've come up with that one."

"Great minds think alike. Come on." He hurried to the door, then eased it open. "All clear."

She took a deep breath. Her heart beat ninety miles an hour. He glanced over his shoulder.

"Ready?"

She nodded, even though she wasn't that sure. They didn't have much of a choice. To stay would be certain death. Beyond this room, they at least had a chance.

"Stay behind me, and if we meet anyone, don't make eye contact. They don't put much value on women here. If they think you belong to me, we might make it out of here alive."

She cocked an eyebrow.

"They're idiots."

She agreed. There was no one in the hall. Roan went to the left. She grabbed his arm and pointed to the right. "This way."

He raised his eyebrows. "And you know this how?"

"I'll explain later." There'd been a docking station not too far from where they were being held. When they were back on Earth, she was going to look into this meditation thing. It could be pretty useful.

Someone turned the corner and started toward them. She looked at her feet, and shuffled behind Roan. As they passed, she saw the scars from the chains the person had once worn. A former slave that had quit trying to escape.

They could've been that person. Still could be.

"There are guards searching the north side and coming this way," the man said.

She glanced over her shoulder, but the man who'd just passed didn't stop. What must his life be like? A shudder swept over her.

They turned south at the corner, going away from the docking station, and traveling down a shorter hall. Dark and dismal didn't begin to describe the hallway. They turned another corner, went down another hall that led to stairs.

"Do we go up or down?" Roan looked at her.

"Up? I'm not sure."

"What does your gut say?"

"That it's hungry so I don't think it would be much help."

"Then we'll go up."

"Are you sure?"

He shook his head. "I'm not sure of anything."

"I think the docking station was on the lower level."

"Then we'll go down."

God, she hoped she was right.

They went down the stairs. There was a door at the bottom. He pushed a button and the door opened. She took a step back. They must be at the back of the castle.

"Wrong direction," Roan said beneath his breath.

"This isn't good," she said as she stared at row upon row of people in chains and men wielding whips. God, it looked as though they'd stepped back into the dark ages.

He reached toward the button and started to push it, but voices sounded behind them.

"Now what?"

"We don't have a choice." He grabbed her hand and stepped outside.

Chapter 29

The only light came from the quarter moon. Dark gray shadows hid in the corners of the courtyard. There was a metal platform in the center of the open area. People milled about as if a party was about to take place.

Roan noted there were different species. Some he knew—Roverts, Adnams, Eidojs, and even a couple he suspected were earthlings. Some he didn't know. They skirted them all, keeping a safe distance.

An Eidoj walked over to one of the men in chains. The Eidoj species were stunning—alluring, auburn-haired delicate beauties—if you didn't mind them having three eyes and a short tail, kind of like a lizard, and the fact they could change from male to female at will.

She slipped her hand between the man's legs and squeezed, then smiled and nodded toward her companion before returning to her place as someone stepped to the platform.

"What's going on?" Lyraka whispered.

"Slave auction."

"You're serious?"

The door they'd exited was flung open and three armed Roverts stepped out.

Roan pulled Lyraka back farther into the shadows until their backs were against the wall.

The Rovert guards looked around, then one motioned for

the others to go back inside. Roan and Lyraka were safe, for now, but they might have to wait for the end of the auction before they could leave.

An Adnam waddled up on the stage and began to shout in a garbled sounding language that Roan couldn't understand, then again in English.

"How come they know our language?" she whispered.

He leaned closer, caught the scent of her hair, and almost forgot what she'd asked.

"I think there have been aliens living on Earth for thousands of years. They stay pretty low key. No one is going to believe their neighbor is from another planet. Strange maybe, but not from another galaxy."

"So, they—we—merged with society."

"And some returned to their home planet and took back knowledge of Earth."

"I think I would've noticed him." She nodded toward the stage.

"Joe was involved in Area 51 for years. They tried to monitor the aliens. When the public started getting wise, they split their investigation areas into smaller sections so they could work below public scrutiny. But what Joe is doing, actual space travel, is limited because of the resources. Some don't think we should be involved."

"Will the team come for us?" she suddenly asked.

He hesitated. "I don't know." He wished he did.

Guards pulled some poor sap up on stage. He downed his head, not even moving when the Adnam jerked away the white cloth that covered the lower part of his body. The bidding was fast and furious. It slowed, then stopped, and the man was led off the stage.

Another Adnam laughed, then grabbed the guy's chain and raised it in the air showing his triumph at having won the bid. Not that he was able to raise it that high. Most Adnams weren't more than four feet tall.

Roan scanned the area, figuring they were safer staying in

the shadows. He might be able to mingle, but he wasn't so sure about Lyraka. Women usually didn't travel to Rovertia—unless they were Eidojs.

They would have to go back the way they came. The guards had already checked the area so maybe they wouldn't return.

"When the bidding starts, let's try the stairs again."

Lyraka seemed to breathe a sigh of relief. Roan knew how she felt. He'd only been on a few planets. Some were okay, some not. He'd never landed on Rovertia and that was fine with him. Some called it a trip to the dark side. The Sodom and Gomorrah of the universe. Anything you wanted, you could find it here—drugs, slaves, a hired gun.

Rovertia was one reason the elite teams were formed, but they were spread thin. For that very reason, he didn't know whether a team would come after them or not. Roan and Lyraka might be on their own.

A female was pulled on stage, head lowered. His gut clenched, but he knew there wasn't a damn thing he could do right now. He silently vowed that ending slave auctions would be a top priority.

"Come on, let's go." He grabbed Lyraka's hand and started to turn away when the woman on the stage raised her head. He froze. Lyraka ran into his back.

"What's wrong?"

He pulled her back into the shadows. "Look toward the platform." Maybe his eyes were deceiving him.

"Oh my God, that's Alesha."

"What the hell is Alesha doing in a slave auction?"

A Rovert stepped up on the platform and grabbed her breast. Alesha kicked him in the balls.

"Touch me again you slimy Rovert and you're dead meat!"

The Rovert quickly backed off the platform as everyone burst out laughing.

"The team must be around here somewhere." Roan scanned the area.

"Do you think they were all captured?"

"I don't know." The team was green. It was possible they discovered who'd taken Roan and Lyraka and attempted a rescue mission. Damn, everything was a mess. It would've been hard enough to get Lyraka out safely. He had no idea how he was going to get a whole team off this godforsaken planet.

"I bid three shuckas!" someone yelled out and everyone laughed.

"What's a shucka?"

"An insult," he said, then looked at her. "Stay here."

"What are you going to do?"

"Try to save her." When she looked as though she'd follow, he continued. "Trust me."

She opened her mouth, then closed it. "I trust you. Just be careful."

He moved out of the shadows, hoping his plan would work. As he weaved through the crowd, he slipped the small knife out of his pocket. He stumbled against an Eidoj, and smiled down into her face at the same time that he cut the strings on the pouch that hung from her waist. He caught the pouch in his hand without blinking an eye.

She smiled, batting her lashes, and biting her lower lip. Looking at someone with three eyes was really weird. He winked and moved farther into the crowd, thankful for the Christmas his aunt had given him a copy of *Oliver Twist*.

He opened the pouch, then dumped the contents into his hand. Three large diamonds, two rubies and an emerald. He knew the Nerakians had gems on their planet, but they were hard to come by on others so they were still worth something.

"I like spitfires," an earthling said. "One diamond!"

"You'll never have me," Alesha said.

"I want to see her breasts," the man sneered.

The earthling was fat, his teeth rotting and yellowed, and it didn't look as though he'd bathed in a very long time. The only ones not keeping their distance were the Adnams.

The Adnam on the platform grabbed the length of chain that held Alesha's wrists and tossed it in the air. It locked against an overhead bar. The Rovert who had reached for her earlier grabbed an ankle chain, someone else grabbed the other. Even though Alesha wiggled, her movements were ineffective. The Adnam reached for her robe.

"No! I don't think she's been bought and paid for yet and I don't like to display my slaves." Roan met Alesha's look of gratitude.

"But then, you haven't bid, either." The earthling turned back to the platform. "Strip her!"

"One ruby and one emerald!" Roan called out and hoped the earthling wasn't rich.

There was a hush over the crowd.

"And a diamond," Roan added.

Roan glanced at Alesha. She was biting her bottom lip and looking worried. He felt as though he was in a poker game and a friend's life was on the line. In this case, that pretty much summed it up.

The earthling opened his pouch, then looked up. "Three diamonds, three rubies and an emerald."

Roan's gaze jerked to Alesha. She must have known by the expression on his face that he'd just been outbid. Her expression turned to resignation. The earthling laughed, sensing he'd won.

"Five rubies, four emeralds, and three diamonds," Ray said as he stepped forward. He was sporting a bruise under one eye and a swollen lip, and carried a pouch that looked a lot like the one Roan had lifted.

"You can't bid!" The earthling argued. "It was between me and that guy."

Ray walked over and clamped his hand on the man's shoulder. "Is that so?"

The man cowered. "I didn't want her anyway."

Force always ruled in places like this and Ray didn't look

as though he'd mind beating the pulp out of anyone who overbid him. Just to make sure, he looked at the crowd. No one offered to dispute his claim.

Ray walked over to the payment desk and dropped a pouch on the table, then strode up the steps of the platform to claim Alesha. He reached up and unhooked the chain from the overhead bar, then glared at the Roverts who still held her ankle chains. They immediately backed away. They didn't want to sport any bruises or broken bones that Ray might inflict.

Alesha glared at the crowd as she followed Ray down the stairs, then she looked at Roan. "Thank God, you're alive. Lyraka?"

Roan looked in the general direction of where Lyraka was still hidden, and keeping his voice low, he said, "Over there. I don't suppose you have a ship close by." She'd trusted him, and not gotten involved. Pride swelled inside him. That, and fear. They still had to get the hell out of here.

"We have a ship at the docking station," Ray told Roan.

"Then let's go. Lyraka knocked Banyon out, but I'd be willing to bet he won't be unconscious long. He'll turn this place upside down looking for us."

"I know a shortcut," Alesha said.

"Figures." But Roan was smiling. "I'll get Lyraka." He hurried over to where he'd left her. "Same game plan. Head down. Don't make eye contact."

"I really hate being subservient."

"I'll let you be in control when we get home." When she bit her bottom lip, he knew she was envisioning exactly what she would do when she had complete control.

They returned to Ray and Alesha.

"Behind the platform is a door in the wall that should take us a different route to the docking station," Alesha said, keeping her head lowered.

"That's how we missed each other," Ray told Alesha as they headed in that direction.

They didn't say anything more until they were safely on the other side of the door, and away from the crowd.

"I was supposed to lead Alesha around on a chain until we found you guys, but some Rovert s.o.b. must've thought we were you two. I punched his lights out, but two more joined in. By the time I had things back under control, some jerk had stolen Alesha."

"Two jerks," she quickly spoke up. "I could've taken one. Anyway, he led me through these tunnels. How'd you two get away?"

"I faked escape, then when Banyon came inside the glass cage, I knocked him out."

"Good job."

They didn't say anything else until they reached the other end of the tunnel.

"We'll look around, make sure everything is safe. That should give you time to help Alesha out of those chains."

"The best idea I've heard all day," she said.

Ray and Roan stepped out into the open and quickly scanned the docking area. There were about forty crafts in all. People were loading and unloading supplies and contraband. Roan didn't see any guards. They made their way back to the women.

"All clear," Ray said. "We have a straight shot to the craft."

Lyraka sighed with relief. "Let's go."

As soon as they stepped from the tunnel, they were surrounded by armed guards.

Banyon stood on the deck smiling. "Did you think you would get away so easily?"

"Why is he talking like Urkel?" Ray said.

Chapter 30

Lyraka had a feeling she was going to pay dearly for slamming Banyon's head into the glass. Not only did he not look happy, but his head was sort of flat on one side, and his nose looked more out of joint—literally.

"You did all that damage?" Alesha whispered.

"Guilty."

"I'm impressed."

Banyon walked across the platform in front of them. Lyraka noticed there was a decided limp in his walk, too. She only hoped he didn't take his anger out on the others. Yeah, like he'd cut anyone slack at this point.

"I'm not going back in that cage," she said. She squared her shoulders and looked at Roan.

"I never did like cages," Ray said.

"Where's the rest of the team?" Lyraka looked around, but didn't see anyone else.

"It doesn't matter. We're outnumbered," Roan said.

He was right. They didn't have a chance of making it out of here alive.

"I say we rush them," Alesha looked at the guns as if they were mere plastic toys.

"We'll never make it," Roan warned.

"Then I plan on taking a few of the bastards with me." Ray hunched his shoulders like a lineman about to tackle his opponent. Lyraka had no doubt he'd take out more than one guard.

"Banyon, Ruler of Rovertia, I hereby place you under arrest," Joe said as the door of a nearby craft opened, and he stepped out. He pointed a gun at Banyon, but Banyon quickly stepped behind two guards and laughed, sounding more like a pig's snort. "Who are you?"

"I'm on the council of humanities for a unified universe and we're cleaning house. You're charged with importing and exporting illegal contraband and drugs, the buying and selling of slaves, and kidnapping agents of the elite force."

"Who's going to lock me up?" He waved his arm. "In case you have bad vision, I have guards with guns. I believe, *you* are *my* prisoners."

Reeka, Warren, and Link stepped from the craft, all carrying guns.

"*We'll* stop you," they said.

Banyon did his snort-laugh again. "I think you're outnumbered. Unless you have an army in the wings." He waved his arm in front of him at the same time twenty craft landed. Nerakian warriors poured out of them. Reeka stood tall as she watched her countrymen, for the first time, ready to fight an opposing force. Pride practically oozed from her.

Not only were there warriors, but Lyraka spotted Sam and Nick, along with Kia. Technically, Kia was her niece, even though Kia was older than Lyraka. Kia was a warrior, and right now, she looked the part, and she'd brought her husband, Nick, with her. He, and his partner Sam, who married Kia's sister, were undercover cops on Earth who knew how to take down the bad guys.

They were so going to kick ass now. Banyon had met his match, and then some with the team and her family.

Aasera stepped between the warriors, directly in front of Banyon. He screamed and did a little jig backwards.

Mom. Lyraka should've known her mother would be in the middle of rescuing them.

"I see you're still a wimp, Banny." Aasera cast a disparaging look at Banyon.

He quickly collected himself and stiffened his spine. "I am Banyon, Ruler of the Roverts."

"I suggest you tell your guards to lower their weapons." Joe smiled, but it held no warmth when he looked at Banyon. "As you can see, we now have *you* outnumbered."

"I refuse to . . ."

Aasera doubled her fist and punched him in the nose.

Banyon grabbed his nose and screamed. "You're going to be sorry!"

"Urkel with a bad cold. Amazing. I didn't think anyone really talked like that," Aasera said.

"He didn't until Lyraka slammed her fist into his nose."

Alesha sniffed. "Does anyone else smell decaying roses? Bleh."

"Surrender or die!" Joe ordered.

The guards all laid down their weapons and dropped to their knees. Sam pulled a pair of handcuffs from his back pocket and handcuffed Banyon. Banyon was still screaming as they led him to one of the crafts.

A heavyset man stepped from the crowd. "I am Kragen, chief advisor. Please forgive us for our leader's faults. He was out of control."

Roan eyed the man with something close to contempt. He didn't like the looks of the Rovert. Something about him said he looked out for himself and no one else.

"We will leave people here to assist in getting Rovertia back in compliance." Apparently, Aasera had the same feeling.

Roan studied her. From what he'd gathered, she didn't like or trust men. He wondered what she would think of him.

Lyraka walked closer to where Roan stood, and touched his arm. He smiled at her. She might make a pretty good agent after all. His heart swelled with pride.

"I love you," he said before he thought, then felt the heat

rise up his face when he saw that most of the people had heard what he'd said.

Lyraka looked at him. "Yes, I know. I love you too."

He grinned, then glanced around and met Aasera's glare. She didn't look too pleased with his declaration.

He took a deep breath. "Traveler, I've fallen in love with your daughter."

Aasera raised an eyebrow and turned slightly, but when she did, her gun pointed toward him. He wondered if it was intentional or by accident.

"It doesn't look as though you're very good at protecting her."

"She's still alive."

Her frown deepened. "You will come with us to Nerak so I can have a chance to talk with you."

"I love him, too," Lyraka said.

"It's not your choice. The elders will need to approve this earthling."

Lyraka stiffened beside him. "Did Mala ask for permission? Or Lara? Mala came to Earth looking for more than what Nerak could offer, but found Mason McKinley. They married without getting permission. Okay, so maybe Sam and Lara had asked, but that doesn't matter. I've never been to Nerak."

"It was too late to get approval for Mala, but yes, Sam had to be approved for Lara. It's not too late with you." She looked at them. "Come."

"Now, Aasera," Joe began.

"You owe me this much," Aasera told him.

She turned and went to one of the crafts. Roan and Lyraka had no choice except to follow her. Roan looked at Joe, who only shrugged his shoulders.

Crap, how the hell had Roan gotten into this mess?

Lyraka bowed her head as she stood in the doorway of Elder Torcara's chambers.

"Enter."

Lyraka looked up and for a moment couldn't move. The woman was regal and beautiful despite her many years. Lyraka took a deep breath and went inside.

"Sit."

Lyraka sat on the chair across from the elder. It was hard to believe she was a part of this great woman through Aasera. Torcara's DNA blended with Lyraka's, even though it wasn't a pure blend. This was another part of who she was. The heritage that she didn't know, the part of herself that had been blank all these years.

"You're very beautiful," Torcara said. "Did you know you were named after my grandmother?"

"Yes."

"She was wise beyond her years."

"Wasn't she the one who altered the DNA so only females were born?" Lyraka squared her shoulders.

"Maybe she wasn't wise in all things, but her heart was in the right place."

"I'm half earthling," she reminded her in case the elder forgot she wasn't of pure blood.

"That must be the stubborn part I see in you," Torcara said.

Lyraka felt duly chastised.

"Do you love this man you call Roan?"

She met Torcara's gaze without flinching. "Very much."

"Why?"

"I beg your pardon?"

"Why do you love him?"

This was some kind of test and she had a feeling if she didn't pass, then she might never see Roan again. She wasn't sure how the elder would be able to pull it off, but Lyraka had a feeling she would.

She took a deep breath, closed her eyes, and thought about her relationship with Roan. When she opened her eyes, calmness had settled over her.

"Roan makes me feel alive. He loves the good in me, but

he accepts the bad, too. When I'm not with him, I feel as if there's something missing in my life, and when he's with me, I feel whole again. I can't imagine life without him."

"Very well said." Torcara nodded, her smile soft.

Lyraka had to ask the question that had been burning inside her. "He's okay, isn't he?"

"He's with your mother."

That wasn't exactly what she'd asked.

"If love is meant to be, it will happen," Torcara said.

Some of her skeptism must have shown. After all, what did Torcara know about love?

"I know what you think. That since there are no men, I wouldn't know what love is, but you'd be wrong." Her eyes took on a far away look. "Before we banned space travel there was a man. A trader. Of course, it would never have worked between us."

"What did you do?"

Sadness seemed to wash over her. "I did the right thing. I banned him, and all men, from stopping on Nerak."

Lyraka could see just how much it had cost the Elder. She doubted she would be able to go through life without ever seeing Roan again. "Was it the right thing?" She couldn't help asking.

"As a ruler I often have to make difficult decisions."

"Like allowing men on Nerak again."

Torcara's smile was soft. "That wasn't as hard as you might think. I rather like Sam's undisciplined nature, and Nick is headstrong and often does things without thinking first. I think we needed more spontaneity."

"Roan is a good man, too."

"He'll need to meet with Aasera's approval, though."

Her mother didn't like men. Lyraka's father had been mean, and when he'd found out Aasera was pregnant, he'd left. Things did not look good for Lyraka and Roan.

The door swished opened and Aasera walked in. Lyraka stood, looking anxiously at her mother.

"What?" Aasera asked. "I didn't vaporize him if that's what you're thinking. He's down the hall in the blue room."

Lyraka didn't move, not sure exactly what that meant.

"Are you going to make him wait forever?"

"Then you like him?"

Aasera shrugged. "For a man, he's okay."

Disappointment filled Lyraka. She wanted her mother to more than just like him.

"He seems nice enough," Aasera conceded.

Lyraka flung her arms around her mother and gave her a quick hug, then ran out of the room. She didn't like these separations she and Roan had had to endure.

Aasera settled herself in the seat across from Torcara only after Torcara motioned for her to sit.

"Times are changing, Aasera." Torcara sighed.

"Sometimes changes are necessary."

"I suppose."

"What will it be like with men on the planet again?"

"I'm sure it will be quite disruptive."

"But there are good men, too. I see that now. Lyraka's father was cruel, but Nick and Sam are good."

"And Roan?"

"I'm not ready to make a final judgment. We shall see." Aasera's gaze met the elder's. "He seemed like a good man."

"And very handsome."

"Looks aren't everything."

"It doesn't hurt, though."

"True." There was Joe. Not handsome like Roan, Nick, or Sam, but he had a way of making her pulse speed up. Maybe it was time to let down some of her barriers.

Yes, times were changing, and maybe, just maybe, it would be for the good.

Roan paced the tiny confines of the room. Would he ever see Lyraka again? Maybe they would just zap him and tell her that he'd left or something. Aasera hadn't seemed that pleased with some of his answers to her questions.

How the hell had he fallen in love with Lyraka in the first place? He wasn't ready to settle down with one woman. He liked his free, easy lifestyle without the clutter of a romantic involvement.

The door was flung open and Lyraka barreled in. His pulse beat faster, his palms began to sweat, and just looking at her made his heart swell with love.

Fool! Of course you can't live without her. She's what makes you complete.

She ran to him. He opened his arms, then wrapped them around her, holding her close.

"I don't care what they think of me. I'll never let you go."

"Aasera approves of our relationship."

He leaned back. "She likes me?" That was a shock.

"I don't think she actually used the word like. She said you were nice enough."

"I'll settle for that." He lowered his head and once more tasted the sweetness of her lips.

How had he ever lived without her?

And don't miss Cynthia Eden's ETERNAL HUNTER, in stores next month from Brava . . .

She reached into her bag and pulled out a check. Not the usual way things were handled in the DA's office, but . . . "I've been authorized to acquire your services." He didn't glance at the check, just kept those blue eyes trained on hers. Her fingers were steady as she held the check in the air between them "This check is for ten thousand dollars."

No change of expression. From the looks of his cabin, the guy shouldn't have been hesitating to snatch up the money.

"Give the check to Night Watch."

At that, her lips firmed. "I already gave them one." A hefty one, at that. "This one's for you. A bonus from the mayor—he wants this guy caught, fast." Before word about the true nature of the crime leaked too far.

"So old Gus doesn't think his cops can handle this guy?"

Gus LaCroix. Hard-talking, ex-hard drinking mayor. No nonsense, deceptively smart, and demanding. "He's got the cops on this, but he said he knew you, and that you'd be the best one to handle this job."

Erin strongly suspected that Gus belonged in the *Other* world. She hadn't caught any scent that was off drifting from him, but his agreement to bring in Night Watch and his almost desperate demands to the DA had sure indicated the guy knew more than he was letting on about the situation.

Could be he was a demon. Low-level. Many politicians were.

Jude took the check. Finally. She dropped her fingers, fast, not wanting the flesh on flesh contact with him. Not then.

He folded the check and tucked it into the back pocket of his jeans. "Guess you just got yourself a bounty hunter."

"And I guess you've got yourself one sick shifter to catch."

He closed the distance between them, moving fast and catching her arms in a strong grip.

Aw, hell. It was just like before. The heat of his touch swept though her, waking hungers she'd deliberately denied for so long.

Jude was sexual. From his knowing eyes. His curving, kiss-me lips, to the hard lines and muscles of his body.

Deep inside, in the dark, secret places of her soul that she fought to keep hidden, there was a part of her just like that.

Wild. Hot.

Sexual.

"Why are you afraid of me?"

Not the question she'd expected, but one she could answer. "I know what you are. What sane woman wouldn't be afraid of a man who becomes an animal?"

"Some women like a little bit of the animal in their men."

"Not me." *Liar.*

His eyes said the same thing.

"Do your job, Donovan. Catch the freak who cut up my prisoner—"

"Like Bobby had been slashing his victims?"

Hit. Yeah, there'd been no way to miss that significance.

"When word gets out about what really happened, some folks will say Bobby deserved what he got." His fingers pressed into her arms. Erin wore a light, silk shirt—and even that seemed too hot for the humid Louisiana spring night. His touch burned through the blouse and seemed to singe her flesh.

"Some will say that," she allowed. Okay, a hell of a lot would say that. "But his killer still has to be caught." Stopped, because she had the feeling this could be just the beginning.

Her feelings about death weren't often wrong.

She was a lot like her dad that way.

And, unfortunately, like her mother, too.

"What do you think? Did he deserve to be clawed to death?"

An image of Bobby's ex-wife, Pat, flashed before her eyes. The doctors had put over one hundred and fifty stitches into her face. She'd been his most brutal attack.

Erin swallowed. "His punishment was for the court to decide." She stepped back, but he didn't let her go. "Uh, do you mind?"

"Yeah, I do." His eyes glittered down at her. "If we're gonna be working together, we need honesty between us."

"We need you to find the killer."

"Oh, I will. Don't worry about that. I always catch my prey."

So the rumors claimed. The hunters from Night Watch were known throughout the U.S.

"You're shivering, Erin."

"No, no, I'm not." She was.

"I make you nervous. I scare you." A pause. His gaze dropped to her lips, lingered, then slowly rose back to meet her stare. "Is it because I know what you are?"

She wanted his mouth on hers. A foolish desire. Ridiculous. Not something the controlled woman wanted, but what the wild thing inside craved. "You don't know anything about me."

"Don't I?"

Erin jerked free of his hold and glared at him. "Few things in this world scare me. You should know that." There was one thing, one person, who terrified her—but now wasn't the time for that disclosure. No, she didn't tell anyone about *him*.

If she could just get around Jude and march out of that door—

"Maybe you're not scared of me, then. Maybe you're scared of yourself."

She froze.

"Not human," he murmured, shaking his head. "Not vamp."

Vamp? Thankfully, no.

"Djinn? Nah, you don't have that look." His right hand lifted and he rubbed his chin. "Tell me your secrets, sweetheart, and I'll tell you mine."

"Sorry, not the sharing type." She'd wasted enough time here. Erin pushed past him, ignoring the press of his arm against her side. Her body ached and the whispers of hunger within her grew more demanding every moment she stayed with him.

Weak.

She hated her weakness.

Just like her mother's.

"You're a shifter." His words stopped her near the door. She stared blankly at the faded wood. Heard the dull thud of her heart echoing in her ears.

Then the soft squeak of the old floorboards as he closed the distance between them.

Erin turned to him, tilted her head back—

He kissed her.

She heard a growl. Not from him—no, from her own throat.

The hunger.

Sure, he made the first move, he brought his lips crashing down on hers, but . . . she kissed him right back.

Some relationships burn WITH EXTREME PLEASURE, so go out and get Alison Kent's newest Dragon One novel today!

He stilled in the act of scrubbing the day's sweat from his face and waited to see if Cady had something to say, or if she'd only come for the facilities because she couldn't wait. He didn't want to make her uncomfortable if she had.

But she didn't say or do anything. Best he could tell, she was standing unmoving just inside the door. And since his clothes were in a pile somewhere near her feet and his towel on the edge of the sink, he needed her to do whatever it was she'd come to do and get out.

So he nudged her. "First my truck, and now my shower. Is nothing sacred?"

"Sorry," he heard her mutter. "The TV wasn't working."

What the hell? "You came to get me to fix the TV? Did you try calling the front desk first?"

"No. I mean, the TV works fine. It just wasn't . . . working. As a distraction." She groaned beneath her breath, the sound giving off an emotion he hadn't heard before. "I needed a distraction."

She had dozens of channels broadcasting more distracting crap than a person could need in a lifetime. She wasn't making any sense. And he wasn't exactly comfortable here with the situation.

"You're looking for a distraction? In here? Where I'm

bare-as-the-day-I-was-born naked? Cady, Cady, Cady." He clicked his tongue. "You devil."

"It's not like that."

"Then what's it like, boo, because you coming in here saying you need a distraction kinda leads me down that road." He stared at the shower curtain where he could see her shadow on the other side. It was the strangest way to be having a conversation, not one he was exactly good with.

The water was beating down on his shoulders as he stood with his hands at his hips, keeping his secrets out of sight the same way Cady was on the other side of the cheap white vinyl keeping hers.

His were of a physically personal nature; he didn't hang it out for everyone to see. But her own package of mysteries was obviously pretty damn heavy. After all, it had sent her seeking refuge in a steamy wet bathroom when she had a perfectly comfortable bed to hide out in.

King leaned into the spray, rinsed the shampoo from his hair, the soapy water from his face, neck, and chest. He was clean and ready to get out, but he was also butt naked, and she was standing between him and his towel.

Except standing wasn't exactly the right word. Even through the curtain he could see her nervous movements, pacing, rocking, leaning over the sink and talking into her hands instead of to him.

He'd had enough. "Cady, either talk to me or get out so I can get out."

"I can't go back out there."

Then talk it was. "Because?"

"I just can't. In the city, I felt safe. The incident with Alice aside," she added. "In the city, I was just another nameless person in the crowd. It was easy to stay out of sight, lost, bland, blending in."

She was not bland. She was anything but. "And somehow that all changed with me taking you home."

"That place is not my home."

No, but it used to be. She had a lot of history there. Was standing out now what was bothering her? "You think the gossip mill is all churned up with tales of your face meeting your mother's fist?"

"It's not the tales and the gossip that scare me."

Scared? That's what she was feeling? He would've thought something like rejected, dejected. Embarrassed. Any one seemed more in order. "Then what scares you?"

"That after all these years, they're finally going to catch me. And kill me when they do."

Okay, now this was getting spooky weird, but the thing about feeling safer sharing a room? If she thought someone was after her, it made sense. Made him glad, too, he'd kept his gun close. At least until he knew more.

Like whether she had a real reason to be frightened. Or whether she was some kind of schizo whack job. "They? Who is they?"

It took her several seconds to respond. He sensed her move again, lean back against the wall beside the door. "I don't know their names, or even who they are except for being friends of the guys who went away for Kevin's murder."

Real enough. So far. "And you think they're after you?"

"They've been after me since the trial."

There were a dozen things he wanted to ask, all related to wondering why she was still living here in this part of the country when she had no ties. Why, if there was a legitimate threat, had she not found out who *they* were and filed a restraining order?

But her fear was immediate, her need for a diversion urgent enough to bring her in here while he showered. He ended up asking, "And you think they're here? Now?"

"I don't know. It's just . . . When I looked out the window, I saw a truck idling behind yours, then rolling forward slowly and stopping as if searching for our room. Or searching for me."

He didn't want to discount what she was feeling, or ignore

what she thought she'd seen. But he'd been the one driving, and nothing about the traffic around them had struck him as strange or hostile.

No, he hadn't been on the lookout for a tail or had any reason to be, but those early years behind bars had left him with a good pair of eyes in the back of his head.

As far as he knew, they were still working, and they hadn't seen a thing. "I'm sure it's nothing."

She bit off some not so nice words. "You're sure I'm hallucinating? Is that it?"

Women. Twist and turn everything a man said. "No, I'm sure you saw what you saw."

"But until you see it for yourself, then it doesn't count."

"I didn't say that either."

"You didn't have to. You don't believe me."

What he believed was that they weren't going to get anywhere with this barrier between them.

He shut off the water, grabbed his wet rag and held it with one hand in the most strategic of locations, then whipped the curtain out of the way and met her gaze.

The hooks clattered the length of the rod, and Cady jumped, her eyes going wide as she took him in in all of his Garden of Eden glory.

Then a smile teased one corner of her mouth upward, and a knowing brow followed suit. "Nice fig leaf."

He glared, moved his other hand to his hip to secure the terry cloth from both sides. "I can't talk to you when I'm naked and you're not."

"Are you saying you want me to take off my clothes?"

That hadn't been the response he was after, but now that she'd brought it up . . . "If you're not up for doing that, then I'm going to put mine on. You can stay and watch, or stay and help, or you can turn your back until I'm dried off and dressed. And we can pick up this conversation then."

She'd lost a bit of her smirk during his speech, and though

she hadn't run screaming out of the bathroom, he wouldn't be surprised if she turned and did.

He wasn't much to look at as it was, but dripping wet and naked save for his terry cloth fig leaf—the rag itself growing wetter with all the dripping going on—he could scare the chocolate out of an M&M candy shell.

So it left him feeling strangely naked and vulnerable when she was slow to reach for the handle, and even slower to open the door, leaving him behind with an expression he swore was tinged with regret.

Check out Terri Brisbin's first book for Brava, A STORM OF PASSION, available now!

Whatever the Seer wanted, the Seer got, be it for his comfort or his whim or his pleasure.

She stood, staring at the chair on the raised dais at one end of the chamber, the chair where he sat when the visions came. From the expression that filled her green eyes, she knew it as well.

Had she witnessed his power? Had she watched as the magic within him exploded into a vision of what was or what would yet be? As he influenced the high and the mighty of the surrounding lands and clans with the truth of his gift? Walking over to stand behind her, he placed his hands on her shoulders and drew her back to his body.

"I have not seen you before, sweetling," he whispered into her ear. Leaning down, he smoothed the hair from the side of her face with his own and then touched his tongue to the edge of her ear. "What is your name?"

He felt the shivers travel through her as his mouth tickled her ear. Smiling, he bent down and kissed her neck, tracing the muscle there down to her shoulder with the tip of his tongue. Connor bit the spot gently, teasing it with his teeth and soothing it with his tongue. "Your name?" he asked again.

She arched then, clearly enjoying his touch and ready for more. Her head fell back against his shoulder, and he moved his mouth to the soft skin there, kissing and licking his way down and back to her ear. Still, she had not spoken.

"When I call out my pleasure, sweetling, what name will I speak?"

He released her shoulders and slid his hands down her arms and then over her stomach to hold her in complete contact with him. Covering her stomach and pressing her to him, he rubbed against her back, letting her feel the extent of his erection—hard and large and ready to pleasure her. Connor moved his hands up to take her breasts in his grasp. Rubbing his thumbs over their tips and teasing them to tightness, he no longer asked; he demanded.

"Tell me your name."

He felt her breasts swell in his hands, and he tugged now on the distended nipples, enjoying the feel and imagining them in his mouth, as he suckled hard on them and as she screamed out her pleasure. But nothing could have pleased him more in that moment than the way she gasped at each stroke he made, over and over until she moaned out her name to him.

"Moira."

"Moira," he repeated slowly, drawing her name out until it was a wish in the air around them. "Moira," he said again as he untied the laces on her bodice and slid it down her shoulders until he could touch her skin. "Moira," he now moaned as the heat and the scent of her enticed him as much as his own scent was pulling her under his control.

Connor paused for a moment, releasing her long enough to drag his tunic over his head and then turning her in to his embrace. He inhaled sharply as her skin touched his; the heat of it seared into his soul as the tightened peaks of her breasts pressed against his chest. Her added height brought her hips level almost to his, and he rubbed his hardened cock against her stomach, letting her feel the extent of his arousal.

As he pushed her hair back off her shoulders, he realized that in addition to the raging lust in his blood, there was something else there, teasing him with its presence.

Anticipation.

For the first time in years, this felt like more than the mindless rutting that happened between him and the countless, nameless women there for his needs. For the first time in too long, this was not simply scratching an itch, for the hint of something more seemed to stand off in the distance, something tantalizing and unknown and somehow tied to this woman.

He lifted her chin with his finger, forcing her gaze off the blasted chair and onto his face. Instead of the compliant gaze that usually met him, the clarity of her gold-flecked green eyes startled him. Connor did something he'd not done before, something he never needed to do: he asked her permission.

"I want you, Moira," he whispered, dipping to touch and taste her lips for the first time. Connor slid his hand down to gather up her skirts, baring her legs and the treasure between them to his touch and his sight. "Let me?"